STONE RIVER ANTHOLOGY

KAY LYONS

Kindred Spirits Publishing

KAY LYONS

Christmas at
HOLLY WOOD

STONE RIVER BOOK FIVE

Copyright

SIGN UP FOR KAY'S NEWSLETTER AND RECEIVE UPDATES ON NEW RELEASES, CONTESTS, PRE-RELEASE BOOK INFORMATION, EXCLUSIVES AND MORE!

CHRISTMAS AT
HOLLY WOOD
A STONE RIVER NOVELLA

SIGN UP FOR KAY'S NEWSLETTER TO RECEIVE
UPDATES ON NEW RELEASES, CONTESTS, PRE-RELEASE
BOOK INFORMATION, EXCLUSIVES AND MORE!

Merry when-will-this-be-over Christmas," Morgan Ashley said with a grumble, peering out her fogged-and-snow-caked windshield. She shut off the radio, sick of the sappy, happy, make-her-gag Christmas carols on every station.

Normally, she was all over the holiday. She wore the sweaters, baked the cookies and cakes and casseroles, decorated the house from top to bottom. She rocked the holidays from Thanksgiving to New Year's, thrilled to do whatever she could in the name of celebrating her Father's birth.

But this year?

She pursed her lips and twisted the heat a notch higher, knowing it wouldn't do any good but hoping all the same. The minivan was twelve years old with two hundred fifty thousand miles on it. It stayed hot in the summer and cold in the winter, and nowhere in between.

She'd complained about it and begged Rory for a new van for the last couple of years, but her now ex-husband had repeatedly said no, that it wasn't a good time for such a huge financial purchase. He'd said things were tight at work with pay cuts and layoffs and the like. Turned out his "pay cut" had come in the form of a leggy brunette with big boobs who danced at the Wild Pony. His business expenses and tax write-offs? The sleazy motel rooms he'd rented for them.

Since she'd had the kids at Thanksgiving, it was Rory's turn to keep them for Christmas. But when she'd walked up the steps carrying Camilla and the bags and holding Caleb's mittened hand, Rory had answered the door with a grin, his Wild Pony bimbo behind him sporting leggings and a thin T-shirt that showcased every anorexic but surprisingly lush curve. The girl—Morgan refused to call her a woman—hadn't looked a day over eighteen.

Morgan grabbed her thermos of coffee and took a long sip, grateful for friends who filled for free. She'd stopped by Cuppa Jo's on the way out of town for one last *Besties* group hug and to rant about having to leave her young children with her ex and his lover. That was not the example she wanted for them, but custody laws no longer cared about right and wrong.

Surprisingly, Tasha was the one who'd managed to talk Morgan out of going back to Rory's with a baseball bat to claim her babies before they were exposed to things they shouldn't see. Tasha had convinced her that while Rory was a cheating, lying, loser of a schmuck, he wouldn't let anything happen to his kids, reminding her that having Big Boobs there for their arrival was a planned move to get under her skin.

And it had definitely worked. Not because she still loved him. That ship had sailed due to all the emotional abuse he'd dished out, not to mention his adultery. She had put up with so much in an effort to make her marriage work, but she could never love or honor Rory again after his treatment of her and the way he'd destroyed their marriage.

"Ten faithful years, two kids, a beautiful home, and how many parties as your trophy wife—and this is how you treat me?" she'd asked Rory after discovering his cheating ways.

"Hate to say it, darlin', but your trophy wife days were over a long time ago," Rory had shot back at her.

Her fingers tightened around the steering wheel as she took the curve a little faster than she should have, given the snowy conditions. Thankfully, the van's worn tires held true, and other than the clatter of her baking pans as they slid out of their box in the rear compartment, the vehicle held traction.

Please help me do this. I can't do this alone.

And if she won—*when* she won—the Cake-Off Competition, she'd have the money to open her own business, maybe even get her own television show if the producers liked her well enough.

But leaving her kids so close to Christmas? With *them?*

Men earned medals in war, but single mothers facing cheating ex-husbands and leggy bimbos…

She deserved the Purple Heart. God knew hers was bleeding from the encounter.

She hadn't wanted to leave her babies. She'd wanted to bundle the kids back into the van and say screw the court-ordered visitation agreement. But she couldn't. Especially not when her parents were both sick with the flu, and Rory had shockingly agreed to take the kids days earlier than expected.

A whimper left her throat before she could squelch it. Her budget was so tight her coupons were cutting coupons, and heading to Holly Wood Resort earlier than planned and having to *pay for a room* at the ski resort for those four extra days would definitely have cleaned out her savings. "If not for my *Besties*," she said. "Thank God for them."

She'd told her best friends about the sudden change in her schedule and how the weather reports and blizzard conditions in the mountain/ski area required more time at the resort. How the television production manager had made it clear if she was a minute late for the photo shoots and festivities leading up to the Cake-Off Competition, she would be disqualified. Period.

So what had they done?

When she'd gone to the bathroom to repair her tear-smudged makeup and have a small panic attack, the *Besties* had run to the ATM on the corner and chipped in more than enough money to cover the extra days at the resort—in addition to the massage and facial they had already given her as part of her Christmas present to both relax and prep her for her time on-camera.

"Go and enjoy and stop worrying," Emma had said.

"We support you, Mo," Jolie had added.

"Don't forget to hang out in the lobby and flirt with the ski instructors. I hear they're hot," Tasha had added.

Tasha had sounded briefly like her old self, despite her worry over her still-missing boyfriend.

So here she was, alone in the dark on the snowy mountain road, praying Big Boobs wasn't teaching her daughter how to pole dance, and so very thankful for her friends that she fought back tears once again.

Please, please, please. I need to win!

Winning the competition would mark the start of her new life. Divorced, yes, but more important, free. Free to be who she was. Free of the consequences of someone else's bad choices.

You can do this. You were born *to do this. You were one of five chosen from how many entries?*

Maybe you don't have a fancy degree from some culinary school, but that just means you're blessed.

Your competitors have no eye. No creativity. That's been drilled out of them and changed by all the schooling. You've got moxie and heart, and no one can take that away from you.

Not even Rory.

And who knew what would happen during her extra time there? Maybe she *would* flirt with a ski instructor.

She nodded to herself at the last bit of her pep talk, hoping something would calm her nerves and lift her confidence level out of the negative zone. "Come on, Mo, just breathe. You can do this."

Morgan continued up the mountain road, the thickening snow and steeper grade forcing her to drive more slowly. The van's tires slipped, but she pressed on. It couldn't be much farther, could it?

The rear of the van slid when she entered a curve, and she slammed on the brake, but it made things worse. The van kept going sideways on the icy road.

Steer into the slide or out of it? She couldn't remember which way to turn the wheel!

Thankfully her low speed meant she barely bumped the

guardrail, but then a loud screech ripped through the air. The van slid backward, the rear passenger side scraping against the railing, before it bounced to a jarring stop. The noise had been loud enough to wake the dead, but she said a litany of prayers, thankful she wasn't still sliding backward down the curvy road—or tumbling over the side of the mountain. "Nothing like a little excitement to get your blood pumping."

Morgan took a moment to gather her frazzled nerves before tentatively taking her foot off the brake and slowly pressing on the gas. The wheels spun, and the van jerked, but something wasn't right.

After a few more tries, she zipped and buttoned her coat and found the hat she'd removed after leaving Cuppa Jo's, as well as the flashlight she kept in the glove box.

The icy wind stole her breath when she opened the door, and she balanced herself along the side of the van as she made her way to the rear. The driver's side was fine, but the passenger's rear tire had slipped off the road and had somehow gotten wedged between the berm and the guardrail, leaving the van sitting at an odd angle like a wobbly table. "Are you kidding me?"

She stared at the wheel, looked up at the sky and the big, fat flakes falling so rapidly, and since no one was around to see her, she stomped her feet and let out a muffled shriek, careful not to be *too* loud in case she was in an avalanche-prone area. "Seriously? What did I do to deserve this? I didn't cheat. I didn't lie and betray my family. I'm already spending Christmas alone. Are you *really* going to deny me a massage and facial? A few days of peace and quiet sitting by a roaring fire? Can't something go right for me for a change?"

"I don't want to intrude but if you're done yelling at God, maybe I can help?" a male voice said from the darkness.

Chapter 2

Knox Stewart watched as the woman searched the road for some sign of him. He had the advantage in that he could see her thanks to the vehicle's lights and the one she held in her hand. "Over here," he said, his boots crunching in the snow and ice as he left his driveway and walked toward her. Puck pulled at his leash, eager to greet the woman, but Knox held the black Lab back so Puck wouldn't scare her.

"Where did you come from?"

"My house. I was out getting wood when I heard the scraping and bang. It's not the first time it's happened on this curve."

"Glad to know I'm not the only one," she muttered. "I don't remember passing a house."

"You can't see it from the road," he said, entering the halo of light around the van. "Looks like you could use some help."

The woman nodded rapidly, and Knox felt her scrutinizing him as he approached her. He did quite a bit of looking himself, noting her long, blond hair and the lipstick darkening her full lips.

Her eyes were huge with her unease, but other than taking things slowly, he didn't know how to show her she was safe. "I'll take a look. You're on your way to the resort?" he asked, smiling at the memory of her conversation.

He'd heard her talking to someone as he'd approached, but it wasn't until he'd gotten closer that he'd realized the woman was in the middle of a good, old-fashioned tantrum, stomping her feet and fisting her hands as she stared at the sky. Obviously she'd had a bad night, and hitting the guardrail had topped it.

"Yes. They're expecting me."

As owner of the resort, he knew for a fact they weren't expecting her. Night travel was never recommended on the mountain road, especially in weather like this. But he let her comment pass and paused as he moved to the rear of the van. "Would you mind?" he asked, holding Puck's leash out for her to take. "Keep a firm grip. He'll either take off on you to explore or lick you to death to say hello."

The woman looked a bit surprised that he was asking her to keep hold of the dog, but she accepted the leash. Puck began an immediate tail-wag-swat against her jean-clad legs that earned him honorary pats on his massive head.

Seeing that they were comfortable, he moved to the end of the van, giving it a light shove. What the—

"The wheel is off the road."

Knox glanced at her before pulling the flashlight from his pocket. He moved toward the wheel in question, frowning at what he saw. He'd known the van kissed the rail, but he hadn't noticed how it was caught beneath the metal.

"Can you get it unstuck?" she asked, bouncing on the balls of her feet as though she tried to keep warm.

"'Fraid not. A road crew is going to have to come out and remove the guardrail so the tow truck can pull you out, otherwise you're going to be minus a wheel and maybe part of the van."

He tried to think of another way of getting the van unstuck, but without quite a few more guys and a lot of luck, lifting the van up and over without catching it on the underside of the guardrail wasn't possible.

"*Really?*"

He turned to see she wasn't asking him but had her face lifted to the sky once more. "You talk to Him a lot?"

"More so recently than in the past," she muttered. "And if you ask my mother, that's why I keep finding reason to do it now, too."

He chuckled at her statement and held out his gloved hand. "Your mother and my mother have a lot in common, then. Knox Stewart."

"Knocks? As in knock-knock jokes?"

"Knox with an x," he clarified.

"Ah," she said, giving him a beautiful smile and her name. "I don't suppose you know how far it is to the resort?"

"I do. I also know you're not going to make it up there tonight," he added. "Didn't you see the flashing sign at the bottom of the road?"

Her gaze shifted away from his. "I thought I could make it."

Yeah, her and every other novice unused to driving mountain roads. They were so focused on getting to the slopes they ignored the warnings about the weather conditions. "Look, you don't know me. But trust me when I say you're not going to make it up the mountain to the resort. How about you come back to my house and warm up, get some coffee, and come up with a plan? Maybe call someone to come get you lower down on the mountain?"

"No, I'm not— I want to go to the resort."

"Then you'll have to wait on a road crew."

She turned and walked several steps away from him, seemingly unaware that Puck followed her as she looked up and down the quiet, still road. Knox waited patiently for her to come to terms with her present situation. She was probably worried about him being a murderer or rapist, but there was always the possibility that he'd just agreed to take a crazy woman home with him. Sadly, it had happened before. Once. Until he'd learned the hard way not to down a few drinks before inviting a woman back to his room.

That's the price you pay for being a face and a name, his attorney and agent had both told him more than once. Winning the Stanley Cup as well as playing on three Olympic teams had definitely earned him some attention from hockey fans and groupies alike.

"I don't have a cell signal," she said, staring down at the device in her hand.

Puck whined and looked at him, no doubt getting cold himself and ready for his cozy bed near the fire. "That's because you're in No Man's Land. I have a landline at the house unless a tree's knocked out service. You can call whomever you like from there. Let them know where you are and what's going on."

She stood unmoving, her expression revealing her indecision and hesitation. "Hey, no pressure from me. If you want to stay and wait with your van, I'd be happy to lend you a couple of sleeping bags."

"A couple?" she asked, her tone dubious.

"I doubt one will be enough seeing how you're dressed. Storm's supposed to last several days," he warned. "Do you have enough food and water? Extra containers of gas? You'll have to keep the tailpipe clear of snow or you'll die of carbon monoxide poisoning."

Her mouth compressed into a thin line, and she hugged her arms around her front, shivering. "I have an emergency kit in the back with a blanket and some supplies. I'll be fine, but thanks for the offer. I'm sure a salt truck or mountain patrol will be by soon."

Her expression made it clear she was pleased with herself for being able to say she'd come somewhat prepared. How prepared was debatable, though. She probably thought some snacks and a bottle of water would get her through.

And it would get her through the night if the temperature didn't drop any more and the mountain road remained open.

But if the weather continued as predicted, the state would completely close the road by morning—not merely post a warning —and no one would be entering or leaving the resort until the storm passed.

"I'll be fine here. Really. I don't want to impose."

He hesitated for a moment before deciding he wasn't going to spend the rest of the night standing out in the cold waiting for her to change her mind. He'd give her an hour or so and check on her again. Maybe then she'd wise up, and if not, maybe by morning she'd be ready to make things easy. "Suit yourself. My house is right down that road," he said, pointing to the snow-covered driveway before taking Puck's leash from her. "It's the only one around, so you can't miss it."

"How far away is the resort? You didn't say."

"It's another twelve miles, all of it uphill," he stressed, wanting to make it clear. Surely she wouldn't attempt to make it on foot?

"I see."

"You're not going to try walking it, are you?" he asked, just to be safe.

"No. I know to stay with my car."

Good. "It's not too late to change your mind," he told her. "Are you sure you're going to be okay out here in the quiet?"

Her smile nearly blinded him, and a warm, rich laugh bubbled out of her throat. "I'm a mom. Quiet is so blissfully rare, I'll think of it as a vacation in my very own snow globe."

Knox smiled at the description, and even though he hated leaving her there, he said good-bye before taking Puck back to the house.

Inside, Puck shook off the snow before he bounded toward the rug in front of the hearth, circling twice and scrunching up in just the right spot. It never ceased to amaze Knox how tightly Puck could curl up for such a big dog, just like he had as a puppy. Between his jet-black color and the habit, the dog had been easy to name.

Knox stoked the fire and added a few logs, then set about preparing the spare bedroom for a guest. He preferred family and friends stay at the resort for convenience sake, but more often than not, his close-knit family wound up hanging out here instead.

The bed linens were changed every week regardless of whether he had guests, but Knox opened the room to let it warm and made sure to stock the bath with towels. That done, he checked the time and went back outside to gather more wood. The generator was prepped and ready in case of a power outage, and barring disaster, he was good to go food-wise for a couple of weeks if he wasn't able to make it to the resort because of sickness or other reason.

He dumped a last load of logs into the container and headed

out the door again to check on Morgan, leaving Puck behind to snooze.

This time he took the snowmobile. Morgan opened the door when he pulled alongside the van, and he noticed she wasn't using the blanket she'd said she had. Her nose was red, the makeup beneath her eyes smudged as though she might have shed a few tears, and though she hugged her arms tight around herself, she couldn't stop shivering. "Something wrong with the blanket you brought?"

"Other than the fact my ex-husband apparently used it to have sex with his stripper mistress because it reeks of cheap perfume, no."

Ouch. "My house is nice and warm. You ready to trust me yet?" he asked, holding out his hand.

"My mother told me never to talk to strangers."

He laughed softly and nodded. "Good advice. We've met, though, remember? About an hour ago? I'm not a stranger anymore."

"That's true." She sniffled and sank her teeth into her lower lip.

"Look, my guest room door locks. You could probably put a chair under the handle if you feel the need for it—not that you'd have any reason to," he added. "But you can stay with me, and I'll get you to the resort as soon as I can."

Seconds passed as she mulled over his words.

"I'll need my bags."

"Plenty of room. Come on." He helped her out and watched as Morgan opened the sliding door behind her. She handed him a good-sized piece of luggage from the seat, as well as a smaller case.

"Sorry. I can't pack light to save my life."

He'd never known a woman who could. "Not a problem. Lock up. You can hold the big one while I drive."

Morgan gathered her purse out of the front and climbed onto the snowmobile behind the suitcase. Knox gripped the smaller case and got them moving, taking things slowly so he didn't dump his cargo.

"Knox?"

"Yeah?"

"You're not a serial killer, right?"

"Wasn't the last time I checked. Are you crazy or anything?"

Her throaty laughter filled his ears, and he smiled at the sound.

"Only if you ask my ex-husband or my mother. You?"

"Depends on what you consider to be crazy." He'd done some crazy things in his life before straightening up his act. Who hadn't?

"This," she said. "This definitely qualifies. I've never gone home with a stranger before, so if you're lying, I'm going to be thoroughly disappointed that my mother was right."

He nodded again, even though he knew she couldn't see him. Yeah, this definitely qualified.

Her mother wasn't going to be the only one disappointed if Morgan Ashley turned out to be a psycho.

The crazy ones never think they're crazy, after all.

Chapter 3

He didn't have a Christmas tree.

That was the first thing Morgan noticed when she entered the warmth of Knox's log home. Modern in design, the two-story home was spacious with an open floor plan that left lots of room for entertaining and movement without being obnoxiously large.

The floors were wood, the walls a pale color that was neither gray nor beige but somewhere in between. Black leather furnishings were oversized to fit the space and Knox's large, lean frame, with some other pieces thrown in casually, as though to add texture, color, and impact. "You have a beautiful home."

"Thanks."

"No one would ever believe this is tucked back here," she said, feeling the urge to ramble. She rarely got nervous, but how could anyone not be nervous in such a situation?

"That's kind of the point." He set her suitcase off to one side and reached out to collect the smaller case from her, adding it to the top. "I like my privacy."

"And here I am intruding. I'm sorry."

"Mother Nature and accidents can't be helped."

He smiled at her as he pulled off his gloves and tossed them onto the bench of a hall tree. He shrugged out of his coat next, removed his hat, hanging them neatly to allow them to dry.

All Morgan could do was stand and watch in awe, wanting to hug the woman who'd taught him to pick up after himself.

"You want to keep that on for a while until you warm up?" he asked, turning to face her.

Morgan stared at him blankly, only then getting her first good look at her host and becoming totally tongue-tied. He was…*gorgeous*. His brown-and-blue-plaid shirt stretched across his broad shoulders and chest and hung open over a dark navy shirt and worn jeans. He looked like he'd stepped off the pages of an advertisement.

"Something wrong?"

She blinked at the question, finally remembered the one he'd asked before it, and shook her head. "I'm still cold."

His hazel eyes crinkled with amusement, like it wasn't the first time he'd struck a woman speechless in his life. But how could he not when so many attributes combined to form… *him?*

Tall, gorgeous, and picks up after himself. You really do have a sense of humor, don't you, God?

She'd always had a thing for tall guys, and Knox fit the description to a T. And his eyes? They bordered on gold, surrounded by thick, tawny lashes that were simply to die for. If that weren't enough, Knox also possessed the most amazing cheekbones above a square jawline with a couple days' worth of scruff on his cheeks and chin, giving him a woodsman-rough appearance. His hair was a little long but not *too* long, just enough to run her fingers through.

As if you'd get the chance.

The former beauty queen and pageant winner inside of her faltered. At one point in time, she would've flashed him a flirtatious smile, given him *the look*, and done her best to win him over, confident in her ability to do so.

But after nearly ten years of marriage to Rory, she quickly stepped back and lowered her gaze.

Dang, Morgan, where's the hot babe I married? Are you sneaking and eating fat-girl food?

You've still got a pretty face, Mo, but your body's shot. Sure wish I'd known kids would do that to you.

The comments... Oh, how they'd made her heart ache. But when it came down to it, words weren't enough to end a marriage over so she'd stayed. And endured. "Where's the, um, phone?" she asked when she finally managed to shake off Rory's obnoxious voice and horrible words.

Knox led the way into the living room and kitchen. He pulled a portable phone off the charging base and handed it to her. Their fingers brushed in the exchange, and she felt ridiculous when a tingle raced up her arm as a result.

After a deep breath, in which she inhaled the tantalizing aroma of Knox's cologne mingled with woodsmoke, she turned away and paced to the window to place the call, frowning when nothing happened. "Um... there's no dial tone."

"Ahhh, I'm sorry. It happens sometimes. If the phone is out already, the power will probably go next. I have a generator, but I don't like to run it all night unless I have to." He waved a hand around the room. "I'm not a candle salesman, in case you were wondering."

He didn't have *that* many candles, but there were a few scattered around the room on various surfaces, along with several battery-operated LED lights. "I understand."

She pressed the button to turn off the phone but didn't return it to him. She faced the window again, shaken from the slide into the guardrail and finding herself here with a too-handsome stranger when she'd just wanted to get to the resort to relax and de-stress.

The light from the house let her see the snow drifting down outside. It really was pretty out there. Picturesque. If only she were at the resort enjoying the view.

"You hungry?" Knox asked from the kitchen.

"I could eat." She didn't want to admit she was famished. The problem with carrying extra weight was being self-conscious about eating in front of people, wondering what they thought of her, her food choices. She'd give just about anything for her seventeen-year-old metabolism and the days when she'd thought stick-thin was "fat."

"Come take a look," Knox said.

Puck wagged his tail as she passed the couch, and she paused long enough to pet the dog's head and ears.

"You're good with him. Some people are put off by his size, but he's harmless."

Puck was an extraordinarily large Lab, but one glance into his near-black eyes made it clear he wouldn't hurt a soul. "Oh, I'm used to them. One of my best friends raises dogs, mostly Labs."

"Ah, that explains it," Knox said. "She's one of us, Puck."

"One of us?" What did that mean?

"A dog person. Not everyone is, but those who are? They're special people."

She'd always wanted a dog to raise with the kids, but Rory had told her how stupid an idea it was when she could barely keep up with the kids and house as it was.

Rory's not there anymore. You want a dog? Get a dog. Merry Christmas.

But how would she care for a puppy with a new business to get off the ground once she won the contest?

Well, at least you're thinking positive.

"So what'll it be? A sandwich? Some muffins? Fruit and cheese? You name it and I've probably got it here somewhere."

"Something simple." She tried not to sound too eager, even though her stomach was about to eat itself. "Anything is fine."

He opened the fridge and pulled out a tray of cheese and fruit and two large bottles of water. "This do?"

"Um… wow. Yeah." How many men had fruit and cheese trays in their refrigerators? "You've hosted a party recently."

"No," he said firmly. "I get some leftovers handed to me, that's all. Grab some plates and napkins, and let's sit down."

She walked to the telephone base to return the portable and noticed a corkboard with photos and notes. "You teach at the resort?" She stared at the pictures of her host, smiling with various groups ranging in age from kids to adults. Not surprisingly, most of his students were female.

"Huh? Uh, yeah."

There you go. A hot ski instructor. Practice those rusty flirting skills.

Morgan could hear Tasha's voice in her head, egging her on. "No wonder you get the leftovers." The female staff at the resort would probably use any excuse for contact with the gorgeous man who'd invited her into his home.

She found plates and napkins on the counter and carried them into the living room.

Maybe it was naive of her, but she knew for a fact the resort vetted its employees very well before hiring them. When ownership of the resort had changed hands a year or so ago, the company had hired Duncan MacGregor's security firm to perform the background checks on the employees. Of course, the *Besties* knew about the process since Emma was now married to Duncan's brother and had shared the news.

Knox's background would have been carefully researched and cleared, especially if he worked with children, and the awareness gave her a sense of peace she hadn't had before, allowing her to relax a bit more.

After spending the last twelve years of her life with Rory, she didn't understand how women could meet a man in a bar and simply go home with him. The thought terrified her.

"Anything extra or left after a conference is fair game for employees. Sometimes I luck out."

"That sounds much better than letting the food go to waste. I'm sure everyone appreciates the extra break on their grocery bill. I know I would."

Morgan set the items on the coffee table and debated the wisdom of removing her coat. She was warming up, but there was something about keeping it on that made her feel better and not so self-conscious about the extra weight Rory pointed out on every occasion.

They settled themselves and tucked into the tray. Morgan perched on the edge of a chair, but Knox seated himself on the floor and leaned back against the couch since Puck sprawled out on the cushions belly-up and looked like the king of the castle. "Do you, um, live here year-round?" she asked, trying to make conversation.

"Yeah. I travel some, but I mostly stay here. What about you? Where's home?"

"Stone River. I moved there when I was a kid and have been there ever since. It's beautiful, though nowhere near as beautiful as it is up here."

"You like the mountains?"

"Yes. I've always thought there was something comforting about them."

"Yeah? How so?" he asked, drawing her attention, not that it was difficult.

"I don't know, I guess because they're massive and protective… welcoming. That probably sounds silly."

"Not at all. Like you said, the mountains are beautiful. And on winter nights like this, it's so peaceful and quiet, everything fades away, and all is right with the world. It is like living in a snow globe. I like your description."

She stared into his hazel eyes and noted the way they crinkled at the corners. Tan as his face was, she could tell he spent a lot of time outdoors, a lot of time smiling. The lines on his face attested to both, and she liked that about him. "So long as there aren't any cracks," she added, smiling ruefully.

He chuckled at her words and leaned an arm along the couch cushions, holding the bottle of water casually from his fingers. "Sounds like your snow globe in Stone River sprang a few leaks?"

"And then some," she said, munching on a grape and thinking about how she'd smelled Big Boobs' perfume on the blanket when she'd pulled it out of the emergency bag. It had been the last straw in a very long, very bad day, but the icing on the proverbial cake was finding the empty condom wrapper in the folds.

Better than finding something else in there.

"Wanna talk about it?"

"Trust me, you don't want to hear about my problems," she said with a firm shake of her head. "And to be honest, I don't want to talk about them. All I wanted was to get away for a few days, but instead…"

"You're here with me."

She winced at the way that sounded. "I'm sorry. That was *not* the way I meant it to sound. I'm grateful, truly."

He chuckled at her embarrassment and the flush she felt rising into her cheeks. "It's fine. I know what you meant. You wanted to get to the resort and kick back, not get stuck with a stranger."

"Exactly. Although so far the company's been okay," she said, smiling at him and wondering if she'd ever get her flirting skills back.

He lifted the water bottle in a salute to her. "The feeling is mutual."

She picked up a piece of cheese and plopped it into her mouth. "So, um," she said, talking around the bite, "what does one do inside a snow globe when it snows?"

A slow, purely masculine smile curled Knox's lips up at the corners.

"You really want to know?" Knox asked softly.

She forced her gaze back to his and nodded.

He set the water bottle on the table between them and got to his feet, moving to where she sat. Morgan stared up at him, barely breathing because of the gorgeous picture he presented when he extended his hand and waited for her to place her palm in his. The moment she did, he drew her to her feet.

Chapter 4

Take it off," Knox ordered once Morgan stood before him. He knew she had to be warm by now, especially sitting as close to the fire as she'd been.

"What?"

"Your coat. Take it off. Get comfortable."

"Oh. Oh…I—"

She began to fumble with the buttons on the front, but once she unfastened them, he stepped behind her to ease it down her arms, moving to hang it by his. "Boots, too. You'll be better off without them."

He didn't know how she'd managed to walk in the spiked boots, especially on the slippery road around her van, but he didn't want her twisting an ankle and injuring herself.

When she hesitated, he gently nudged her backward into the chair once more and knelt in front of her to gently tug off the impractical footwear. "Nice socks," he said, smiling at the black socks dotted with smiling elves.

"They were part of a gag gift. I didn't— I didn't think anyone would *see* them," she said, her cheeks rosy.

He tugged her to her feet again, wanting to erase the sadness and embarrassment in her expression. She had the biggest blue eyes, the most beautiful skin. She wasn't stick-thin like so many of the women who came to the resort to see and be seen by his athlete friends, hoping a hookup would lead to more. Nor was she one of the slam-bam groupies who'd hung around after a game hoping to get picked to go back to a hotel room. Morgan's beauty was full-figured and bountiful, and her spirit radiated from within, flickering despite all she'd been through. "Shove the table out of the way and clear the floor while I get things ready."

"Shove the— Um… I beg your pardon? Ready for what? Knox, I'm not sure what you're thinking but—"

He'd turned away, having a pretty good idea of what she thought he was thinking, and grabbed the game controllers in both hands, reminding himself that he never wanted to see the inside of another courtroom again. "I'm thinking bowling, but there's also skiing— which I'm killer at— or you can choose another," he said, grinning innocently at the befuddled expression on her face.

She really thought he was going to put the moves on her—and he would have, in a different lifetime. But now his moves were strictly G-rated.

"You want us to play video games?"

"You have a better idea?"

A huff of a laugh burst out of her chest before the tension left her body in a visible rush. "No. No, that— Bowling is fine. Bowling is actually… perfect."

They shared a smile, and in short order, they had the floor cleared and the game system running. Knox preferred the Xbox over the Wii system for combat games, but when it came to sports games, the Wii system kicked some serious butt, as his ten-year-old nephew liked to say, which was why Knox kept it there and with a ready supply of entertainment. Name the gaming system and he probably had it.

"Ha! Strike!" she cried, doing a victory dance after her second consecutive win.

He took the score in stride, enjoying the show way more than he should. If nothing else, he liked it that he'd managed to change the pinched look she'd worn into one of happiness. "You're pretty good at this. I have a feeling I've been had."

"You're not the only one with nephews," she said. "My kids aren't old enough to know what they're doing, so guess who gets to play in their place?"

Knox smiled at her cheesy grin and prepared for his turn, surprised to discover he'd had more fun in the last forty-five minutes playing a video game with Morgan than he'd had on his last date with a Turkish model his agent had insisted was perfect for him.

The system timed out for a moment to load the next round, and he handed her his controller. "I'm going to get some more water. Want one?"

"No, thank you, but, um, where's the bathroom?"

"Down the hall, first door on the left." He went to the fridge, vaguely aware of Puck following. The dog demanded food with a nose-nudge of his stainless steel bowl, and after feeding Puck and getting the canine more water, Knox washed his hands and grabbed a glass for tap water.

Morgan didn't linger in the bathroom and returned to the living room while he let Puck outside. On a cold night like this, the dog didn't take long and was soon barking at the door to be let back in.

Knox returned to the living room, water in hand, only to discover Morgan grinning from ear to ear, in the process of changing the appearance of his Wii Mii, the self-made miniature every player created and used to play the games. "Hey!"

Morgan laughed and dodged his grab for the controller. "I'm tweaking it," she said, putting some distance between them.

He quickly set the water aside and stalked her with lazy steps. "You aren't allowed to tweak when you won't create one for yourself," he told her, reminding her of the fact she'd used his sister's Mii instead of making her own. He'd no sooner said the words than he spied the controller she'd used sitting atop the game console. "Ahh. Now we can both 'tweak.'"

"No. No, don't do that." She rounded the couch and moved closer to him. "Knox? Here. Take it back."

"Nope." He was already backing out of the system to the point where he could make a new miniature Mii.

"Knox, I'm sorry. I shouldn't have— Please, don't."

Something in her tone cut through the fun he was having and put an instant stop to it. He frowned at her expression, the unease and— "Hey... What's wrong?"

She shook her head, her blond hair falling forward to cover her face until he reached out and gently nudged it up. Her skin really was as soft as it looked.

"I don't like pictures o-or images of me. That's all." She smiled, but it was a horrible attempt. "It's a weird pet peeve."

It was. Especially when she was beautiful. "Why?"

She shrugged and avoided eye contact.

"Don't give me that. We were having fun. Goofing around. How can making a cartoon image change that?"

"Can we just go back to bowling?"

"No." He nudged her chin up another notch and bent his knees until he managed to catch her gaze with his. "Tell me."

"You wouldn't understand."

"Try me."

"It's no big deal. Really. I just...used to be different."

It was a big deal if she couldn't even make a game character. "Different how?"

She looked away from him and shook her head. "Please, just forget I mentioned it?"

"Don't give me that, darlin'. Different how?"

"Gah, fine. I used to be a beauty queen and pageant winner. I was also runner-up for Miss Georgia and did some modeling."

"Those are some great accomplishments." But the way she'd said it made it seem as though she was embarrassed.

"Not really. Not now."

"What do you mean?"

"Are you really going to make me spell it out?" she asked. "I mean, what does it matter now? Especially when I don't look like that anymore."

"Is that what your ex said to you?" He could tell his words hit home by the way she flinched.

"Rory liked *that* me," she whispered, the words low, husky. "Not this one. Please. Please just forget it. I'm sorry. I've ruined everything."

The thought of a man criticizing her about her beauty based on her size ticked him off. Yes, she was rounded and lush. Maybe not modern day's typical definition of thin, but—

"C-can we just go back to the game? We're in the snow globe. It doesn't matter now."

It mattered to him. Whatever her jerk of an ex had said to her had turned a beautiful, confident woman into someone who no longer saw herself as worthy of love or attention. He might not have known her long, but he'd glimpsed her humor, her intelligence. Her gentleness with Puck. Dogs read people way better than humans, and Puck liked their guest. That said something to him.

But how could he prove to Morgan that she possessed all those qualities?

Unbidden, he ran his knuckles over her cheek, amazed at the silky texture. Warnings sounded in his head. Debates took place. But all he could think of was her smiles during the game and how beautiful and happy she'd looked when she'd performed her victory dances.

"Knox?"

"You still hung up on your ex?"

"No," she stated in no uncertain terms. "This sounds awful, but I'm so happy to be free of him."

"You're sure about that?"

"Yes. I can forgive him—somehow—eventually, but I will never trust or forget how he betrayed me and our marriage vows."

"Good. Because he obviously doesn't deserve you." He brushed his thumb across her lips.

"What? Why are you looking at me that way?"

"You don't seem crazy."

She laughed, a frown pulling her eyebrows together. "Why do you keep saying that?"

"So many questions. Maybe I'll tell you sometime," he said.

"Knox…?"

He shook off the thoughts of what he'd like to do and focused instead on getting the fun and laughter back. "What would you say if I told you I've been taking it easy on you?"

"What? No way! That's a lie. I won fair and square!"

"Well, there's only one way to find out, isn't there?"

Chapter 5

This had to be a dream. Right? She'd hit the guardrail. Wrecked. Hit her head or something? No way could this be real.

Because if it was real...

She couldn't remember ever having this much fun with Rory. In high school, fun had consisted of Rory talking about football, attending games, and—truthfully—making out after the games because it seemed like the thing to do. Dating had consisted of hanging with Rory's friends and getting made fun of because her grades had suffered because he'd demanded so much of her time and attention when she wasn't on the pageant circuit.

She'd found it...sweet at the time. Thought it meant Rory felt the same way for her as she did for him. But she knew now Rory had considered her arm candy and his "prize" for being the football star. Marriage, college, kids... Once the kids came first and she wasn't as slim and put together as before, Rory's interest had dimmed, and the comments had gotten worse.

Morgan shook her head at her thoughts and focused on winning the game. She and Knox were tied for the lead, and while maybe —*maybe*—he had cut her some slack on previous games, she held her own with this one. All the way up to— "Noooo!"

"Ah! I win!" Knox cried, flashing a pleased grin in her direction.

She sank back amongst the cushions and watched as Knox stood and proceeded to do his own victory dance. "Yeah, yeah. Gloating isn't attractive, you know." Though with his looks, he could gloat all he wanted and never be *un*attractive.

"What's next? Play this one again or are you ready for some hockey?"

Oh, no. Knox had already proclaimed his proficiency at hockey, and no way was she going to walk into that spider's web. "How about"—she slid her hand under the cushion next to her, where she'd hidden the game she'd found during Knox's turn in the down-stairs bathroom— "this one?"

She held it up with a challenging grin.

"Oh. Game on. I get Mario."

"Fine. Princess Peach is my kind of girl, anyway."

He chuckled, and she liked the sound of his amusement. The low, masculine sound filled her with warmth and even gave her a sense of safety. She knew—deep down—that Knox was just a nice guy. And accident or no accident—this was a great way to have her faith in the male sex restored.

"Come on, slow poke, pick your Peach and let's get to racing."

Morgan leaned forward once more and went through the steps to choose her character. "I should probably warn you," she murmured, "I may drive a minivan now, but once upon a time, I dreamed of becoming a Nascar driver."

THE NEXT MORNING, Knox stared at his guest from across the kitchen table. How could anyone not think she was beautiful?

They'd stayed up into the early hours of the morning playing video games and talking. They had discussed everything from favorite foods and movies to best childhood memories, steering clear of the topic of her ex husband and why he'd mentioned her not appearing crazy on more than one occasion.

All said and done, it was the most innocent, completely

platonic *fun* he could ever remember having with a woman since… well, forever. And it would go down in memory as one of the best nights he'd ever spent with a member of the opposite sex.

He had questions he wanted to ask, things he wanted to say, but considering the nature of their "relationship," he forced himself to remain quiet.

"It's still snowing," she murmured.

He followed her gaze and took in the thick wall of blowing snow outside. "Not supposed to stop until tomorrow evening. Are you okay with staying here with me and the generator, or do you want me to try to get you to the resort?" Her gaze met his, and he saw the wheels turning behind her eyes.

"Um… I don't mind the candles and generator if you— That is… I don't want to impose or make you try to navigate the mountain in dangerous conditions. I don't *have* to be there until Thursday, but I'm not sure if—"

"I want you to stay," he heard himself say. Morgan had proven herself to be as sweet and normal as any woman would be post-divorce from a jerk of a cheating husband, unlike his previous experience, in which he'd woken up the morning after handcuffed to the bed by his "biggest fan" like some sick and twisted Stephen King character.

"Really? Knox, be honest. I don't want to intrude."

"I want you to stay," he repeated. "If you want to, that is. The guest room is yours," he said, just in case there was any question as to how things would go.

"I'd like that," she said with a shy smile.

He placed his elbows on the table and leaned his chin against his fists. "Even though I can't give you the facial you complained to God about missing?"

Morgan's eyes sparkled even as her face flushed with her embarrassment.

"Gah, I was having a moment. I hope you don't think too badly of me for that rant. Trust me, it came at the end of a *really* bad day."

"I gathered that. So since we have hours to kill, want to help me put up a tree?"

"A Christmas tree?"

"I haven't taken the time, but with my family coming in to visit…. You interested?" It dawned on him in a terrifying moment that he liked her. A lot. So what was wrong with her? Because something had to be wrong, right? Her showing up like she had, them getting along… The proverbial shoe had to drop sometime.

Morgan was smart. Funny. Beautiful. And when she left here, he wanted her to leave with the awareness and memories of how something bad had turned into something amazing.

"I'd love that."

"Finish up. I'll go get you some warmer clothes." He stood and moved across the floor, surprising himself and apparently her when he paused long enough to bend low and brush a kiss against her forehead as he passed by.

He kept waiting for the novelty to wear off and for her to at least try to seduce him like so many others before. There were a lot of single women in the world today, but *good* women were hard to come by—at least in his circles.

Could she be the real deal?

Without a word about the forehead kiss, he forced himself to step away and walked to the mudroom closet to search out a snowsuit for her, something else he kept on hand for when his family visited so they wouldn't have to pack so much through the airports.

His mother and sister inevitably left additional items behind, adding to the collection of more feminine-looking gear, and he chose those, knowing from Morgan's taste in clothes she would prefer them.

Knox carried an assortment with him back to the living room and found she'd gathered the dishes and stood at the sink, washing them. "You should have left them," he said, dumping the snow gear and moving toward her. "I would've done them later."

"It's, uh… I want to pitch in."

The kiss had made her nervous. Him, too, truth be told. A kiss on the forehead was a kiss, after all, but it wasn't a *kiss*.

He placed his hands on her shoulders and gently squeezed, feeling strangely domestic and settled and drawn to the woman who'd literally crashed into his life. If his mother could see him like this, she'd be over the moon.

"Done. Quick and easy." She released the water and dried her hands before turning to face him, avoiding his gaze when the move required he release her.

He didn't want to make her uncomfortable and he certainly didn't want her to feel any pressure. It had just seemed like the natural thing to do as he'd walked by so he'd done it. "Then let's go find that tree and get to decorating, shall we?"

While she dressed in a snowsuit, he found a chain saw, and together they headed out with Puck to search for a tree. The snow floated down in big, fat flakes, and he had to stop a few times to wait on Morgan because she'd paused to lift her face to the sky, smiling when the snowflakes hit her nose and lips.

She looked so beautiful standing there. An ache formed in his chest, and he realized he was going to miss her when the snow stopped and the road cleared for her to make it the rest of the way up the mountain. He couldn't see her during her stay at the resort. Not without his employees noticing and inquiring why the boss was allowed to break the rules. So was it really going to end here? Was he going to allow it to?

Awful serious thoughts for a woman you've only just met.

They resumed their trek through the woods and found a seven-footer Morgan declared perfectly proportioned. He set to work and downed the tree, dragging it back to the house while watching Morgan toss sticks for Puck to fetch along the way. The dog was falling for her, too, if his big, dopey dog grin was anything by which to judge.

He set the tree in a stand and retrieved ornaments from storage with Morgan's help. The generator was running, so they plugged the lights in to test them before they added them to the limbs but unplugged them to save power. The only exception to this was Morgan's phone, which she charged and used to play Christmas carols.

"These ornaments are gorgeous."

Knox hung a snowman high on a limb. "I can't take credit. One year my mother and sister visited over the holidays and purchased everything you see so I'd have it for when they were here. Same with the snowsuit you wore, in case you wondered," he added, figuring most women wouldn't like the thought of wearing an ex's left-behinds.

Morgan didn't say anything but he thought he saw a small smile flash over her lips.

"Are you close to your family?" She frowned in concentration as she stacked several of the oddly shaped boxes atop one another.

"Yeah. They're coming in for the holidays. Maybe you'll meet them while you're here."

The boxes fell with a crash, and her eyes flared wide at his words. He'd said too much and reminded himself that she'd just gotten out of a lousy relationship not that long ago.

Besides, he might be breaking the rules now, but he knew the drill. Once the snow ended, if he was serious about getting to know her better, there were certain steps he had to follow, just to be safe. Steps now necessary because he refused to risk repeating the mistake of falling for someone wanting to take advantage of him for his name and money and what he might be able to do for them.

Now, after a few short hours, he was talking about her meeting his family?

Who was the crazy one here?

Chapter 6

Morgan stacked and restocked the oddly shaped ornament boxes, trying hard not to think about Knox's words or the impact they'd had on her.

Meet his family? That implied… well, serious things. Didn't it?

But they were strangers. Friends, now, yes, but relative strangers who'd hit it off and— Meet his *family?*

"You going to play with those all night?" Knox asked, still wrapping the lights around the tree limbs.

"The lights aren't fun to do. And I'm trying to get the boxes to stay upright."

"Angle them more," he said from his position behind the tree.

"Like this?" She adjusted the boxes, but they still tipped and fell. Just like her cake design would do because it was top-heavy. She had to either find a way of balancing them better or use her Plan B design, which was okay but nothing competition-worthy.

She gathered the boxes and tried again, liking the fact that Knox continued to work on the lights and didn't immediately come to take over the way Rory would have done, scoffing at her attempts to do it herself.

Morgan stacked them again, almost succeeding. But one of the boxes wouldn't hold to form and shifted. She would have dowel rods securing the layers of her cakes, but they had to remain invisible or be incorporated into the design to look natural. How could she make it work?

Growing frustrated, she lifted her hand, about to purposely knock the stack over when Knox caught her fingers with his and carried them to his lips.

"Don't tell me you're giving up," Knox said.

"That side is too, um… unstable."

"So put another one in there," he countered.

She shook her head. "No. Then it's too crowded. I want it here."

Knox released her now-tingling fingers and braced his hand on the table to study the stack. "Widen the base to counter the expanse. They should stack and stay in place."

She did. And he was right. The boxes stayed put without a wobble. Not only that, the adjustment gave her plenty of room to add another dowel rod, which would help better secure the heavier side. Could it really have been such a simple fix? How could she have missed that all this time?

She pictured her cake design in her head instead of the boxes in front of her. Her hands trembled a bit, but she sketched imaginary dowel rods here and there at various angles. It worked. It totally worked!

She flew out of her chair and flung herself against Knox's chest, hugging him tight. His arms wrapped around her and lifted her off her feet, until her mouth was level with his.

"You like playing with boxes that much?"

She laughed and kissed him on the cheek in her happiness. "It's the simple things. Come on. Let's decorate this tree."

Morgan didn't remember tree decorating ever being so much fun. Knox sang along with the Christmas carols, and every now and again, they'd stop decorating the tree to slow dance. Face-to-face, body-to-body. They'd move for a bit in tune to the song and then slowly separate when it was over to begin decorating again.

Now, she stepped back and declared the tree perfect.

Knox seconded her statement and escorted her to the couch beside two mugs of hot cocoa he'd retrieved sometime when she wasn't looking because she'd been fussing to get things just right.

Somehow between sips and talking and getting comfortable amid the cushions, she wound up snuggled with her back against his side, the heat of his body warming her as much as the fire in front of them.

This was perfect. He was perfect. It was almost the best Christmas ever.

Chapter 7

Morgan liked life in their snow globe. It was quiet and peaceful and just what she needed before the Cake-Off Competition began. *I'm sorry I yelled at you, God. This is perfect,* she thought as she held on to Knox's waist while he guided the snowmobile around his log home and into the woods nearby.

Knox had left Puck at the house, afraid the dog might wander off after an animal or that his paws would sustain frostbite from exposure if he were out too long.

Morgan pressed her face into Knox's back as they sped along the snow, knowing Emma would approve of Knox's care of Puck and how Knox had put his animal's safety above the dog's whining desire to come with them. Knox had petted the dog's massive head and promised a walk later as a reward.

They rounded the top of an incline, and Knox cut the engine. It took her a moment to realize why, but when she turned her head, she gasped at the sight spread out below them. The mountain valley wore a blanket of pure, pristine white with a gorgeous little red church in the distance, surrounded by towering evergreens standing guard. "Oh. Oh, it's *beautiful.*"

"My grandparents were married in that church," Knox said. "Long, long time ago."

The peace and serenity of the location overwhelmed her, and she lifted her face to the sky and closed her eyes, letting the snow land on her cheeks, nose, and lips.

"You like it here."

She opened her eyes and focused on Knox. "I wish I'd brought my phone so I could take pictures. Capture the quiet and simplicity. I *needed* this," she told him. "I needed to be reminded of what's important and… that there are gentlemen left in the world who value their families and aren't jerks to all women just because they can be," she added softly. "Thank you for bringing me here. For showing me this and… sharing it with me."

He twisted a bit more on the seat and placed his hand behind her, leaning into her. Morgan didn't hesitate but met his kiss with her own, unable to deny Knox anything when he'd given her so much in such a short amount of time.

Their cold noses warmed against each other's cheeks as they kissed in the snowfall until Knox pulled away, nuzzling his lips against hers.

"Ready to keep going?"

Her lips tingled and her body temp had shot up a good twenty degrees at his touch. "I can't wait to see more."

Knox showed her his favorite spots, the last being the resort atop the mountain, which she couldn't make out due to the blowing snow. "I thought you said it was twelve miles away?"

"It is by road. By snowmobile, it's a lot closer, though a hard, uphill ride. But on a clear day, you can see it from here."

Even though she couldn't see it, the thought of the resort and the competition left her feeling a bit ill and uneasy. If she screwed up, if she failed… The thought nearly sent her into a panic attack.

Please, let me win. I need to win.

"Hey, you okay?"

She battled the rush of anxiety. *Focus.* "Yeah, just getting cold."

"Ready to head back to our snow globe?"

And watch another movie or play video games with him? Forget that her whole world depended on the competition? "Yes. But will you go slow? I want to savor the peacefulness here." Because it was the calm before the storm. Before everything exploded and her life got very real, very fast.

"I can bring you out again tomorrow."

Would she still be here tomorrow? "Yeah, sure. Maybe." Reality was closing in. And even though she'd only met Knox last night...

How was it possible for her to feel this way? Torn between this snow globe fantasy they had created and the absoluteness of her life?

Let's see, on the one hand, you have pressure, chaos, and stress of single parenthood, divorce, and starting over—and on the other hand, you have a gorgeous hunk who seems to like you for you and has the ability to make you forget your own name.

But it was more than that. Wasn't it?

She still pondered the question when they arrived back at Knox's home. The moment Knox opened the door, Puck came bounding outside, and they spent some time playing with the rambunctious dog to ease their guilt over leaving him behind. Puck loved the snow and would dive headfirst into the drifts, rising up and looking like a bearded Santa wearing a white hat.

Finally remembering her phone, she walked inside long enough to grab it to take a few photos of the dog and of Knox. Knox looked uncomfortable at first, which she found strange, seeing as how she was the one with the issues, but then he agreed—so long as they took a photo together.

Her body image was still a hot button with her, but she chose to fixate on the moment and not her insecurities. Besides, she'd be lying if she said she wouldn't like to have a picture of them to keep as a memento of their wonderful time together.

They took pictures with her standing in front of Knox, smiling and laughing as they tried to get a good shot. After that, they knelt in the snow and posed with Puck before she insisted on taking a couple of Knox and Puck alone.

The snowfall had started to dwindle by the time they entered the house. The first thing she noticed was that the electricity had come back on. And even though she knew she ought to be pleased, she'd liked the candlelight meals and couch snuggling with Knox.

The electricity was the first step back to reality, and she wasn't sure she was ready.

"Hey, are you sure you're okay?"

She turned to find Knox watching her, his expression concerned. "Fine. Just… feeling the stress, knowing the snow globe is about to crack," she said dryly. "I have to leave soon. Tomorrow at the latest."

He moved toward her and tugged her against his chest. Neither of them spoke for a long while. They held each other, and Morgan wondered if Knox was relieved by her statement or feeling the same sense of dread churning in her stomach.

Their time together was never meant to be more than short-term and friendly, two people sharing space during the long, cold nights of the storm. But somewhere along the way, she'd connected with Knox because he'd given her back a piece of herself she'd lost over the last ten years of marriage.

She inhaled and closed her eyes at the delicious smell of his cologne mingled with the fresh air and woodsmoke from the hearth. "You know how to show a girl a good time, you know that?"

Knox shifted and nudged her face upward.

"It's not over yet."

Knox left Morgan to sleep in the spare bedroom the following morning and headed out into the bright sunshine and blinding snowscape on foot to check on the road conditions. He heard the road crew before he saw them and rounded the curve shielding his home from passersby in time to see them removing the guardrail to free Morgan's van.

One of the crewmen spotted him and lifted his hand in greeting. "Looks like you got another one, Eagle-eye."

Knox nodded, recognizing the man's voice even though he was too far away and the man too bundled up against the cold to be recognizable. George Plunket was a hockey fan. "That I did. Can we get it out before the cops get here? I don't want the owner getting a ticket."

George chuckled. "That pretty?"

Knox grinned, closing the distance between them. "A guest at the resort. Tickets are bad for business."

"Uh-huh," the man said, motioning for more of his men to come and aid in the process of getting the van unstuck, an easy task once the guardrail was out of the way.

While the crew replaced the guardrail, Knox shook George's

hand and thanked him and the crew for their help. "Once you get to the top, stop in to warm up. Lunch is on me." A round of thanks and back claps left Knox smiling. "No problem. Just showing my appreciation for your hard work on days like this."

He called Puck to his side and said good-bye to the crew, making his way back to the house. Knox carried some more wood in on the way, having gone through most of the supply last night keeping the room warm enough for Morgan while he grilled steaks on the stove and made them dinner.

"Where were you?" Morgan asked from behind him.

He took in her long sweater, dark jeans, and low-heeled boots that looked a little more practical than the ones she'd worn the first night, liking the fact that while she wore a little bling, she dressed modestly compared to most of the women who approached him. "Checking on the roads. The crews are out, and your van is free. I didn't think to grab your keys, but the crew slid it into the end of my driveway."

"Oh, wow. Thank you."

"You're welcome. It will take them a while to get to the top of the mountain. Have you eaten?"

"No. And I can't. I'm too nervous," she said, moving to where he stood.

"Why?"

She smoothed her hand over his face and stared into his eyes.

"Because my future awaits me at the resort."

Knox frowned down at her, confused by her words and more than a little uneasy. "What do you mean?"

She flashed him a proud grin. "I'm one of the five contestants in the Cake-Off Competition that's taking place there. Have you heard about it?"

"Yeah. I have." He turned away from her and frowned, anger fueling his blood. "I didn't know you were part of the competition. It's a big deal."

And a part of him couldn't help but wonder if she knew more about him than she pretended to. Had he been used again? Did she know who he was? Want him to pull strings to make sure she won?

Was she going to try to use their snow globe relationship to gain favor?

"I know, right? Well," she drawled sweetly, moving around him to snuggle close, a soft smile on her lips, "I'm one of five who made the cut. *Me.* Out of I don't know how many entries. Can you believe it? This means everything to me. I've worked so hard on my designs. My family thinks I'm crazy. My ex… He can't *wait* to see me fail. But I'm going to prove him wrong. I'm going to do this," she said with a confident smile.

"Why haven't you mentioned this competition before?"

"Because I'm so stressed about it. It's the last thing I wanted to think about, you know? Especially after the van got stuck. I thought it was another sign I wasn't meant to be there, but I'm glad I wound up here with you." She smoothed her hand over his head and nape. "Does it matter that I didn't tell you?"

He gazed into her eyes and realized how screwed up his thinking had become. For the first time in a long time, he realized there were still people—women—in this world who were smart and beautiful and giving, and they didn't want anything from anyone other than to be treated with respect and kindness. Morgan was one of those people. "For a second there, I thought you wanted me to help you win somehow, but I have nothing to do with the contest."

She stepped back, looking insulted. "I would never ask you to do that. If I win, it will be because my designs are the best, not because you— Why would you think that?"

The hurt she felt reflected in her eyes, her expression. Her ex-husband had treated her badly, and the time she'd spent here had bolstered her confidence, something Knox had been more than happy to do. But with his accusation, he'd clearly destroyed something precious. "Someone did that to me once, set me up to make it look like I had taken advantage of them instead of the other way around, which it was. It took a long time and a lot of legal bills to get it straightened out."

Her expression softened. "I'm sorry that happened to you. Sounds like we've both been burned by people we trusted."

He smoothed his hands over her hair and used his hold to bring her close. "I'm sorry I thought that of you."

"Knox… I swear to you, I'm not that person. I don't expect you to put in a good word for me or to pull strings. But I wouldn't mind a kiss for luck, especially since leaving our snow globe won't be easy. Being here with you, talking and watching movies, playing video games… I haven't had that much fun in *years*. I won't ever forget how you took me in and… You've helped me so much. In ways you can't imagine."

"I had fun, too." It was true. Crazy as it sounded, he shared more affection for Morgan than he did for women he'd considered girlfriends in his past. There was something about her. Special and earnest. She was a woman to be treasured.

He lowered his head, and she rose onto her toes, their lips meeting in a slow, sweet kiss. Until she pulled away with a sad smile, making it clear their snow globe had finally sprung a leak.

Chapter 9

Morgan arrived at the resort an hour later and checked into her room, her heart heavy with regret. She hated that something so wonderful had to come to an end, but she'd kissed Knox knowing nothing would come of it. Still, the time she had spent in his company had restored something within her and given her back some of the confidence she'd lost due to Rory's emotional and verbal abuse.

She leaned against the shower wall and closed her eyes, imagining how it had felt earlier when Knox had held her. She'd never kissed a man so accepting of her body, as though he didn't see her flaws at all. Like they didn't matter to him and she was enough as she was. Men tended to pick and choose when it came to acceptance. And women—herself included—tried too hard to please them. Why was the world so mixed up?

Knox's kindness and tenderness, his interest in her as a person had freed her from her doubts and insecurities. Given her the confidence and awareness she needed to let go and move forward. She could do this. Win the competition.

It's time to focus, she told herself. *Get your head where it's supposed to be.*

But maybe afterward... She would see Knox again?

An hour later, she was dressed and ready, her hair dried and styled to one side in a long braid to keep it out of her way as she entered the elevator and followed the map she'd been given to the stage where the Cake-Off would take place.

She'd brought her own cake pans and utensils just in case, but the show insisted on using sponsor products provided to them. Still, she wanted to run through her station and make sure everything was there before she began to work so that she wouldn't find herself lacking an item she needed.

"Ah, the wildcard has arrived," a female voice stated when Morgan entered the staging area.

Morgan searched until she spotted the woman dressed in a chef's smock replete with a tall white hat. Morgan disliked the woman instantly. She wore a superior sneer on her narrow, unmade face and looked as pleasant and friendly as a feral ferret.

Besides, like her granny always said— *Don't ever trust a skinny baker.*

Pulling out her practiced smile from her pageant days, Morgan stepped forward and held out her hand, knowing the quickest way to combat women like the one in front of her was to blast them with compliments. "Andrea Costina, right? *The* youngest up-and-coming cake designer from the West Coast?"

Andrea's handshake resembled a lump of too-dry bread dough. The woman really needed to invest in some hand lotion.

"That's me," Andrea said, visibly taken aback by Morgan's friendliness.

The door behind them opened again, and seconds later, a man entered, also wearing a chef's smock. Morgan thought of the suffocating, too-tight-in-the-boobs smock she'd brought with her and frowned. She preferred to wear aprons over her clothes, but apparently that was a no-no.

More and more people arrived, including some of the production crew who'd left for lunch. After introducing herself, she puttered around her chosen station trying to figure out what some of the fancier things were, as well as what they were used for. She baked cakes out of her kitchen. Kept her designs simple and focused on beauty and the fine details, not… all the gizmos here.

Lights clicked on. Not regular lights but *camera* lights. The production team tested their equipment. She watched the process, and it suddenly hit home that she was going to be doing this not only in front of the audience at the resort but also the thousands—millions?—of people viewing on TV.

Panic stole over her, taking her breath and leaving her motionless, unable to do anything but gawk as the other contestants arrived. A low laugh huffed out of her chest as she saw them. She stood on stage in a tiny, teeming sea of white smocks. Two men, two women, all of whom looked at her as if she were the biggest joke on the planet.

Maybe she was. She'd dressed for the camera in slimming black, with her hair and makeup perfect, even though it wasn't a day of shooting.

While they grew chummy and showed her their backs, Morgan reconsidered Knox's offer. Right now, she'd much rather be there in their snow globe with him than here.

Spit and fire and sweet kiss-my-sass, that's what southern girls are made of, she reminded herself, quoting her granny again.

Let them wear their smocks. Paula Dean didn't need no stinking smock, and neither did she.

"Ms. Ashley?"

Morgan turned and startled when she found herself facing a camera lens.

"We'd like to interview each contestant throughout the process, and we'd like to begin with you," the show's host said.

"I see. Um, sure. Okay." *Shoulders back, head tall. Think thin.*

"Great. So tell us— How does it feel to be the only non-professional contestant in this year's Cake-Off Competition? Do you feel like you have a chance at winning the prize?"

Ah, crud. "Well, it feels like a challenge," she said, struggling to keep her smile in place. "But I'm *always* up for a challenge."

MORGAN WAS EXHAUSTED by the time she stepped onto the elevator that would take her to her room. The on-camera interview had unnerved her, and it seemed as though the interviewer had been watching her and had picked up on her insecurities, because he'd kept jabbing at them with his barbed questions.

She leaned against the elevator wall and waited for the doors to close. Just as they were about to, a man stuck his hand between them and quickly jumped on. Great, now she'd— "Knox?"

He pressed the button for the doors to close and inserted a key, pressing several more. Suddenly the elevator wasn't going up, and the arrow changed direction. "What are you doing?"

"Stealing you."

"Oh, o-okay." That was all she managed to say before she lowered her head to his chest and fought off the sting of tears.

"Hey." He wrapped his arms around her and squeezed. "Hey, what's wrong?"

"I don't know if I can do this," she whispered. "They're all so… so… They're *not* nice."

He kissed her cheek, his chuckle warming her ear.

"Don't *laugh!*"

"I'm not, sweetheart."

"I heard you," she said in a low voice, basking in the scent of him. He smelled so good. Like spices and fresh mountain air.

"So you wouldn't mind getting out of here for a while?"

"Snow globe?" she asked hopefully.

"Whatever you want."

Chapter 10

Knox walked the interior of the resort the next morning, nodding and smiling at employees and regular guests and checking to make sure there weren't any complaints.

"The hermit returns," Don, his daytime manager said, greeting Knox. "I heard you were in last night."

"Only briefly. And watch it. The hermit is your boss," Knox reminded the man. "How'd you do with the snow?"

"Party central. Everyone had a good time, I think. Only had a few hardcore Internet junkies going through withdrawal because of business, but we fired up the karaoke and drinks and they were fine."

"Any other issues?"

"Your agent called a few times before the phones went down."

"Besides him," Knox grumbled. He didn't want to do whatever it was the man wanted, considering it was so close to the holidays. His family had made plans to spend Christmas at the resort, and he wasn't about to go jetting off to do a commercial just because someone in some advertising group didn't believe in Christmas. He did. And he planned to celebrate with his loved ones.

And Morgan?

"The cake competition people have had a few fits. They're set up in the arena," Don said, referring to the stage area where entertainment performed. "Production has started, but only two of the judges have arrived, so the manager is freaking out. The flights were delayed or cancelled, but with the phones out, they can't get status reports."

Knox welcomed the distraction from his thoughts. "Did they forget they were filming on top of a mountain in winter? Snow happens," Knox muttered with a disgusted shake of his head. "Keep me posted."

"Will do. You'll be in your office?"

"For a while, but don't disturb me unless it's an emergency. I want to get some work done so I can watch some of the taping later." Knox walked toward the private offices, Puck at his side. He didn't want to distract Morgan from the competition, but he'd be lying if he said he didn't want to see her in action.

He spent the next hour or so catching up on work, continuously distracted by thoughts of Morgan and the time they'd spent together last night. He'd driven her down the mountain, made dinner and listened to her talk about her day, and reluctantly returned her to the resort so she could get some much-needed rest.

Knox got up and paced to the window. Morgan hadn't asked him for help with the competition, even after the bad day she'd had yesterday with the elite chefs looking down their noses at the mother of two who baked from her kitchen. The fact that she hadn't asked for help reinforced his feelings for her, making him actually *want* to throw his weight around and make sure she stayed in the running, for a while at least.

He knew nothing about cakes, nothing about the process, but Morgan had taken enough blows emotionally. She didn't need another. But how could she compete with professionals? Maybe he *should* talk to the production manager?

He shook his head at himself, drawing a lazy head-lift from Puck, who lay curled atop the leather love seat in the corner of the room. "What do you think, Puck? Crazy, right? Is she really as good of a woman as she seems?"

Puck let out a rare whine, drawing Knox's attention. He walked over to the dog and sat down, petting Puck's head and ears. "She got to you, too, didn't she? Not everyone makes homemade dog treats." But Morgan had, just for Puck.

Puck licked his chops and whined again, like he'd understood the question and agreed.

Knox inhaled and tried to get a grip on his rioting emotions. Crazy was falling in love with a woman over a couple of days. Nobody did that. But he'd never felt such a connection before. "You're going to have to stay here, bud. One bark and you'd get us both kicked out."

The Lab put his head down with a grunt.

Knox gave Puck a final pat and moved toward the door, wondering what his hockey buddies would think of his sudden interest in cake decorating.

It took him a while to get to the taping area. First he ran into guests who recognized him and wanted to chat or score an autograph, then two employees asking about various maintenance and ski issues.

Finally he stepped into the arena, but to his embarrassment, his arrival drew applause and too much attention from everyone there, including Morgan, who looked confused.

"I see our illustrious host has arrived," the production manager said, clapping loudly and grinning from ear to ear. The man moved close and held out his hand, shaking Knox's with enthusiasm. "So good to see you again. I was just about to send someone to your office."

"Is there a problem?" Knox glanced at Morgan and made eye contact, then had to force himself to look away. Man, she looked beautiful.

"Yes, there is, I'm afraid," Barry Winchester said. "I'm short a judge, and considering you are the owner of the resort, not to mention your name recognition among sports fans, we want you to be our fill-in until our third judge manages to escape Europe and make her way here."

They wanted him to be a judge? For the competition? "Uh…"

"Come, Mr. Stewart. It's a piece of cake," the man said, laughing at his pun. "This part of the competition is easy and focuses on flavor and texture, originality of recipes. All you have to do is follow your taste buds and decide which cakes you like the best."

He liked cake as well as everyone else, but he couldn't be a judge. Not when Morgan was a contestant. "I'm sorry, but I can't."

"I don't understand," the man said. "Your agent cleared it already. He assured us you would be happy to do it."

Of course, Marty would clear the event because Marty didn't know what had happened in the last few days. Didn't know about Morgan. "Barry, can I talk to you? Privately?"

The man glanced at his watch. "We're already behind schedule. Can't it wait?"

"I'm afraid not." He didn't look at Morgan as he passed by her, following Barry across the floor to a more secluded area.

"What's going on?" Barry asked, staring up at Knox from behind his pointy, black-rimmed hipster glasses.

"I can't be a judge," Knox said simply. "I haven't talked to Marty, and I'm sorry he made the arrangements and agreed to this, but I have to decline."

"I don't understand the problem. Why can't you?"

Knox turned his back to the stage, lowering his voice even more. "Because I have a… personal connection to one of the finalists."

Barry blinked twice behind the thick lenses and gaped at Knox in horror. "Please, tell me you're joking."

"I know this puts a kink in your plans, but to keep things fair, I'm staying out of it."

Barry's mouth dropped open, and the shorter man turned and threw his clipboard, yanking the headset off of his ears and tossing it aside as well. "I think it's a bit late for that."

"Hey, calm down," Knox said, aware they were being watched. "I'll find you another judge. There's always a celebrity of some sort here. I'm sure I can talk one of them into doing it."

"You have no idea what you've done, do you? You have ruined this competition. Set us back even more!"

"I'll find you a judge," Knox told the man.

"I suppose you'll find us a new contestant, too?" Barry glared at Knox and then sidestepped to stare up at the stage. "Which one of you is sleeping with Mr. Stewart?"

Knox grabbed Barry's arm, but he pulled away.

"The Cake-Off Competition rules state *specifically* that no one related to or having an association with a production member of the Cake-off Competition *or* the Holly Wood Resort was allowed to enter the competition. They most certainly would not have been chosen as a finalist. Now, Mr. Stewart has just admitted to a personal relationship with one of you to explain his inability to judge," Barry said. "Which one of you is it?"

Knox looked at Morgan, his heart in his throat at what he'd done, and noticed that she'd paled to match the color of the ruffled white apron she wore.

"Its... me," Morgan whispered, the words barely audible. "But we're not— I mean, we haven't—"

"Ms. Ashley, you are hereby disqualified from the Cake-Off Competition. *Leave the stage.*"

Chapter 11

Morgan raced for the elevator, vaguely hearing her name being called by Emma and Jolie. She'd been so surprised when she'd arrived for the taping of the show and found her friends there, grinning from ear to ear. Tasha wasn't able to leave her veterinary practice, but Jolie had managed to find help to cover things at Cuppa Jo's and had driven Emma from Stone River to the resort so they could cheer her on.

But now?

"Mo, wait!" Emma said.

She pressed the button to close the elevator doors, but in a sick twist of déjà vu, a hand managed to grab the door at the last second and keep it from closing. In seconds, Emma and Jolie were on the elevator with her, and Morgan covered her face with her apron.

"Oh, Morgan. I'm so sorry," Emma said, wrapping her arms around her.

"Me, too."

Morgan felt Jolie joining in on the hug, and even though *Bestie* hugs normally made her feel better, this time it made her feel worse. "Disqualified," she whispered, barely able to get the word out.

"It will be okay. It will all be okay," Emma said.

Morgan shook her head. No. No, it wouldn't. She had no money. She'd burned through her savings keeping up with the bills in the last couple of months, and now that she'd lost—*been disqualified*— she had nothing. "I feel sick."

"Deep breaths," Jolie said. "It's okay."

The elevator dinged, and the doors slid open. Emma and Jolie wrapped their arms around Morgan's waist and helped her stumble into the hall.

"Which room is yours?"

"Four-eighteen." Oh, no. The room. She had to check out. What time was it? She'd be charged for another day if she stayed past eleven. "Help me pack," she said once they were inside. It was ten forty-eight. Maybe they could make it. "Hurry."

"Morgan, calm down."

"No! I have to get out of here," she said, barely able to hold in the sobs clawing to escape her chest. "*Please.* Help me pack."

She saw Emma and Jolie exchange worried glances before they scrambled into motion. They grabbed toiletries and clothes, her suitcase and toiletry bag, throwing everything in as quickly as they could.

"Hurry, hurry, hurry." She had to get out of there. Had to leave. She couldn't stand the thought of paying three hundred dollars more than she already was—all to be *disqualified*. Because she'd stupidly thought one thing—*one thing*—could go right in her life. *What did I do? I've tried so hard!*

"Morgan, we'll help you," Emma said. "Calm down."

"Yeah," Jolie added. "Mo, we'll—"

"No. I have to get out of here. I'm so embarrassed. I feel so *stupid*. Tasha said to flirt with a ski instructor, so I did! And now I've ruined *everything*." Morgan slammed the suitcase lid closed and zipped it, yanking it off the bed. She turned and discovered why things had gotten quiet, other than the frantic sound of her breath chugging in and out of her lungs.

Knox stood inside her room, a key card in his hand. His gaze lowered to the suitcase and toiletry bag before returning to her.

"Morgan—"

"No. I don't want to hear it. I don't. I'm *leaving*," she said, cutting off whatever he was about to say. Sorry wasn't enough. Rationally she knew it wasn't his fault, that she was just as guilty as he was about what had—*hadn't!*— taken place between them. She'd certainly never said no to the kisses they'd shared. But had she known the consequences…

What? Would you have refused? Missed out on life in the snow globe?

She shook her head at her thoughts and fought the emotions wreaking havoc on her. Overwhelming her and stealing every ounce of happiness she'd had with him.

"Should we wait outside?" Emma asked.

"Please," Knox said.

"*No.*" Morgan glared at her friends. "Stay." Because if they didn't stay, she would wind up letting Knox hug her, comfort her. And wasn't that how she'd gotten herself into this mess in the first place?

"Morgan, I had no idea about the contest rules. Did you?" he asked.

A laugh bubbled out of her chest, and she could practically *hear* Rory crowing. "I read them. I read all of them, but I didn't think about it when we… I didn't—" Her voice broke, and she quickly stopped and cleared her throat, shook her head. "I guess I am like that person who hurt you because I know it's not right, and it wouldn't have been fair or honest, but a part of me just wishes you'd have done it. That you would have kept quiet and voted me down, but at least that way I could've had a shot at winning."

"Morgan, don't leave. We'll work this out. There's a lot you don't know."

She shook her head, wishing with all her heart that they could. That she could. "I *can't.*"

Morgan would have sworn she felt her heart ripping in two when she walked by Knox and out of the hotel room. She hadn't felt this much when she had ended her marriage. Such a contrast. Such a telling difference.

She went downstairs to the desk, but when she walked up to the clerk, she noticed the clock behind the woman read five after eleven.

The woman rang up her bill, and sure enough, an extra day's charge appeared on the screen until a man with a name tag reading Don murmured something to the woman and took over. He smiled at her, rapidly clicked some buttons on the computer after inserting a key into the machine, and printed off a zero balance.

"Merry Christmas from Holly Wood Resort. We heard about your accident on the way up the mountain, so please accept your time here on us."

The air left Morgan's lungs in a rush. They weren't going to charge her? Really? "Does this have something to do with Knox Stewart? I'm not going to sue the resort, because your ski instructor took me in out of the cold. There was a blizzard. I would have frozen to death."

The man's eyebrows rose high on his wrinkled forehead before he smiled at her. "It's taken care of, miss. Have a nice day."

Morgan watched as Don walked away before she gathered up the slip of paper and tucked it into her purse. Fine. Whatever. She wasn't going to turn it down. Especially not now. The resort owner probably was trying to cover his butt, fearing some sort of lawsuit.

Did that mean Knox might lose his job?

Let him worry about that. Get out of here before you're humiliated any more than you've already been.

Why, why, why had she already signed those release papers? They could still use the footage of her, still show her onstage *getting* disqualified.

God, I know you get a lot of requests for these at this time of year but... help!

Chapter 12

Morgan blessed the fact it was dark by the time she made it back to Stone River and on to Rose Hill, where she lived. Emma had ridden with her down the mountain with Jolie following behind, and they'd stopped for lunch and lingered over dessert.

Her friends had asked very pointed questions about Knox and what had transpired between them. Morgan had been honest about the kisses and how being with him had felt. When they'd offered to follow her home, Morgan had sent them on their way.

She'd waited until the sun had gone down, blessed the darkness, and pulled the van into the garage to hide it from her neighbors' eyes, hoping no one would see her return and know she'd failed so quickly.

You didn't fail. You were disqualified. There is a difference.

Maybe. But the end result was the same.

Her front entry floor was littered with mail the postman had slid through the door slot. She left her suitcase and toiletry bag by the stairs to gather up the bills, a few Christmas cards, more bills. Several days' worth of newspapers.

She dumped everything but the newspapers on the desk in the

kitchen and grabbed a pen, moving through the dark house using the night-lights to guide the way.

How pathetic. How desperate did she have to be to stay in the dark to keep from having to answer her door? To hide inside her own home?

She walked into the downstairs bathroom and closed herself inside before turning on the light. Back to the wall, she sank to the floor and used her teeth to pull off the pen cap before opening the newspaper to the Help Wanted section.

SHE FELL asleep on the bathroom floor and woke up with newsprint on her cheek. Morgan glared at her image in the mirror.

Not quite the pageant queen now, are you?

She picked up the papers with jobs she'd circled, few though there were, carried them with her through the house to the kitchen. Coffee first. Shower. Maybe then she'd be awake and sociable enough to call for interviews.

Or not.

Her heart wasn't in any of the job listings. She didn't want to be a grocery checker, a bank teller, or a receptionist. They were perfectly wonderful jobs. Just not the job she wanted.

She moved to the coffee maker and waited impatiently for the brew to appear. How was she going to face everyone? Her parents? Her ex and his stripper?

A knock sounded on her door. Not her front door but the kitchen door a few feet away. She gasped and jumped back, banging her hip against the countertop. She couldn't hide, though. The paned glass of the French doors wouldn't allow it.

When she didn't move to unlock the door, Knox frowned and knocked again. When that didn't produce results, either— because really, what else was there to say— he held papers up for her to see.

Her designs!

She'd been so desperate to get away yesterday she hadn't even realized she'd left her designs at her cake station. But to get them, she had to open the door. And opening the door meant…

"Sweetheart, are you going to make me stand here all day? Because I will."

The way he said it, so calmly, put her feet into motion. "Fine."

She moved to the door and unlocked it, letting him inside.

"What happened to your face?"

Her face? *The newspaper.*

She licked her fingers and began to scrub at her cheek, only then remembering she not only had ink on her face but *bathroom*-head instead of bedhead.

"Stop. Let me."

Knox grabbed her fingers in his and pulled them away, replacing her hand with a paper towel he'd dampened while she'd been frantically spit-scrubbing like any mom would. "What are you doing here?"

"You left your sketches."

"You could have mailed them."

"I wanted to see you and hoped you'd listen to me now."

It was amazing how his words could bring such joy and happiness but be layered with such sadness, too. "Knox, my life is such a mess right now. I loved spending time with you, but I have to find a job and—"

"I might be able to help you with that."

She grasped his wrist to still the wiping motions. "What do you mean?"

"There's an opening at the resort. We need someone who specializes in desserts. Interested?"

"Who's we?" Good grief, she needed coffee. The cobwebs in her brain made thinking difficult, but toss Knox into the mix and she was lucky to breathe properly.

"Morgan, Don told me what you said."

"Don?"

"The man at the desk when you checked out yesterday. Sweetheart, I'm not a ski instructor. I teach skiing sometimes, when I have to, but that's not my job."

"I don't understand," she whispered, finally finding her voice. "What are you saying?"

"You're not a hockey fan, are you?"

She shook her head. "I watch ice skating." Knox grimaced so much at her statement that she laughed. "I'm sorry? Why does it matter that I'm not a hockey fan?"

"Because I used to play."

"Were you any— Professionally?" she asked, finally getting a clue.

"Yeah."

Things finally began to click in her brain. "Emma told me once that the owner of the resort was a professional athlete. That wouldn't be… you?"

"And if it is?"

If it—oh, boy. "So you want me to work for you?"

He tossed the napkin aside. "Yes. And not because it's my fault you were disqualified."

"No. No, I was angry yesterday, but I'm the only one to blame. I read the rules. I just didn't think, which is something I have a bad habit of doing sometimes."

He drew her close and tucked her hair behind her ear. "Well, I can't offer you a television show, but— I can offer you space inside the resort for a small shop where you can sell your cakes and desserts and whatever else you like. Puck's preference would be your dog treats, of course. You can also handle the special occasion cakes for the resort. I looked at your design sketches. They're amazing."

Her pulse raced at the thought. Was this really happening?

It was a dream come true. It was everything she could really ask for and yet— "What about…us?" she forced herself to ask. "You said the resort has a policy against employees fraternizing with the guests. Does it also have a policy against its boss dating employees?"

"It does."

"I see. So the shop is the consolation prize, right?" she asked, pulling away from him.

Knox tugged her right back into position against him. "No. There's a technicality," he murmured.

"I don't understand."

"Morgan," he said, "the boss can do what he likes—which includes changing the rules."

The air whooshed from her lungs. "So you're saying…?"

He tilted his head to one side. "Do you want things to be over between us?"

"No," she whispered. That was the last thing she wanted. "I just can't believe you're going to such lengths to help me and… be with me."

He lowered his head and took her lips in a slow, heady kiss. "Sweetheart, when will you realize you're worth it?"

Epilogue

Two days before Christmas, one year later…

MORGAN STARED out the window of Knox's home—their home —watching as Knox, Puck, and Caleb built a snowman in the yard. She and Camilla had come inside a little while ago, and Cam was fast asleep on the couch, worn out from their adventures in the snow.

Knox grabbed Caleb beneath his arms, lifting him up so Caleb could place the snowman's eyes and nose. When Caleb finished, Knox shifted his stepson against his chest and held him there so they could stand back and admire their handiwork.

Morgan lifted the mug of hot chocolate to her lips, pausing to hold out her hand and admire the wedding set Knox had given her over the summer.

They had married in the little red church where his grandparents had tied the knot and held the reception at the resort with her *Besties* by her side. She'd made their wedding cake— and garnered a lot of business afterward as a result.

Knox's family had accepted her as one of their own, and her parents couldn't be more thrilled with the marriage now that they saw the difference between happy—and going through the motions for the sake of her family.

The video of her being disqualified had aired, but once the media had gotten wind of the reason *why* she'd been kicked out of the competition, their romance had received some press, earning her some offers as a plus-size model, as well as Rory's jealousy and upset. After all, if a former professional hockey player and the media could find her attractive just as she was, well…maybe he'd acted in haste and done some things he shouldn't have. In the meantime, Big Boobs wasn't amused by Rory's distraction and had dropped Rory for a man with deeper pockets.

Caleb's laughter filtered through the windowpane, and Morgan smiled at the sound. So many changes in a year. So many *good* changes. It had taken long hours and hard work, but her snack and dessert bar was up and running inside the resort and doing very, very well.

She slid her hand over her stomach and sank her teeth into her lower lip, barely able to contain her excitement at being able to tell the *Besties* her news when they got together at Emma and Ian's to exchange gifts on Christmas Eve.

Knox caught her watching him and lifted his hand to blow her a kiss. And because his stepfather had done it, Caleb had to do it, too, and threw multiple kisses her way. She made a show of gathering them up and hugging them to her chest.

Her men went back to playing with Puck, and she lifted her gaze to the sky. "The worst things had to happen in order for me to get the best. I get it now," she whispered.

WANT MORE OF STONE RIVER? **READ ON BELOW FOR A SNEAK PEEK AT TASHA AND OWEN'S STORY IN THEIR CHRISTMAS MIRACLE!**

Just call me Scrooge, Tasha thought as she watched the *Besties*, her friends since elementary and high school, and their significant others laugh and talk with each other in Emma and Ian's living room.

Emma had gone all out decorating the house for her and Ian's first Christmas together, and the home was ablaze with lights and color. Every mantel, tabletop, and doorway had some type of decoration, and the tree… For someone who'd spent the last fourteen years blind, Emma had an eye for decorating.

A burst of laughter drew her attention back to the couples gathered in the room. She was happy for them. Her friends *deserved* happiness and love, but watching it happen and being surrounded by their smiles and the loving glances they sometimes exchanged reminded her that it sucked that *her* significant other was MIA. And thought to be…

Dead. Just say it. Duncan thinks it. Owen's sister, too. They've given up. They're all waiting for you to come to your senses, so just say it. Owen's dead.

She tried to accept what her mind told her, but her heart refused. Life couldn't be so cruel. She'd lost her state trooper fiancé several years ago. To finally fall in love and have it happen *again*?

But because Owen's whereabouts remained unknown and the trail Duncan had attempted to track had gone cold, she was left with little hope she would receive *her* Christmas wish.

Tasha turned and set her drink aside, wondering if she could slip from the house unnoticed. She hadn't wanted to come tonight. Wasn't in the holiday spirit *at all*. How could she be?

Three months had passed since Owen Redd had disappeared while investigating his younger sister's ex-boyfriend's alleged death. Now Owen's sibling sat across the room, holding her baby girl cradled against her chest while Duncan MacGregor doted on mother and baby both with unprecedented attention.

Duncan and Bethany had married in a quiet ceremony in Atlanta, and Hollyn MacGregor had been born days later. The couple's whirlwind relationship had left everyone with doubts, but once they saw Duncan and Bethany together, it became perfectly clear the two had simply met their match in one another.

It was quite a sight to see. Special. Just like Emma and Ian's newly wedded state, and Morgan's taking-things-a-step-at-a-time dating strategy with her love interest.

"Hey. You okay?" Morgan asked.

Tasha faced her friend and saw Morgan's silver Christmas tree earrings swinging from her ears like chandeliers. "Yeah. Fine," she said, forcing a smile because she didn't want to bring everyone down. They all struggled to cope with Owen's disappearance and absence in one way or another.

Morgan glowed like the sparkling lights circling the tree in the corner, all thanks to finding the man of her dreams after a heart-breaking divorce. Morgan had been devastated by the results of the Cake-Off Competition, but things had turned out better in the long run. Amazing how that happened. Morgan and Knox Stewart, former professional hockey player turned entrepreneur, seemed made for each other.

"You sure?" Morgan asked.

Tasha lifted her hand to her temple and rubbed the tight muscles and skin. "Headache. I think I'm going to head home."

"So soon? But we only just exchanged presents. Won't you stay a little longer?"

Not when she was the seventh wheel. Ninth if she counted Emma's sister, Laney, and her husband, Rand, who talked to Jolie and her fiancé, Nathan Quinn, in the corner.

Oh, *why* had she agreed to come tonight?

"Tash, please. You've barely left the clinic in months."

"I'm not fit company," she said to Morgan. "You guys will have more fun without me."

"That's not true," Morgan argued. "We love you. We need you here."

"And I need some headache meds and my pj's. Mo, I'm going home. Don't make a fuss, and give my excuses to Em after I leave. Please?"

Morgan opened her mouth to argue, but thankfully something stopped her.

"Fine. But text me when you get home so I know you made it safe?"

"Sure," Tasha murmured, slipping away from Morgan and into the hall to hurry out the door before Em or Jolie saw her and required a repeat of the same argument.

Crisp, December air filled her nose and cooled her hot face as she made her way to her Jeep and climbed in. The road down the mountain was curvy and dark, but the drive didn't bother her.

On the other hand, carols on the radio annoyed her, so she hit the button to turn off the noise, preferring the hum of the motor and silence that allowed her to think.

The streets of Stone River, Georgia, were quiet but beautifully decorated. Another reminder of the holiday she would spend alone by choice. Normally, she had fill-in coverage for her veterinary clinic, but the other vet had decided to travel north with his family for Christmas and New Year's, and she'd volunteered to cover his emergency calls while he was gone. Her family wasn't pleased she wouldn't be joining them in Florida at her parents' condo, but thankfully her father, a retired vet himself, understood.

The brightly lit storefronts looked festive, but she passed by without giving them much attention, not stopping until she pulled into the drive next to the clinic. Her house was small but perfect for her needs, with white siding and a burgundy roof, matching shutters on the windows.

After a quick text to Morgan, Tasha let herself in and was immediately greeted by Dexter, her one and only feline guest at the moment. She'd had a total of five cats earlier in the summer, but four were fosters she'd eventually found homes for. "Hey, Dex."

Tasha dropped her purse and keys onto the table by the stairs and turned toward the kitchen for a glass of water. To her left, a shadow shifted along the wall.

Tasha gasped and stumbled away from it, fumbling for a weapon and lifting a lamp. The shade was loose and clattered to the floor. "Who's there?"

"Me. Instead of beaming me with that, why don't you turn it on."

The voice was husky, male. Scratchy and low and pained. Familiar?

Her heart pounded against her chest as she felt for the switch. The bright light left him closing his eyes against the glare. Not that closing them was much of a stretch since they were both bruised and swollen, as was his face. *"Owen?"*

She barely recognized him. Wouldn't have recognized him had he not spoken to her first.

He wore stained, filthy clothes, and his face and hands looked dark with grime and bruises, his beard straggly and thick with gray. Gone was the athletic, kick-butt man with a ready smile, and in his place sat a man nearly starved and visibly broken. Owen looked to be homeless, one of many in this day and age on the city streets begging for money. "Is it really you?"

I HOPE **you have enjoyed CHRISTMAS AT HOLLY WOOD. Listed below are links to the rest of the books so you can continue reading about Tasha and Owen and all of their friends.**

Word of mouth and reviews are the two best ways an author has to gain attention for their books. While you're browsing the titles, please consider taking a moment to leave a short review of this book.

Thank you,

Kay

The Stone River Novels

WORTH THE WAIT

NOT BY SIGHT

MORE THAN LOVE (FORMERLY THROUGH THE VALLEY)

TO PROTECT HER (FORMERLY LEAD ME NOT)

CHRISTMAS AT HOLLY WOOD

THEIR CHRISTMAS MIRACLE

SECOND CHANCES

SIGN UP FOR KAY'S NEWSLETTER AND RECEIVE FREE BOOKS, UPDATES ON NEW RELEASES, CONTESTS, PRE-RELEASE BOOK INFORMATION, EXCLUSIVES AND MORE!

Kay Lyons Books

MAKE ME A MATCH SERIES:

- ROMANCE RESET
- RULES OF ENGAGEMENT
- THE MATCHMAKER'S SECRET
- PERFECTLY MISMATCHED
- BY THE BOOK

MONTANA SECRETS SERIES:

- HEALING HER COWBOY
- IT HAD TO BE YOU
- HERS TO KEEP
- MILLION DOLLAR STANDOFF
- HIS CHRISTMAS WISH
- THEIR SECRET SON

THE SEASIDE SISTERS SERIES:

- THE LAST GOODBYE
- LATTES AND LULLABYES
- MAP OF DREAMS
- WORTH THE RISK
- LOST LOVE FOUND

TAMING THE TULANES SERIES:

- SMALL TOWN SCANDAL
- THEIR SECRET BARGAIN
- CROSSING THE LINE
- THE NANNY'S SECRET
- SOMEONE TO TRUST

The Stone River Novels

- WORTH THE WAIT
- NOT BY SIGHT
- MORE THAN LOVE (FORMERLY THROUGH THE VALLEY)
- TO PROTECT HER (FORMERLY LEAD ME NOT)
- CHRISTMAS AT HOLLY WOOD
- THEIR CHRISTMAS MIRACLE
- SECOND CHANCES

SMALL TOWN SCANDALS SERIES:

- BRODY'S REDEMPTION
- FALLING FOR HER BOSS
- WITH THIS MAN

SECRET SANTA SERIES:

- SECRET SANTA
- SECRET SANTA II: A CHRISTMAS TO REMEMBER

SIGN UP FOR KAY'S NEWSLETTER AND RECEIVE FREE BOOKS, UPDATES ON NEW RELEASES, CONTESTS, PRE-RELEASE BOOK INFORMATION, EXCLUSIVES AND MORE!

Author Bio

Kay Lyons always wanted to be a writer, ever since the age of seven or eight when she copied the pictures out of a Charlie Brown book and rewrote the story because she didn't like the plot. Through the years her stories have changed but one characteristic stayed true—they were all romances. Each and every one of her manuscripts included a love story.

Published in 2005 with Harlequin Enterprises, Kay's first release was a national bestseller. Kay has also been a HOLT Medallion, Book Buyers Best and RITA Award nominee. Look for her most recent novels with Kindred Spirits Publishing.

For more information regarding her work, please visit Kay at the following:

www.kaylyonsauthor.com

@KayLyonsAuthor (Twitter)

Kay Lyons Author (Facebook)

Author_Kay_Lyons (Instagram)

Kay Lyons, Author (Pinterest)

SIGN UP FOR KAY'S NEWSLETTER AND RECEIVE FREE BOOKS, UPDATES ON NEW RELEASES, CONTESTS, PRE-

RELEASE BOOK INFORMATION, EXCLUSIVES AND MORE!

NATIONAL BESTSELLING AUTHOR
KAY LYONS
Their Christmas
MIRACLE
STONE RIVER BOOK SIX

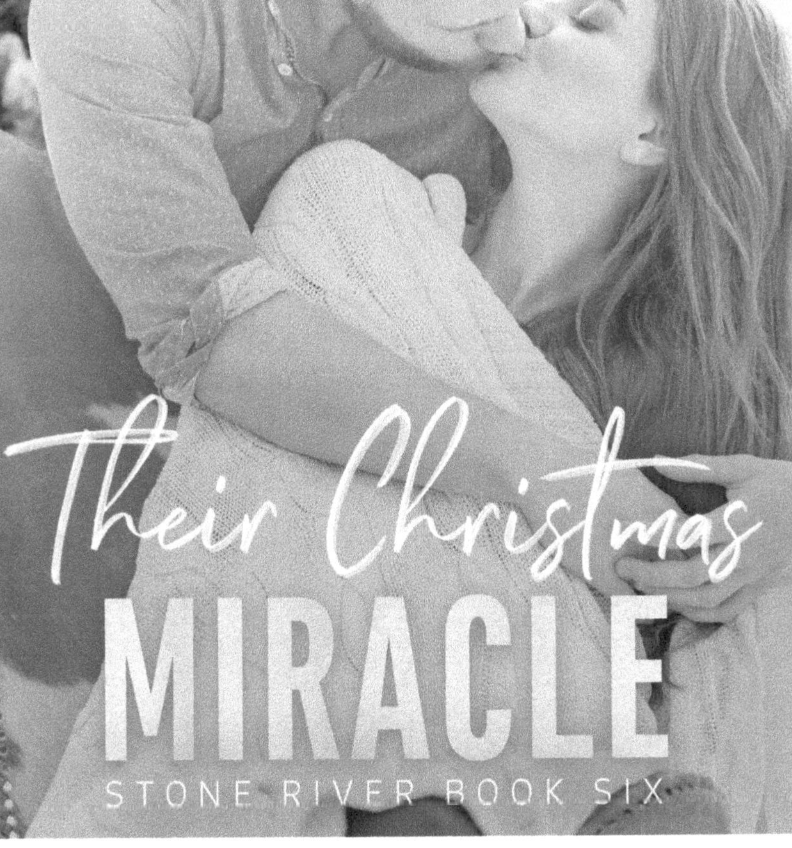

Copyright

Chapter 1

Just call me Scrooge, Tasha thought as she watched the *Besties*, her friends since elementary and high school, and their significant others laugh and talk with each other in Emma and Ian's living room.

Emma had gone all out decorating the house for her and Ian's first Christmas together, and the home was ablaze with lights and color. Every mantel, tabletop, and doorway had some type of decoration, and the tree… For someone who'd spent the last fourteen years blind, Emma had an eye for decorating.

A burst of laughter drew her attention back to the couples gathered in the room. She was happy for them. Her friends *deserved* happiness and love, but watching it happen and being surrounded by their smiles and the loving glances they sometimes exchanged reminded her that it sucked that *her* significant other was MIA. And thought to be…

Dead. Just say it. Duncan thinks it. Owen's sister, too. They've given up. They're all waiting for you to come to your senses, so just say it. Owen's dead.

She tried to accept what her mind told her, but her heart refused. Life couldn't be so cruel. She'd lost her state trooper fiancé several years ago. To finally fall in love and have it happen *again*?

But because Owen's whereabouts remained unknown and the trail Duncan had attempted to track had gone cold, she was left with little hope she would receive *her* Christmas wish.

Tasha turned and set her drink aside, wondering if she could slip from the house unnoticed. She hadn't wanted to come tonight. Wasn't in the holiday spirit *at all*. How could she be?

Three months had passed since Owen Redd had disappeared while investigating his younger sister's ex-boyfriend's alleged death. Now Owen's sibling sat across the room, holding her baby girl cradled against her chest while Duncan MacGregor doted on mother and baby both with unprecedented attention.

Duncan and Bethany had married in a quiet ceremony in Atlanta, and Hollyn MacGregor had been born days later. The couple's whirlwind relationship had left everyone with doubts, but once they saw Duncan and Bethany together, it became perfectly clear the two had simply met their match in one another.

It was quite a sight to see. Special. Just like Emma and Ian's newly wedded state, and Morgan's taking-things-a-step-at-a-time dating strategy with her love interest.

"Hey. You okay?" Morgan asked.

Tasha faced her friend and saw Morgan's silver Christmas tree earrings swinging from her ears like chandeliers. "Yeah. Fine," she said, forcing a smile because she didn't want to bring everyone down. They all struggled to cope with Owen's disappearance and absence in one way or another.

Morgan glowed like the sparkling lights circling the tree in the corner, all thanks to finding the man of her dreams after a heart-breaking divorce. Morgan had been devastated by the results of the Cake-Off Competition, but things had turned out better in the long run. Amazing how that happened. Morgan and Knox Stewart, former professional hockey player turned entrepreneur, seemed made for each other.

"You sure?" Morgan asked.

Tasha lifted her hand to her temple and rubbed the tight muscles and skin. "Headache. I think I'm going to head home."

"So soon? But we only just exchanged presents. Won't you stay a little longer?"

Not when she was the seventh wheel. Ninth if she counted Emma's sister, Laney, and her husband, Rand, who talked to Jolie and her fiancé, Nathan Quinn, in the corner.

Oh, *why* had she agreed to come tonight?

"Tash, please. You've barely left the clinic in months."

"I'm not fit company," she said to Morgan. "You guys will have more fun without me."

"That's not true," Morgan argued. "We love you. We need you here."

"And I need some headache meds and my pj's. Mo, I'm going home. Don't make a fuss, and give my excuses to Em after I leave. Please?"

Morgan opened her mouth to argue, but thankfully something stopped her.

"Fine. But text me when you get home so I know you made it safe?"

"Sure," Tasha murmured, slipping away from Morgan and into the hall to hurry out the door before Em or Jolie saw her and required a repeat of the same argument.

Crisp, December air filled her nose and cooled her hot face as she made her way to her Jeep and climbed in. The road down the mountain was curvy and dark, but the drive didn't bother her.

On the other hand, carols on the radio annoyed her, so she hit the button to turn off the noise, preferring the hum of the motor and silence that allowed her to think.

The streets of Stone River, Georgia, were quiet but beautifully decorated. Another reminder of the holiday she would spend alone by choice. Normally, she had fill-in coverage for her veterinary clinic, but the other vet had decided to travel north with his family for Christmas and New Year's, and she'd volunteered to cover his emergency calls while he was gone. Her family wasn't pleased she wouldn't be joining them in Florida at her parents' condo, but thankfully her father, a retired vet himself, understood.

The brightly lit storefronts looked festive, but she passed by without giving them much attention, not stopping until she pulled into the drive next to the clinic. Her house was small but perfect for her needs, with white siding and a burgundy roof, matching shutters on the windows.

After a quick text to Morgan, Tasha let herself in and was immediately greeted by Dexter, her one and only feline guest at the moment. She'd had a total of five cats earlier in the summer, but four were fosters she'd eventually found homes for. "Hey, Dex."

Tasha dropped her purse and keys onto the table by the stairs and turned toward the kitchen for a glass of water. To her left, a shadow shifted along the wall.

Tasha gasped and stumbled away from it, fumbling for a weapon and lifting a lamp. The shade was loose and clattered to the floor. "Who's there?"

"Me. Instead of beaming me with that, why don't you turn it on."

The voice was husky, male. Scratchy and low and pained. Familiar?

Her heart pounded against her chest as she felt for the switch. The bright light left him closing his eyes against the glare. Not that closing them was much of a stretch since they were both bruised and swollen, as was his face. "*Owen?*"

She barely recognized him. Wouldn't have recognized him had he not spoken to her first.

He wore stained, filthy clothes, and his face and hands looked dark with grime and bruises, his beard straggly and thick with gray. Gone was the athletic, kick-butt man with a ready smile, and in his place sat a man nearly starved and visibly broken. Owen looked to be homeless, one of many in this day and age on the city streets begging for money. "Is it really you?"

She stood rooted to the floor, too afraid she imagined him lying there on her floor because of the loneliness of the night. Too scared he would disappear if she breathed or moved or—

A sound burst out of her. She didn't remember moving. Didn't remember crossing the floor or falling to her knees. She was only aware of the moment her body slammed against his.

Owen's grunt of pain blew into her face. He looked awful. He smelled worse. He was injured and in pain, but she didn't care. He was there. In her house. Right now.

Alive.

A brief hint of a smile curled the corners of his lips.

"Ah, sweetheart. Did you miss me?"

"Miss you?" she asked, barely able to get the words out over the lump in her throat. *"Where have you been?"*

Chapter 2

Owen watched as the storm gathered behind Tasha's eyes. Man, she was beautiful. Even more beautiful than he'd remembered.

He should have gone to the MacGregor house first to clean up, should've made use of Tasha's shower while he waited for her to appear, but he'd made the mistake of sinking down onto her floor so as not to mess her furniture, and then... he hadn't been able to get up.

"Let's get you to a hospital," she said, tugging on his arm.

"No. I'm good."

"Owen—"

"No hospitals. But I wouldn't mind a long soak in that tub of yours." He could see the questions she wanted to ask, the ones she buried behind her concern and the need to help him.

"Of course. I take it this means Duncan doesn't know that you're here? I should call."

"Not yet," he said, then softened his tone to add, "I'll contact him tomorrow. Just help me to the tub. Please." He'd waited too long to be here, with Tasha, and he didn't want Duncan keeping him from her. Tasha's presence in his life was the only thing that had gotten him through the last three months. The only person who'd kept him alive when he'd wanted to give in to the pain and the darkness, escape the suffering. Instead, he'd prayed. Pictured her in his mind and the future they'd have together if he stayed alive.

Tasha took a steadying breath before crouching down to wrap the arm he lifted around her shoulders to help him stand. Despite the forty or so pounds he'd lost, he still outweighed her, and she staggered a bit as she straightened with him leaning so heavily against her.

He limped his way to the bathroom and leaned his hips against the sink while she turned on the shower to let it warm.

"You can sit in the tub and shower, then soak. I'll get towels."

He reached out a hand to stop her and found himself staring down into her face. Her beautiful eyes.

Owen lifted his hand to her cheek and started to stroke his fingers across the expanse only to pause when he saw the contrast between his dirty fingers and her pale skin. He didn't want to sully her with all that had happened to him, all that he carried on him, so he let his hand fall to his side. "Towels," he said, hoping the single word got her moving again.

It did. But once again, he could feel her watching him like she did the animals in her care. Like she was afraid to move too quickly and risk scaring him— or expected to be attacked as a result.

Owen ignored the glances she sent him from beneath her long lashes and began to shrug off his clothing. The bulky coat he'd been given at a shelter in Arkansas. The sneakers were from a border town in Texas.

The button-down shirt and pants had been taken from one of his "guards," and the dirt that stained them helped disguise the blood splatters on the hem of the once-white shirt and the left thigh of the pants.

Tasha dug around in the linen closet, and he took advantage of her inattention to step into the tub, the act of lifting his feet over the side and lowering himself down bringing out every aching joint and muscle he possessed.

Water dripped from his too-long hair, but he blinked it away and saw Tasha's reaction to the sight of him. He'd left a man, but he'd returned a shell. Dangerously thin, bearing open wounds from blisters and cuts, a bullet. He had to give her credit, though. Despite looking like she wanted to hurl, she swallowed hard and carried the towels and soap from the closet to the tub. "Thanks."

"I'll help you."

"I can bathe myself."

"I'm a doctor—"

"Of animals."

"—and I can do it better than you at the moment," she finished. "Stop being stubborn and let me help you."

He was too tired to argue. Mostly because she was right, much as he hated to admit it.

Tasha folded a towel and placed it on the floor by the tub before lowering herself to her knees. She deemed his hair needed attending to first and doused the sopping mess with shampoo. Her fingers worked into the matted tangles, her nails lightly scraping against his scalp. He closed his eyes in bliss.

"Owen… Where were you?"

"Tomorrow. I'll tell you tomorrow." He could feel the tension rolling off her at being put off, but she didn't ask again.

She washed his hair and let it soak while she grabbed a loofah and liquid soap and began lathering his shoulders and neck.

"What bit you? Tell me that, at least."

He closed his eyes and reveled in her ministrations, feeling like one of those old, foreign lords who managed to find themselves bathed by the women of the house. "Rats."

Her hands paused momentarily before returning to their task. She washed his back, moved around him, and scrubbed his chest, then his legs, one at a time.

"You were shot?"

"It wasn't fatal."

"Not yet, but it's infected. Is the bullet still in there?"

He shook his head. "Through and through."

Her attention turned to his feet, and he winced when she ran the loofah over the multitudes of blisters there from his journey. He could have called Duncan for help at any point after he'd escaped, but he'd hoped Duncan's attention would be focused on protecting Bethany.

After the brief voice mail message he'd managed to leave Duncan before going missing, he'd known Duncan would go to the farmhouse looking for him. Known Duncan would find Bethany there and quickly discern the level of danger she faced.

He couldn't risk his sister being taken by the same men who'd held him the last three months, and with people thinking him dead… It was safer to travel as a homeless person. No one paid him any attention, especially not in his limping, weak condition.

"Oh, your poor feet. Owen, why? Why didn't you call? Why didn't you—" She lifted her gaze to his. "Are they still out there? I thought Duncan took care of everything. I mean, the men involved in Redemption are in jail, awaiting trial. Bethany's ex-boyfriend is testifying against them. Isn't it over?"

He lifted his head and stared at her in surprise. "He's alive?"

"Yes. He faked his death. He claimed he hoped it would keep Bethany safe, but… long story short, Charlie tried to blackmail his boss, who laundered money for a drug cartel and was skimming from them. When that backfired, Charlie left Redemption and faked his death to protect himself even though it put Bethany and his mother in danger. They…killed his mother. Bethany's fine, though. She's safe."

Good to know. But Tasha's explanation infuriated him.

The last three months of hell were for nothing? Owen leaned hard against the side of the tub to stay upright, trying to take it all in.

Owen needed to talk to Duncan. Figure out what was going on.

Three months of his life were gone, all for a man who wasn't dead.

What else had changed?

Chapter 3

Tasha gently scrubbed the dirt and blood from Owen's body, her hands trembling from the awareness of what he had been through. She was a vet. She'd seen plenty of bruised and broken animals in her practice. But Owen's battered body was the worst she'd ever seen.

She had so many questions. So many. But first he needed food and sleep and antibiotics to help him fight off the infection weakening him.

Once she'd bathed him as thoroughly as she could, she plugged the tub and let it fill, adding a sprinkle of Epsom salts to aid in his recovery, all the while avoiding eye contact and averting her gaze from his nudity.

They had... She had...given into the chemistry before he'd disappeared, and while she would always cherish the intimacy with Owen, she regretted letting her guard down.

She knelt by the tub a long time, simply staring at his bowed head and closed eyes, unable to believe he had returned. Was she dreaming?

So many emotions fought for control inside of her. Joy and

happiness, relief. Empathy. Bitterness. An anger so deep and so profound she struggled to contain it until the appropriate time.

Tasha left Owen to soak and went to her clinic long enough to retrieve some meds for him. If he refused to go to the hospital, he didn't leave her much choice but to medicate him herself. The infection could prove fatal still, given Owen's weakened state.

Back in the house, she prepared a syringe and grabbed a sports drink from the refrigerator. Owen had fallen asleep in the tub, his head propped against the tile wall behind him, his long legs scrunched to fit inside the enclosure. He'd draped a towel over his hips for modesty's sake. And hers, no doubt. "Owen?"

"Stop worrying," he murmured, the words slurring with his fatigue. "I'll be fine. Just need to sleep."

She fought the urge to be sick at how bad he looked and moved toward him. "Drink this first," she said as she handed him the bottle. She pulled the cap off the syringe and saw him eyeing it warily. Owen didn't like needles. "Antibiotics. You know you need them."

He nodded once and lifted the drink to his lips.

"This is going to sting," she said needlessly, swabbing his upper arm and quickly administering the shot.

Owen caught one of her hands in his when she started to turn away. He carried it to his face and held it against his cheek.

"I'm sorry I scared you. I'm sorry I didn't—"

"Let's get you to bed," she said, her voice husky and rough from the lump in her throat.

She dried Owen while he held on to the sink to stay upright. He was so weak. Weaker now that he'd sat in the warm water so long.

Tasha guided him to her bed and raced to pull back the covers. He sank onto the sheets, and she helped him lift his legs onto the mattress. He was asleep before she got him covered up.

She'd never seen anyone fall asleep like that, but it was like his body had simply hit a wall and shut down. The awareness of his exhaustion scared her so much she placed her fingers on his wrist to check his pulse. Strong, steady. Thank God. As a doctor— even an animal doctor— she knew rest was the best thing for Owen. His body needed to heal. But the irrational, impatient side of her wanted answers, and she wanted them *now*.

Turning away from him, she returned to the bathroom and took her anger out on the tub, scrubbing it down before stripping and showering herself.

She needed the sting of the spray in her face, her eyes, because she refused to release another tear over the man in her bed. She'd shed far too many as it was, battling the doubts and fears of his demise.

Tasha donned comfortable sweats and a long-sleeved shirt before taking a seat in the chair along the wall of the bedroom. She drew her knees up and looped her arms around her legs, the light from the bathroom just enough to allow her to see Owen's gaunt face.

He was home. Alive. And she was grateful.

Unsure of their future… but grateful.

SHE MUST HAVE DOZED OFF, because when Tasha opened her eyes, the first rays of sunshine were leaching beneath the curtains of her bedroom windows.

Her gaze shifted to the bed, and she saw Owen still slept, in virtually the exact same position as when he'd first collapsed there. Her lungs seized until she spotted the rhythmic rise and fall of his chest, and she scolded herself for panicking. She couldn't go around checking his pulse every time the man closed his eyes. But that was exactly what she wanted to do. That, and never let him out of her sight again.

Yeah, that's a healthy relationship.

She shoved to her feet and left the bedroom, using the half bath in the main part of the house. Thankfully it was Sunday, her day off unless called out for an emergency, so she didn't have to worry about her practice. Church was a scheduling issue, and she regretted missing the special service, especially today of all days, but it would be over by the time she'd arrive.

She washed and cut an apple into slices and added peanut butter to a small bowl but stared down at it, not the least bit hungry. She'd lost weight herself in the last few months, her worry over Owen's disappearance taking a toll.

She set the bowl aside and made herself a cup of tea, carrying it with her to the living room and curling up on the couch while she waited for Owen to wake up.

Duncan would be angry with her for not immediately informing him and Bethany of Owen's return.

Not that she cared.

She liked Duncan, but she didn't want the man coming into her home and taking charge. Owen needed rest and proper care, and he would be more comfortable here than a hospital room or at the MacGregors' house atop the mountain. Bethany was a new mother, still recovering from birth and dealing with her newborn. Owen's sister had her hands full and didn't need to add caring for her very weak brother to the list.

Maybe it was selfish of her to deny them the knowledge of Owen's return, but given all she'd been through after Owen's disappearance, she figured she'd earned the right to be selfish. They'd given up on him, but she hadn't.

At least not then.

Guilt left her scrambling off the couch and pacing the floor. It was too soon to make any decisions about her relationship with Owen. The time would come for that, but that time wasn't now, when the man was so exhausted he'd practically passed out in her bed.

She walked to the bedroom door and stood there for a long time, watching him sleep, her heart breaking because of what she had to tell him the moment he was well enough to hear it.

Owen's return changed things…because nothing would ever be the same.

Chapter 4

Owen opened his eyes and squinted into the darkness surrounding him. He knew without checking that the space next to him was empty, cold, and he was alone.

He ran his hands over his face and scrubbed hard, wiping away the sleep and exhaustion that lingered. Shoving the blankets aside, he rolled to the edge of the mattress and waited for the waves of dizziness to pass before standing. "Natasha… Tash?"

Not getting a response, he made use of the bathroom before moving to the closet to look for clothes. A knot formed in his gut when he realized the items he'd left there for convenience's sake were nowhere to be seen. Only Tasha's clothes hung on the closet rod.

He turned to search out Tasha when a box on the floor of the walk-in snagged his attention. His clothes? He loosed the folded flaps and saw that his guess was correct.

So she'd considered him gone… but not forgotten? He wasn't sure how to feel about that or the fact she'd packed up the few things he'd left behind after workouts at the gym or those worn covered in dog and cat hair while helping her out at the clinic. She'd boxed them up because she'd believed him dead.

Owen pulled out a pair of jog shorts and a long-sleeved shirt, wincing at the pain and soreness he felt when he pulled them on. Presentable enough to be seen by her neighbors in case he had to leave the house, he went in search of Tasha, finally finding her in her clinic next door.

"You're awake. Hungry?" she asked, sliding him a glance that could only be described as "doctor assessing."

"I could eat. Need some help?"

"All finished. Let's go back to the house, and I'll get you some dinner."

"Dinner? How long was I out?" His gaze locked on a calendar across the room. That couldn't be right, could it?

"It's Monday evening. Had you slept another day, I was going to hook up an IV."

He'd slept for forty-eight hours straight? "I didn't mean to scare you."

A wry twist formed on her beautiful lips. "Your sleeping didn't scare me. Taking off without a word of where you were going or how we could find you if you got into trouble… that scared me. Not that you cared."

Tasha walked away from him without glancing back, her shoulders tight and nearly pinching her ears.

Ticked. That's the only word he could think of to describe her attitude now that he was back on his feet. She was ticked off. "Tasha—"

"If you're about to make some excuse, I really don't want to hear it," she said, cutting him off. "I don't, so just save it."

"Tasha, I'm sorry for putting you through that."

Tasha grabbed her keys from the counter and waited for him to walk through the door, then shut and locked it behind them. Marching past him, Tasha made her way back to the house in record time.

Owen limped along behind her, trying to figure out how to make amends and keep his own temper in check. This wasn't quite the welcome home he'd expected. "I'm sorry for scaring you, sweetheart."

She glanced at him from within her small kitchen and shrugged. "Sit down before you fall down. I'll get you some dinner."

He hobbled to the couch and sank into the soft leather cushions. Dexter the cat immediately jumped off his perch by the window and wandered over for a scratch behind his ears, moving so that Owen also rubbed his back and then the cat's long tail.

Through the open passageway between the snack bar and the living room, he saw Tasha retrieving items from the fridge and pantry, moving about in a rush as was her normal speed. He'd never seen her not going full speed ahead, rushing from room to room in her clinic to treat animals.

"You should call Duncan," she said. "Bethany will want to see you. The baby is fine, by the way. She had a girl."

He'd just leaned back against the cushions but lunged forward on the couch. "What did you say? She had a *baby*?"

Tasha poked her head into the opening over the bar.

"You didn't know she was pregnant?"

He sat back against the cushions and shook his head. When he'd left Redemption, Bethany had been sick with worry. Unable to eat… Quiet. "Please tell me her ex isn't the father."

Tasha's wince gave him the answer. But then he couldn't be surprised by the paternity, either.

Still… Monkey Wrench had gone and had a baby? He was an *uncle*? A smile formed— until he remembered Beth's idiot ex-boyfriend was alive. "Where's Charlie?"

"Charlie turned state's evidence and is in some safe house somewhere waiting to be a prosecuting witness. Once he does that, he's going into Witness Protection. He tried to get Bethany to go with him, but she refused."

"Thank God." Witness Protection couldn't protect the guy, not against the men he'd crossed. Charlie would be on the run forever. Not the kind of life to be dragging along a family.

"Um… Owen?" Tasha said, staring down at her cell phone. "Em just texted me. She wants to stop in. I think Em was going with Bethany to a doctor's appointment, but sometimes Quinn and Ian take the dogs to the medical campus for training. They're probably all together. Oh, and call your parents. Your father took your mother on a cruise for the holidays, but leave a message for them in case they check in. They've worried themselves sick about you."

"I will. But what's Beth doing here in town?" he asked.

"Uh… Just… call Duncan," she ordered, not elaborating further as to why his family would leave Redemption to travel to Stone River for Christmas.

He frowned at the order and her avoidance of the question and grabbed the portable phone off the base near the couch. He'd wanted to talk things out with Tasha before dragging the entire MacGregor household and Tasha's *Besties* into the mix, but that wasn't going to happen.

The call rang twice and clicked. "MacGregor."

The sound of his best friend's voice filled his ear, and sappy as it seemed, Owen grinned. "It's Owen. I'm at Tasha's."

There was a split second of silence. "About time," Duncan said, his voice sounding a bit thick. "Be there in ten."

Owen relayed the news to Tasha, who frowned and hurried even faster to prepare a tray and used the task to avoid answering any other questions about Bethany. "I can wait and eat afterward," he told her.

"There's no telling how long they'll stay. No, you need to eat before they get here. Otherwise I know you won't."

She carried the tray over to him, and he stared down at the bowl of soup, a thick hunk of warmed bread, and a glass of juice.

"Eat. Then take those," she said, pointing toward two horse-sized pills also on the tray. "And before you ask, I bought the soup. It's safe to eat."

He vowed then and there he would never complain or tease her about her cooking again, not after the months of eating— or not eating— whatever slop his captors had fed him to keep him alive.

Owen tucked into the food, his stomach clenching in greed when the soup warmed his insides. Wolfing it down was easy enough to do, and he was finishing off the bread when Tasha's front door opened without so much as a knock.

Chapter 5

Tasha settled herself in a corner of her living room and watched while Duncan wrapped Owen in a bear hug and pounded him on the back. She winced at the expression Owen wore as a result and was glad when Duncan stopped the pounding.

"You don't look so good," Duncan said to Owen. "But, man, am I ever glad to see you. What happened?"

Owen spared her a glance and shrugged his shoulders.

"Emma is on her way here. I doubt she'll be alone. I'll tell you all at once so I'm not repeating myself."

Duncan locked gazes with Tasha. "How is he?" the man asked.

"Infected and dehydrated, exhausted, malnourished, with a bullet wound and multiple lacerations and bruises."

"I'm fine," Owen countered. "I'm here, aren't I? I'm good."

"He slept forty-eight hours and just woke up thirty minutes ago," she added, wanting to make it clear to Duncan and anyone else who walked through the door that Owen was weak and couldn't be expected to do much of anything.

"You keeping anything down?" Duncan asked next.

"Just ate. I'm on the mend."

Owen attempted to make eye contact, but Tasha avoided his

gaze, unwilling to be drawn in. She was glad he was back. Thankful he was alive. But it didn't change things between them.

A knock sounded on her door, and she got to her feet to answer it. Em hugged her the moment Tasha swung the door open, and Tasha held on a few seconds longer than necessary, needing her best friend's embrace.

"Hey, you okay?" Em asked, always able to read Tasha's emotions.

Tasha stepped back to let Emma and Ian inside. Ian followed Em with his hand on his wife's shoulder, his white stick cane held out to the right to make sure he didn't bump into anything.

Tasha turned back toward the door and saw Bethany on the porch, holding the baby carrier. Quinn was behind her, and as Tasha had suspected, two of Ian and Quinn's Mad Dog Security dogs-in-training eagerly stared out the window of the oversized SUV parked in her driveway. "Come in," she said, ushering everyone inside the house.

Em's shocked gasp emerged first, before Bethany let out a cry and raced toward the couch. Owen barely had enough time to stand before Bethany barreled into him, a choked sob tearing from her chest.

"What's happening?" Ian growled, his impatience with not being able to see what was taking place revealed in his tone.

"Owen," Emma whispered. "He's *here*. He's *alive*."

Tasha watched as Bethany fussed over Owen, and seeing them together, she was finally able to pick out subtle similarities between the siblings. Their noses, the shape of their eyes as well as the blue-green-swirled-with-gold color. Bethany's hair was an auburn-brown, while Owen's dark hair burned like fire in the sunlight.

"Start at the beginning," Duncan said to Owen once everyone was settled around the room.

Tasha positioned herself on one of the stools at the snack bar and waited impatiently.

"I was investigating Bethany's boyfriend's—"

"Ex-boyfriend," Duncan and Bethany said in unison.

Tasha noticed Owen looked taken aback by their intensity, but then he wasn't yet aware of the fact Duncan and Bethany were now a couple. How would Owen feel about that?

"Yeah, ex," he corrected. "I didn't believe the guy committed suicide. After checking into his job and nosing around town, I thought I had a good idea of what he might have stumbled on. I believed Charlie was dead— but I thought he'd been murdered. Tasha told me he faked his own death."

"He did. Owen, I'm so sorry," Bethany said, leaning her head against Owen's shoulder.

"Not your fault. Glad he's not going to be around, though, and that you didn't go with him into Witness Protection." Owen bussed a kiss on Bethany's forehead and turned back to the crowd of people in the living room. "Anyway, I went to the dock where your ex rented the boat the Coast Guard found floating and started asking around. Apparently I wasn't the only one interested in why Charlie disappeared, though. Someone had beaten me to it. One of the dockworkers pointed me toward a bar down the street. I started walking there, and next thing I knew, I was in a van. I came to in Mexico."

"Mexico!" Emma said.

"Vargas?" Duncan asked.

"You're saying this *does* have something to do with Kara Winston's rescue?" Ian asked, referring to the nineteen-year-old girl Duncan's security company had been hired to retrieve from a drug lord's hacienda earlier in the year, the same event that had ultimately ended with Ian being blinded.

"I didn't think so," Owen said. "But apparently Vargas was tired of having his possessions taken from him. I heard the guards talking, and from what I could understand, we weren't the only ones in Mexico relieving Vargas of women. Vargas's wife managed to escape his control. That's where he'd gone, who he had gone after, while we were getting Kara out of the compound."

"Did the guards say anything else about him?" Duncan asked.

"Again, my Spanish is pretty rusty, but from the way it sounds, Vargas is a time bomb with major anger issues. He's tired of being made to look like a fool," Owen told them.

"Which means he's going to be even angrier when he finds out what happened in Redemption," Tasha said, her fear tripling at the thought.

Owen glanced from her to Duncan for an explanation, and his boss filled him in on Vargas's massive meth lab and money laundering operation being discovered.

"Wait," Bethany said. "Does that mean Vargas knows Charlie was the one who exposed everything? Because he tried to blackmail Mr. Warren?"

"I doubt there is much Vargas doesn't know when it comes to his business," Owen told her. "Now tell me what else I've missed," Owen ordered, his gaze on Duncan. "How did Charlie surface, anyway?"

"Quinn and I found him when we went looking for you," Duncan said. "As far as I knew, Beth's ex was dead, but when things in town weren't adding up, I followed your footsteps around town checking out the businesses."

"He said he thought by faking his death it would be over," Bethany added. "But the guys after Charlie didn't believe he'd committed suicide, either, and since they hadn't killed him, they wanted to use me as bait to draw him out of hiding. But... Kyle couldn't bring himself to kidnap me."

A low sound emerged from Owen. "*Kyle?*" he asked, referring to a childhood friend from Redemption.

Bethany nodded. "Owen, you wouldn't believe how many people were involved in some way or another. So many of the businesses in town were going under; the families had to have a way of supporting themselves so... Anyway, Kyle wound up sneaking into Mom and Dad's. He tied me up and took pictures of me when I was pregnant to prove to Charlie I was, and threatened me so Charlie would return the information he'd stolen."

"It wouldn't have been a problem at all had her ex not planted it on her in the first place," Duncan said, still sounding angry and bitter.

"*On you?*" Owen asked Bethany, receiving a small nod.

"Owen, what about you? How did you escape?" Emma asked,

bringing the group back on track. "No offense, but you do look… awful."

Tasha watched as Owen stared at his sister for a long moment before he dragged his attention away and focused on Em. "None taken. As to how… The guys guarding me got careless once Vargas wasn't there. I was able to get away. I laid low and managed to hitch a ride to an area I'd heard of back when we were preparing to go after Kara. I made it back into the States there."

"Why not call for help?" Duncan asked.

"He's right," Emma said. "We could've helped you and brought you home."

"I needed to clear my head," Owen said simply. "The walk helped."

Tasha sat there and stared at Owen. Glared at him. *The walk helped?* She'd been worried out of her mind over him, and he couldn't contact them because he'd needed a *walk to clear his head?*

"All that matters is that you're here now," Bethany said.

"She's right," Duncan agreed. "The Feds managed to connect the locals laundering money for the cartel thanks to the intel Charlie had copied and hidden on Bethany's cell phone, but everyone sitting here knows you got lucky getting out of there alive."

Tasha stared at her sneakers, unable to look at the others in the room. Mexico. They would never have found Owen there. Never known what had happened to him.

"Why take you from Virginia Beach to Mexico?" Quinn asked, joining the conversation.

"Good question," Duncan said. "Owen? Any ideas?"

"Bad timing," Owen said. "Vargas was on his way out of the country when they discovered my interest in Charlie. They didn't have time to stay and question me, so they took me with them."

"Vargas won't risk traveling north given all the heat on him at the moment," Ian said. He sat in a chair near the couch, his eyes hidden behind dark sunglasses. "Every agency is looking for him, and the price on his head has quadrupled. With Charlie turning state's evidence to avoid charges, Vargas will focus on tracking Charlie and eliminating the evidence."

Tasha glanced at Bethany's face and saw the woman swallow hard. Ian hadn't stated anything they all hadn't already figured out, but hearing that the biological father of her child had a death sentence had to frighten the woman.

"In case there is any doubt, *you* are safe now," Duncan said to Bethany. "I'm not going to let anything happen to my girls."

Owen pulled his gaze away from the sleeping baby and glanced toward his sister before shifting his attention to Duncan.

"*Your* girls," Owen murmured, his eyebrows drawn low. "Am I missing something?"

Bethany nudged Owen with her shoulder to get his attention, but Owen didn't budge nor turn to look at her. He kept his focus entirely on Duncan, much to everyone else's amusement.

"We're together," Bethany said simply, holding out her left hand and the simple platinum wedding band on her ring finger. "Duncan and I are married."

Owen stared at his little sister and then his boss, unable to comprehend the details. *"Married?"*

Married," Owen repeated again. An hour had passed since everyone had left Tasha's house, but he still couldn't wrap his mind around Duncan and his baby sister. *Married.*

"They're happy," Tasha said from where she sat curled up in a chair. "Duncan and Bethany got really close as they… searched for answers, and Bethany and the baby were in danger. It happened fast, but it's not one of those fly-by-night marriages. I see them going the distance."

Something about the way she said it made him think she referred to their relationship, and he didn't like it. They weren't casual, and he certainly planned to go the distance. "You're still mad at me."

Tasha got to her feet and retrieved the tray he'd left on the coffee table, carrying it to the kitchen and placing the dishes in the dishwasher. Dexter followed her, meowing every step of the way.

"Hungry, Dex? What will it be tonight?" Tasha asked, opening a cabinet door to pick out a can of chow for the cat.

"I'll take that as a yes," he said, sighing and rubbing his tired eyes. How could he be tired after sleeping so much?

"I'm not going to argue with you, Owen."

In all the time they'd spent together, they'd never argued. Not really. They'd had a few spats over the remote control and hadn't agreed on whether Ian was being a jerk or Emma too emotional back in the days before the couple had married, but never anything hardcore. But this... "Tell me why you're so upset so we can deal with it."

She glared at him from above the kitchen pass-through, her mouth open. "Seriously?"

"Yes, seriously. Why are you angry? Because I'm still alive?"

"*No!* How could you think I'm upset about that?" she asked, looking appalled.

Her expression gave him some comfort. "I can't read your mind, sweetheart. If it's not that, then what? Because I *thought* you'd be happy to see me." He waited impatiently for her to respond, but she just continued to glare at him in between body-swivels to load the washer. "Tasha—"

"How am I supposed to feel?" she demanded. "Yes, I'm angry! You took off after dangerous criminals you believed had murdered Charlie— all on your own, without anyone to help you if something happened. Then, something *did* happen. You could've died in *Mexico,* and we would've never known! Never found your bo—"

Her voice broke, and she couldn't finish the sentence. Not that she needed to. Yeah, he could've died in Mexico. Almost had. But to him, it was all part of the job. "Tasha..."

She turned her back to him. While she cleared her throat and banged dishes together, he got to his feet and made his way to the kitchen. She jumped when he placed his hands on her shoulders.

He was obviously more sleep-deprived and exhausted than he'd thought if he hadn't considered what his disappearance had done to her, reminded her of. "I'm sorry. Sweetheart, I'm still foggy, and I wasn't thinking about what happened with your fiancé. But I'm here, Tasha. I made it home." He lowered his mouth to her forehead to kiss, inhaling the smell of her shampoo.

"This time," she added softly. "But doing what you do, how many more times am I going to be left to wait and worry and wonder if you're dead? Hmm?" She turned to stare up at him, her eyes glittering with tears she refused to shed. "How many times are you going to go rushing off to chase danger because of a case, or to protect someone for money? How many times will you endanger yourself for someone you don't know?"

He brushed his knuckles over her cheek, hating that she flinched again and turned her face away before he could make contact. "It's my job. You knew that when we got involved."

"I did," she agreed, the words hoarse and low. "But now I know what it feels like to lose you, too, and… I refuse to go through that again. I *can't*," she said, pulling away from him and avoiding his gaze as she slammed the dishwasher door closed. She slipped by him in the narrow, galley-style kitchen. "Go to bed, Owen. You need to rest."

He watched as she hurried into the spare bedroom off the kitchen and firmly shut the door behind her, a distinct *click* sounding as she locked the paneled wood for good measure.

Owen fought his frustration and wiped his hands over his shaggy face again, unable to deny her words when his body craved the soft mattress of her bed. The only problem was that he wanted her there beside him for the rest of his life.

With that goal in mind, he limped toward the bedroom door and knocked once.

"Owen, please. Leave me alone. I can't— I can't deal with any more tonight."

He pressed his forehead to the cool wood and sighed. "Tasha."

"What?"

"I love you. I fought my way out of there. I fought my way back here because I love you. I know you're scared, but remember that."

Owen went back to the bedroom and fell atop the mattress, staring up at the ceiling in the dark room. Something was wrong. Something he couldn't put his finger on. More than just her fear of losing him like she'd lost her former fiancé.

But what?

Chapter 7

Tasha stared down at the plate in front of her inside Cuppa Jo's, Jolie's coffee house, fighting the roll and pitch of her queasy stomach.

"Something wrong with the bagel?" Jolie asked. "You wanted your usual, right?"

"Right," she said between her clenched teeth. The smell of the bagel and the powerful smell of coffee and chocolate mingled— and not in a good way. In fact, another whiff left her racing toward the ladies' room.

"Tasha!"

Tasha ignored Jolie's cry of alarm, more concerned with upchucking the half bagel and coffee she'd managed to get down all over Jolie's pretty, shiny floors, and in front of customers. She burst into the bathroom stall just in time, and the breakfast she'd just paid for returned for a second visit.

Hot prickles seared her skin, and Tasha groaned when she felt Jolie gathering fistfuls of hair and holding it out of the way. Her rolling stomach finally calmed. Jolie dampened a towel, pressing it to Tasha's neck.

Tasha turned and leaned weakly against the brick wall beside her, using the towel to wipe her mouth and cool her face. "Thanks." She felt a lot better, in fact. Now that she wasn't struggling to hold down her food, the queasiness was abating rapidly.

"Tasha, is there any chance that you're... pregnant?" Jolie asked.

"What?" Even she heard the high-pitched squeak to her voice. "No. I probably have that flu that's going around," she said, glancing quickly at Jolie before looking away.

"Have you taken a test?"

"No need," Tasha said. "Why would I? It's just all the stress."

Jolie helped Tasha stand. Together they walked to the sink for Tasha to splash her face and repair the mascara smudged beneath her eyes. When Tasha finished, Jolie opened the restroom door and steered Tasha to the office rather than the seating area in the front of the store.

"Let's sit in here for a bit," Jolie said. "Lie down."

"When did you get so bossy?" Tasha grumbled, feeling foolish now that her episode was over.

"When I realized bossiness has its benefits," Jolie countered, gently pushing Tasha down to the love seat lining the short wall by the door. "Stay put. I'll go get your purse and be right back with something to settle your stomach."

Not about to argue because she needed some time alone, Tasha nodded and closed her eyes until Jolie left the room, then she stared up at the painted ceiling as abject terror set in.

When was her last cycle? How much longer was she going to deny the truth? Was the queasiness stress-induced?

It was possible. God knew she'd certainly felt an abundance of it with Owen's disappearance and now his return. In and of itself, Owen's return was a happy stress, but it also brought home the very real decision that had to be made before things between them went any further.

Maybe if Owen had been able to escape sooner, she wouldn't have had so much time to think, so much time for the fears to settle deep and take root, grow. Maybe if he hadn't gone missing at all but had sought help from Duncan and the security company, she wouldn't fear her future with Owen.

"Here. Sip this," Jolie ordered. "I found some crackers, too. Wait, I'll help you sit up."

Was she pregnant? "I've got it," Tasha murmured, pushing herself upright. "I'm fine. Seriously. Don't fuss."

Jolie tore open the plastic wrapper and waited for Tasha to take one of the saltines.

"Tash…"

"You know what all's been going on. It's just stress."

"It could be," Jolie pressed. "But are you saying there's absolutely, positively no way you could be pregnant? You and Owen haven't…?"

They had. She and Owen had made love before he'd left… Dinner and a movie had turned into more, and even though she'd told herself their relationship was one of companionship…. "It's… possible."

"Bethany said she didn't realize for several months," Jolie said. "I'll drive you to get a test, and we can come back here for you to take it."

"No."

"Tasha—"

"I'm *not*. I can't be."

"You just said there's a possibility," Jolie argued.

"There's no need for a test. Besides, even if I am…" She let her words trail off, wondering if she shocked her friend. But she had to be honest. She worked long hours six, sometimes seven days a week. And she loved it. But given her current relationship with Owen and her inability to accept what he did for a living, bringing a child into her life was not a good idea.

"You'd… *abort?*" Jolie whispered, barely able to say the word.

Tasha winced. "*No,* I couldn't, because it's certainly not a baby's fault that its parents were irresponsible. It's like killing kittens because the cat followed the natural course of nature or the owner didn't get it fixed."

"You're not a cat, Tasha. And this baby has two very wonderful people as parents."

"*If* there is a baby, which there *isn't*, who's to say it wouldn't be better off... put up for adoption? There are a lot of really good people out there wanting children who can't have them."

"And what about Owen? You don't think he'd want a say in this? In whether he gets to raise his baby and be a father? I know Quinn would."

Tasha munched on the cracker to keep from saying something she might regret to Jolie and pondered her friend's words. "How could he raise a baby with his job? How can I raise a baby working my job, and him working his?" Yeah, in her heart of hearts, she knew Owen would want to raise his baby. He'd demand marriage. Want them to start a life together. But how could she be with him, have a baby with him, when she couldn't be with him now? After nearly losing him? When the thought of losing him *again* ripped her apart and shredded her soul? "What am I going to do?"

"Oh, Tash," Jolie murmured, her voice soft and tender. So Jolie. "I know it's frightening, but you know we're here for you. A baby is a *blessing*—"

She shook her head, a near-hysterical laugh bubbling out of her throat. "No. No, I'm not even talking about that. What am I going to do about Owen?"

"What do you mean?"

Tasha met Jolie's gaze, desperate to confide in someone. "He came back. He's *alive*," she whispered. "It's a Christmas miracle. But instead of being happy— and I am, don't get me wrong— I don't feel the way I should, Jo-Jo. I don't. And that's messed up. *I'm* messed up."

"You're scared," Jolie countered, covering Tasha's hands with her own. "Anyone who has been through what you've been through would be. It's normal. But you can't let the past dictate your future. I'm a perfect example of that, and you know it," she said, referring to her once-secret habit of cutting that had come to light in recent months.

"It's not the same," Tasha argued.

"Why isn't it?"

"Because... Quinn left that life and now works training *dogs* while Owen chases bad guys with guns. If I'm pregnant, that's not the occupation I want for m-my— For Owen. For my child's *father*. I can't— I *can't* be that woman pacing the floor and looking out the window every five seconds waiting to see if I'm a widow."

Jolie was silent a long minute, her eyes, her expression sad but understanding. "So...what are you going to do?"

Chapter 8

That same morning, Owen opened Tasha's front door and spotted Duncan on the other side. "Hey. Wasn't expecting you. Come in."

Duncan held up a set of keys but didn't step forward. "Thought you might be needing this now that you're back."

"Those aren't my keys."

"They are now. Take a look."

Owen stepped outside and spotted a black Denali similar to the one he'd driven for the security company, only newer. "What happened to—"

"It was burned out in Virginia Beach."

Something else he hadn't been made aware of. "Ah, man, Duncan. I'm sorry. I didn't think to ask about it when you were here yesterday."

"That's what insurance is for. I'm just glad you're back to drive the replacement."

"Me, too." They stood there admiring the new purchase for a long moment before Duncan sighed.

"Got time to talk?" Duncan asked.

Owen headed toward the door, dread filling him.

"Tasha over at the clinic?"

"I don't know where she is," Owen said, the words emerging a little more heated and revealing than he'd have liked. He led the way to the living room and the chair he'd vacated when he'd heard Duncan arrive, not in the mood to deal with his boss turned *brother-in-law* at the moment. How was this going to work? He and Duncan worked well together, but that had been before Bethany was involved. He wasn't sure how to feel about that.

"Trouble?" Duncan asked.

"Only if you think Tasha waking up and hightailing it out of here without so much as a note qualifies as trouble." He sat in the recliner and lifted the footrest. "Help yourself to a drink if you want it. You already helped yourself to my sister." Maybe taking his bad mood out on Duncan wasn't such a good idea, but at this point, Owen didn't care.

Duncan stood still as stone before moving to the window facing the backyard.

"I knew you'd be upset."

"Didn't stop you, though."

"The question is why?" Duncan continued, shooting Owen a quick glare. "I love her. Never thought I'd see the day when not one but two little women have me wrapped around their fingers. Isn't that enough to see it's real and know I'll do everything I can to make them happy?"

Owen rubbed his fingers against the beard he had yet to shave and frowned. "Maybe it would be if I didn't know for a fact you had a crush on Emma before she and Ian got together. Wasn't that long ago, either. How do I know Bethany isn't just a fill-in?"

"She's not."

Owen waited for Duncan to continue.

"She's not. And for the record, I *admired* Emma. We all did. She kicked butt as a blind chick. Are you really gonna sit there and tell me you didn't have a little crush on her yourself before Ian staked his claim?"

They locked glares for a long moment before grinning. "Women," Owen said.

"Got that right," Duncan agreed, nodding.

"Treat my sister right, or so help me— boss."

"Understood. Now what's going on with you and Tasha? Got anything to do with you looking like a mountain man?"

"I was just thinking of going to the barbershop when you knocked."

"You sure you're up for that?"

Probably not. "I need to get out of here before I put a hole in one of her walls."

"On your feet then. I know just the place."

Just the place was The Shake Shak, the local diner owned by Emma's father. It was the second stop Duncan made after driving Owen to the barbershop long enough for a shave and a haircut. Owen had tipped the barber well in consideration of the mess he'd had to tackle, and now he and Duncan walked into the Shak and chose a booth near the billiard tables.

"I thought I spotted you two coming in," Emma said, rounding the corner with a smile.

"What are you doing here?" Duncan asked.

"I could ask the same of you," the pretty brunette said with a grin. "I'm filling in for one of the waitresses so she can get some last-minute Christmas shopping done. What about you two? You out shopping for my girlies?"

Christmas. It was only a few days away, and yet he hadn't given it any thought at all. "Duncan and I need to talk business," Owen said, making up an excuse.

"I see. Well, what will you have? On the house to celebrate your return."

He and Duncan ordered an appetizer plate along with steaks and their favorite beer.

"Gotcha. Be back soon," Emma said. "By the way, Owen, you look much better without the wild-man look."

"Thanks," he said, watching as Emma left to place their order for food and fill their drinks.

"Bethany asked to stay on the mountain for a while," Duncan said casually. "She likes it here, especially with all the girls fussing over her and the baby. But now that you're back, I couldn't drag her out of town if I tried. You and Tasha need to drive up this evening and visit."

"Here you go," Emma said, returning with their drinks and the appetizer plate. "Enjoy."

When she'd unloaded her tray and was gone again, Owen forked one of the loaded potato skins onto his plate. "Not sure what we'll be doing, but I'll make sure to spend some time with Beth." Around a mouthful of food, he added, "Tasha and I got into it last night," he said, relaying all that had gone down. "Things are different now."

Duncan sat back in the booth, his silence allowing Owen to ramble.

"Maybe one of these days, I'll be ready to take a desk job and coordinate bodyguard schedules and security system installs, but I'm not there yet."

"You tell her that?" Duncan asked.

"No. I reminded Tasha that she knew what I did for a living when…we got together." Duncan winced at the news, and Owen shrugged. "I wasn't thinking at the time."

"Obviously," Emma said as she rounded the corner of the booth. "Yes, I was eavesdropping, but only because I heard Tasha's name mentioned," she said, lowering another tray and balancing it on the edge of the table to deliver their food. "Owen, you have no idea what a wreck Tasha has been these last few months, not knowing what happened to you… I know it's hard, and as happy as she is that you're here, she's probably pushing you away with both hands right now, but cut her some slack."

"I'm not sure that's what she wants," Owen admitted, the words hard to get out. He stared down at the drink in his hand, unable to look at his friends. "Tasha's the one who has to make a decision, Emma. I'm in this for the long haul, but I'm not sure I'm the man she wants anymore. Or if I can be that man."

Chapter 9

Tasha returned to her clinic and spent the rest of the day and most of the evening in a total daze, her thoughts racing from panic to fear to amazement at the thought of carrying a baby inside her.

She'd never given much thought to kids, to be honest. She'd always assumed that when the time and the marriage were right, things would take their natural course. But here she was without a ring, potentially without a man, and possibly knocked up.

Oh, go buy a test already.

She locked up the clinic and returned to her quiet house, taking a quick shower to remove the ever-present dog and cat hair. She dressed in her softest, most comfortable sweats and foraged in the kitchen for something to eat besides leftover pizza and half of a sub sandwich. Her stomach rolled at the thought, and she quickly closed the refrigerator door, pouring herself a glass of water instead.

Em had texted her from the Shak to let her know Owen and Duncan had stopped for lunch and that Owen was going to spend the rest of the day with Bethany after getting a new cell phone to replace the one taken from him when he'd been kidnapped and held.

The reprieve was welcome, given her mood, but she wondered

what, if anything, Owen was telling his sister and his best friend. That was a lot of hours to fill, and she knew she had to be the topic at some point.

Em had given no indication of when Owen would return. Maybe he'd choose to spend the night atop the mountain, in the empty apartment above the kennel, where he'd stayed while helping Duncan transform the house for Ian.

Her phone chimed, and she walked to the table to pick it up.

Coffee house. Now. Em told me you're alone, so don't you dare not come, Jolie texted.

Realizing she didn't really want to be alone in the house right now, she slipped on a pair of shoes and grabbed her keys. Owen could come or go. He would do as he pleased, anyway. Wasn't that the way things were with men?

Five minutes later, Jolie unlocked the door of Cuppa Jo's, and Tasha stepped inside. "What's up?" She'd no sooner asked the question than she noticed Emma and Morgan seated behind the pretty wall and fireplace. "Jo-Jo, what have you done?"

"Emergency meeting of the *Besties*," Jolie replied, wrapping her arm around Tasha's shoulders and steering her toward the others. "And don't pretend you're surprised."

Surprised. Ticked off. More than a little vulnerable and nauseated. "Don't do this," Tasha begged, the words a hoarse whisper.

"You aren't alone in this, no matter how much you think you are. Sit down," Jolie ordered. "I've already told the girls."

"What?" Tasha glared at Jolie in horror.

"Would you really not tell us?" Emma asked. "We share everything."

Yeah, and sometimes they shared a little too much. But she wasn't Morgan, who spilled every secret, or Em, who'd needed their take on things in the past because she'd missed so many cues while she was blind. Jolie—Jolie liked to *cut* herself when things got really, really stressful and she freaked out, a habit she'd thankfully conquered of late with help from Quinn, but one she'd kept secret from the *Besties* for years. "I'm leaving."

"No, you're not," Jolie said, quickly blocking the exit.

"We knew you couldn't go into the drugstore to buy a test without everyone in town knowing about it so…" Emma scooted a brown paper bag across the table toward Tasha. "No one will say a word to me, or Ian, since it will look like we're trying or something."

Her eyes prickled with the hot sting of tears, and Tasha blinked rapidly, willing them away. Because it was true. She'd resigned herself to the fact she'd have to drive a few towns away to purchase a test or else face the small-town gossip that would result from Stone River's single, female vet purchasing a pregnancy test.

"It says for best results to take it in the morning, so I bought a couple of them," Emma added. "But you're not leaving this building until you take one."

A huff left Tasha's chest. "Falling in love has made *all* of you bossy," she said in complaint. But when they continued to stare at her, she rolled her eyes. "Fine. Whatever. Give me that."

She swiped the bag from the table and carried it with her into the restroom closer to the front of the store, aware that she was being followed. "I can do this alone, you know."

"It's tradition," Morgan said with a snicker. "Don't we always go to the bathroom together when we're hanging out? Why stop now?"

The four of them entered the two-stall restroom, and Tasha shrugged off her coat, handing it to the first pair of hands that reached out to take it. "I can't believe you're forcing me to do this now."

"No better time than the present," Em said.

Inside the stall, Tasha ripped open the box and quickly scanned the instructions before shoving her sweats low and sitting on the toilet only to find the urge to pee nonexistent.

"Let loose," Morgan called, snickering a bit more.

Em shushed Morgan with a murmur, adding, "Need me to turn on the water?"

"This is so not cool," Tasha grumbled, knowing the *Besties* didn't care.

"I can sing the potty song I made up for the kids," Morgan called out, a definite smirk in her voice. "Or what about Christmas carols?"

"Water, please," Tasha called quickly, wanting to bang her head against the stall wall. "Turn on the water."

She ignored the snickers and nervous laughter of her friends, knowing deep down they were almost as anxious and nervous about the outcome of the test as she was. *Almost.*

What if it was positive?

Thanks to the water, she was able to take care of business, and the longest two minutes of her life began.

"You can't be serious," Morgan said loudly. "You are not going to wait in there while we're out here dying to know."

"Come out, Tash. You know if you don't, we're not above crawling under the stall," Emma said.

Muttering under her breath because she knew good and well they would do just that, Tasha yanked up her sweats and left her temporary safe haven. "You call this friendship, but some would call it abuse."

"Consider it tough love," Emma said, stepping close and giving Tasha a hug. "Whatever it says, we're here for you."

"Even if I decide not to raise the baby? Or— Or not to raise it with Owen?" she pressed, needing the reassurance that she had their complete support since Owen and Duncan and Ian were all so close.

"I hope that's not the case, but, yeah," Em replied.

Silence filled the bathroom, broken only by the jangling, jingling sound Morgan's bracelets made when she fluffed her hair with her fingers.

"So… how's things going with you and Mr. Hockey?" Em asked Morgan. "Give us a two-minute update."

Tasha was thankful their attention shifted to Morgan as she filled them in on the latest developments between her and her new love.

"Can we expect wedding bells?" Jolie asked, her eyes wide at the thought.

Morgan gave them an unapologetic grin.

"We're not rushing into anything but— I wouldn't mind wearing

Knox's ring on my hand. *One day.* He's the best thing to happen to me short of my kids. And totally different from my ex."

"Well, that's good, at least," Em murmured, her gaze shifting to the pregnancy test stick lying on the sink.

Em's glance caused them all to look at the plain white stick that could change Tasha's life forever. Tasha took a step closer, but she had deliberately laid the stick result-side down so that she had a moment to prepare herself.

"Has it been two minutes?" Jolie asked.

"I think that's a suggested time," Morgan said, her voice lowering to a gentle whisper. "I could never wait the whole two minutes and looked early. It was always right, one way or another."

Well, Morgan ought to know, considering she had two kids underfoot.

Tasha inhaled and took another step toward the sink and counter, hesitantly reaching out to grasp the thin, white plastic.

"Tash, whatever it is, we've got your six," Em said.

Tasha pursed her lips in a wry smile and met their gazes one by one in the mirror in front of her. "You've been hanging around with Ian too much. The military jargon is rubbing off on you."

"Will you look already," Morgan ordered, her southern twang becoming more pronounced with her agitation. "The suspense is killing me."

"Wait," Jolie said.

"What? *Why?*" Morgan cried.

"Tasha, remember what I said. A baby is a blessing. Some things are meant to be, which is why they happen— or not."

Nodding her understanding, Tasha rolled the plastic between her fingers, feeling her friends crowding around her to see the results.

Two bars.

"You're *pregnant!*" the *Besties* screamed.

Chapter 10

Owen waited up for Tasha to return. Through Ian, Owen knew the *Besties* were getting together tonight after hours at Jolie's coffee shop.

Seeing as how he and Tasha had been separated for so long, he wondered at the reason behind the gathering— and had to believe he was part of their blitz session.

After driving up the mountain to visit Bethany and his newborn niece, he'd had the opportunity to see Beth and Duncan interact. It wasn't hard to tell the two were in love, and Owen had to give Duncan credit for seemingly being unable to take his eyes off Bethany.

He'd been surprised the two had hit it off, but he couldn't have picked a better man for his little sister. So long as Duncan treated her right, he'd live.

Beth had even asked his opinion on what she should buy Duncan for Christmas. That in itself wasn't unusual because Beth had always loved Christmas and giving presents. No, the comical part had come when Duncan had also yanked him aside and asked the same question in regard to Beth.

With Christmas closing in on them, Duncan, Beth, and the baby were going to stay at the house with Emma and Ian until the New

Year then return to Atlanta, where Duncan's security company was located. Beth would eventually open a second Redd Hott Restorations location in Atlanta, but first she was planning to enjoy being a mother.

Owen gave his sister a month, two tops. No way could she stay out from under a muscle car any longer than that. His sister had been born with motor oil in her veins, and he didn't doubt his little niece would be under a car with her mama before she was a year old.

A vehicle pulled into the driveway, lights flashing into the interior of the small house before shutting off with the engine.

Dexter jumped off of Owen's lap and stretched as only a cat could, then padded over to the door to greet his mistress.

"You shouldn't have waited up," she said by way of greeting.

"I didn't want to go to bed without kissing you good night," he said, eyeing Tasha as she stood there in her sweats, her hands clasped in front of her belly as though to keep herself from flying apart. "Are you all right? Something happen tonight with your friends?"

She shook her head, her hair falling forward over her face. "No, I'm just really tired, that's all."

That wasn't it, although he could tell she was more tired than usual. Her veterinary practice kept her busy during all hours of the day and night, but the few days he'd been back, he'd noticed the shadows under her eyes. Put there because of her worry over him? Probably so. "Come here."

He pulled her into his arms, held her against his chest. The scent of her hair enveloped him in comfort.

Owen lifted her face to his and brushed his mouth over hers in a soft kiss. Once. Twice. A third time. He pulled her closer when he felt her melt against him.

And then she pushed him away.

"No."

Chapter 11

Seasick. That's the only way she could describe her condition after Owen kissed her.

She raced toward the bathroom with an excuse that she needed more time, and prayed Owen didn't follow.

Tasha locked the door, flipped on the faucets, and blasted the iPod to drown out the sound of her hurling into the toilet, all the while praying for forgiveness, redemption, for answers as obvious as the positive pregnancy test.

Owen didn't knock on the door. She flushed and showered, her mind whirling with scenarios about how she would tell him.

But the timing… It couldn't be any worse. She couldn't ruin Christmas, but that was exactly what she'd be doing if she brought up the subject.

She darted into the spare bedroom and locked the door without saying good night. She needed time. More time to pray, to think, and to find a solution she could live with…

THANKFULLY TASHA'S four-legged patients kept her busy the following day and forced her to focus on their ailments versus her own. This time of year, she saw all kinds of injuries, from broken Christmas bulbs embedded in paws to the wrong things being eaten because candies and nuts and fruits were abundant around the house.

There was also a new baby about to be born to a prized Arabian out on Cooper's Ridge. It was the horse's first, as well as the very anxious owner's, leaving everyone on edge while they waited for the birth. Winter wasn't an especially good time of year for such things to take place, but sometimes nature had a way of making things happen when they were least expected.

Tasha's lips twisted with wry irony several hours later. Actions had consequences, and hers was no different. Sighing, she lifted an old-fashioned clipboard from the file holder outside one of the exam rooms. Ah, little Penelope.

Tasha knocked on the door before letting herself into the room, immediately spotting the Yorkie/Maltese mix trembling in her owner's arms. "Miss Penelope, you're not feeling well?"

The dog's owner greeted Tasha with a worried frown.

"She hasn't eaten anything today, and barely anything yesterday."

"Any vomiting?" Tasha asked, beginning her examination of the dog while the Morkie was still in her owner's arms.

"Yes. Once today," the woman said. "And a couple times in the last week. She's vomited before when she's gotten into something she shouldn't, but she bounces back so quickly. All she wants to do lately is sleep."

Tasha listened to the dog's heart as well as her stomach but heard nothing out of the ordinary. "And you're sure you don't have any food lying out that she might have gotten into? Plants used for decorating?"

"No. I'm so careful about both those things."

"Any new pets or people in the house that might upset her?" Tasha asked next, knowing dogs, small dogs especially, were very possessive of their humans and homes.

"Well, I have kept my daughter's dog a few times lately while she worked, but Penelope didn't seem to mind."

Frowning, Tasha opened Penelope's chart and took a quick glance at the main sheet. "She's never been fixed."

"No, but— Oh, do you think?" the woman asked, her eyes widening at the possibility. "She was at the end of her cycle the first time I kept the other dog. I thought it would be okay."

"Well, a blood test will tell us and rule out some of the other possibilities." She grabbed a syringe and murmured soothingly to Penelope while drawing blood. "Hang tight, and I'll be back in as soon as we know something."

"Thank you. Oh, Penelope, did you let Zeus get to you? Did you?"

Tasha shut the door to the exam room and leaned against it momentarily, her body wracked with fatigue.

"You have a call on one. It's Emma. Anything I can do?" her assistant asked.

Tasha handed off the syringe and asked for the appropriate tests, dragging her tired body down the hall. "Is it lunch time yet?" she called out along the way, not really hungry but wanting a few minutes alone in her office.

"Ordering now," her billing clerk called in response. "Your usual?"

"Sure," she said, knowing she had to keep up appearances until she figured out what she was going to do. Inside her office, Tasha collapsed into her chair before grabbing the phone. "Hey, Em."

"Did you tell him?"

"No."

"What?" Emma cried. "Tasha, you *have* to tell him."

"I will."

"When?"

Tasha closed her eyes and leaned her head against the tufted leather seat. "When I know how to handle it myself."

"Oh, Tash. I know it's a surprise, but surely you and Owen can work something out."

"I really can't talk right now, Em. Did you need anything else?"

She couldn't discuss the subject of her and Owen's relationship…or whatever it was they shared.

"Yeah, actually. I'm hoping you'll agree to spend Christmas afternoon with us at the house. Dinner with all the trimmings. Please say you'll come. Everyone is going to be there."

"I don't know. I'll be on call. And it just depends," she added. "I'm not really in a social mood at the moment."

"I know. But you realize not being social and celebrating Owen's miracle return is only going to draw more attention to you, right?"

Oh, that was true. "Em… I'm drowning here. I don't know what I'm doing yet. I just… I just can't think about Christmas right now, on top of everything else."

"I understand. Just remember these things happen and we all understand. We're human, too. Now, have you bought anything for Owen?"

A moan left her. "When have I had time?"

"I was just asking. Besides, you know Owen certainly doesn't expect gifts, and even if he does, you're going to give him the best gift of all. *When you tell him.*"

"You have a one-track mind," Tasha grumbled.

"Yeah, well, you're too stubborn for your own good. Someone has to watch out for you when you're too hormonal to take care of yourself."

"You know why I have issues with this, Em. Don't make me out to be the bad guy."

"Oh, sweetie, I'm not. Really. I just wish you could see the potential and come up with a compromise. Every day is a new beginning. Remember that, and maybe that will spark something between you two and you can talk about the future."

The future. Did she and Owen have a future?

The kiss last night had been wonderful. Magical.

But it was also the perfect way to say good-bye.

Chapter 12

You're in a good mood," Duncan said the moment he spotted Owen entering Cuppa Jo's for a coffee fix.

Owen couldn't have stopped the smile that formed even if he'd faced a firing squad. "It's Christmas. Who doesn't love Christmas?"

"Ahh," Duncan said. "His coffee is on me," he said to the girl behind the register.

Owen placed his order and leaned against the counter to take the weight off his injured leg. The bullet wound had healed nicely, but the cold weather was making it ache.

"So does your good mood mean that things are better with Tasha?" Duncan asked.

"No, not really. But I hope they'll be better soon."

"And you're out and about because…?"

"I'm behind on my Christmas shopping. Speaking of which, you busy? I could probably use an opinion from someone who's already been there." Owen accepted his coffee from the barista and took a careful sip of the hot brew.

"Been where?" Duncan asked.

"The jewelry store's ring section." Owen watched as his friend's eyebrows lifted at the statement, but he chose to ignore Duncan's surprise. "I thought about waiting, but why should we? After every-thing that happened, I think it's more reason to jump in with both feet."

"You sure that's wise?" Duncan asked once they had moved away from the counter toward an empty part of the coffee shop.

"What do you mean?"

"Owen, I get where you're coming from. You love her, and you can't wait to make her yours and show her how much you want to be with her. But Tasha had a rough time of it while you were gone."

"I know that."

"And you're sure you aren't pushing things a little too fast?" Duncan questioned.

Owen thought about his suspicions and just as quickly shook his head. Did Tasha really think he wouldn't notice all the changes in her body? Her behavior? Thin though she was, he had definitely noticed the slightly larger, firmer curve of her stomach.

She'd tried to hide the sound of her retching with music, but he'd heard. She'd hurled yesterday morning, too, though at the time, he hadn't been sure. Pregnant or not… "I love her. I want to marry her. The entire time I was rotting in Mexico, it's all I could think about. How I'd had my chance with her, and I hadn't taken it as seriously as I should. I wasn't much of a religious man before but I prayed in that cell. Prayed hard. Can't help but think God's given me a second chance, and I'm not going to waste it."

Duncan accepted the words with a nod. "Any idea of how you're going to propose?"

"Yeah, and if you're not doing anything, I may need your help and Beth's, too. Got any plans for the rest of the day?"

COME ON, what's taking so long?" Owen murmured that evening after he'd stood and retrieved the switch he needed for the first part of his surprise.

The moment Tasha's key slid into the lock and the door opened, he pressed the button, and the interior of the house lit up with bright white lights.

Tasha gasped and stared at him, the fire burning in the hearth, candles atop the mantel, then at the six-foot blue spruce he'd picked up on the way home. Duncan and Bethany had arrived soon after, and they had gone to work decorating for Christmas. "Well? What do you think?"

Tasha looked paler than normal, and he chalked it up to not enough sleep. At least, that's what he hoped it was. Did women get morning sickness in the evening? Was she carrying his child?

"It's… pretty. You shouldn't have gone to the fuss, though. Christmas will be here and gone in a couple of days."

But he wouldn't be, and that was the point he wanted to get across to her with his spur-of-the-moment romantic evening. He'd meant what he'd said to Emma at the Shak. He was in this with Tasha for the long haul— if she'd have him. "The house was the only one on the street without a tree. I didn't know where you stored your decorations, but I'll get them out tomorrow."

She set her purse and keys on the table by the door, shrugged off her coat, all in silence.

"You must be tired. Have a seat," he said, turning to grab the two glasses of champagne he'd poured, another small test to find out if she was keeping him in the dark about a possible pregnancy or if she even knew herself. Could it be that she didn't know? Hard as she worked, and with so much going on, he supposed it was possible. Maybe the champagne wasn't such a good idea?

Out of his peripheral vision, he saw her move closer to him with slow steps, but the moment he faced her with the champagne, she stopped as though rooted to the floor. "Champagne and chocolate-covered strawberries. Your favorite." He waited for her to take the flute, but she didn't. "Tasha?"

"I'm pregnant."

He quickly set the flutes aside and wrapped her in his arms, lifted her off her feet in a bear hug. "Oh, baby, that's fantastic," he said, murmuring the words against her cheek before he kissed her soft skin. He shifted to kiss her on the lips, but at the last second, she turned her head.

"Owen, put me down. Please."

The second her feet touched the floor, Tasha straight-armed him and shoved him away.

"I can't believe you're happy about this."

"Of course I'm happy about it," he countered. "Tash, look, I know it's not the best of circumstances or the way we'd have liked things to go but—"

"I thought about giving it away," she said, turning her back to him and moving to the kitchen. She pulled a mug from the cabinet and poured herself a glass of filtered water. "But then I thought of how it would feel to know I was handing a child over to total strangers and counting on them to care for and love and raise him or her… I realized I couldn't do it."

"I wouldn't have let you," he told her, following her as far as the entry to the galley kitchen.

She stiffened at his statement, her back and shoulders pulling tight.

"But," she continued softly, "I also know I can't raise a baby with a man who risks his life for a living. I know it's not fair," she said, sliding around so that she leaned her hips against the counter behind her. "You were right when you said I knew what you did for a living before… But now that it's… *confirmed*, it's up to me—"

"Us," he quickly corrected.

"—to protect this baby from harm. That means protecting it from the pain and loss and *devastation* it would feel to love a father who won't be here for him when he needs it."

He fisted his hands at his sides and fought the rage boiling to the surface. "You are not going to keep me from my child, Tasha. I don't even know why we're having this discussion. I love you," he said quietly. "I know you're scared, but are you really going to stand there and pretend you don't feel the same about me?"

She wouldn't look at him.

"I do love you," she finally whispered. "You know I do."

Relief left him weak. "Then work with me here, sweetheart. Tasha… We'll figure something out. We'll get married, and—"

"No."

"Tasha—"

"I *refuse* to go through what I've been through the last few months every time you walk out the door." She crossed her arms over her front and shook her head, her eyes sparkling with tears. "We're both adults, Owen. We both know that sometimes love isn't enough to make something work. I can't *do* this. It's not fair to you, and I am sorry, but I can't. I won't change my mind, either. I'm *not* marrying you. I won't. You need to leave."

Chapter 13

Tasha scooted by him and left the tiny kitchen, but Owen followed her into the living room.

"You want me to quit my job."

She glanced at him over her shoulder. "How many times have you been shot at?" she asked, knowing the number was far, far too high. "Or, just answer this—how many times have you *been* shot? Faced a knife, or a weapon, or been in a fight in the name of duty?"

Considering he still carried the bruises, cuts, and a bullet hole presently healing, she didn't really expect an answer.

Owen raised his hands and took a step closer.

"I'm still here, sweetheart. I know I'm not invincible, but I am careful. I take every precaution I can. Last time… I thought Charlie's disappearance was open and shut. I would have waited had I dug deeper and known what was going on."

She closed her eyes at his response, and a muffled sound left her throat. "Owen, I *love* you. I love you so much I resent you asking me to marry you knowing I could very well have to watch you die. It's not *fair*. It's not right, and I can't do it. I won't do it. Please, just forget I told you about the pregnancy. This baby is *mine*."

She attempted to escape into the spare bedroom after her declaration, but Owen caught her and blocked the way with his body.

Despite the weight loss and treatment he'd received at the hands of his captors, he was still strong, still intimidating to those who didn't know him well. Still handsome, his looks striking.

She stared up at him in the tree-lit hallway and fought the pull of attraction she always felt whenever he was near. Fought the pain ripping her to pieces.

It was better to hurt now than later. How much worse would she hurt having lost him, gotten him back, only to lose him again when he raced out the door for a job? Like his Viking ancestors, Owen relished the thought of battle, of taking on the bad guys and winning.

"Ours," he said simply, the word accompanied by the slightest shake of her shoulders.

He did nothing to hurt her or scare her, but she recognized it as Owen trying to make his point. Still, she blinked, unable to think straight when he stood so close. "What?"

Owen lowered his head until she had to meet his gaze, his nose nearly rubbing against hers.

"The baby is *ours*. Sweetheart, I can tell this has taken you by surprise. Me, too. But it's a *good* surprise. Tash…" He lowered his head even more. "Give it some time. Give us some time. Don't do this. I dreamed of coming back to you. I prayed to see you again, to be with you. *Marry you.* Loving you kept me alive when I was away. Now you're trying to end us?"

Her heart broke at the anguish in his tone. She didn't want to hurt him. "I don't want to. I *have* to. You don't understand."

"You're scared."

"Of course I am! Owen, I know animals, pets. I don't know anything about kids except— I know they have to be protected."

"Not from me."

"Yes, from you," she said, the tears she fought so hard to hide leaking from her eyes. "From the danger you seek out every time you go to work. You *run* toward trouble, not away from it. This whole thing with Bethany… It's a perfect example."

Owen inhaled a ragged breath and pressed his forehead to hers.

"Bethany wouldn't have had any problems at all had her ex not tried to blackmail a money launderer."

"And you wouldn't have gone missing had you simply gone to see Bethany as you said you were, instead of turning it into an investigation."

"You can't ask me to give up my job."

A huff of a laugh left her, and she made a face. "I'm not. That's just it, Owen. I know you don't want to quit. And I know you would resent me if I asked you to. That's why… I'm asking you to leave," she said, barely able to get the words out. "And to leave us—the baby and me—be."

"You don't mean that."

He stood over her, crowding her against the wall. His hands cupped her face and nape as he stared down at her, and with the light of his surprise Christmas tree, she saw every line and shadow of his features. The remainder of the bruises marring his skin, the cut slicing his eyebrow. Her eyes blurred with tears she blinked away, desperate to memorize every detail. "I do," she whispered, well aware that it wasn't the "I do" he wanted.

She wet her lips, waiting, hoping he would kiss her good-bye. One last kiss, one last bit of comfort and love and treasure to hold her in the years to come. Instead, he simply lowered his hands to his sides and took a step back, straightening to his full height.

"This isn't over, Tasha. I'm not giving up on you. On us. We have a life now, one we created together."

Tasha leaned her shoulders against the wall behind her and welcomed the support keeping her upright. "I'm not going to change my mind. Some things are just too hard. I can't work full-time and be a full-time mom and always wonder if you're coming home or not. And I won't be that woman you hate because you gave up something you love. Owen, don't you see? We can't win here."

Owen glared down at her but finally broke away to grab his keys from the table, his coat from the hook by the door.

"This isn't over."

After the door slammed shut behind him, she closed her eyes

and hugged her arms around her front, her legs folding beneath her so that she sank to the floor. She opened her mouth to cry, to release the sobs building in her chest, but no sound emerged, the pain too great.

The old-fashioned clock in the hall clicked and began to chime. Midnight.

It was officially Christmas Eve.

Her phone rang, startling her. The *Besties* or Owen knew to use her cell phone if they needed her. The calls from her clinic forwarded to a service in the evening hours, but in case of emergency, the service rang her here at the house.

She hurried to the base and picked up the portable phone, pressing it to her ear and welcoming the distraction. "Dr. Carter."

Chapter 14

Owen stared out the windshield of the Denali as he drove through town on his way up the mountain to the apartment above Emma's kennel. Every storefront was lit up and decorated for the holiday, every house with a tree shining bright in a window or even out on the porch, welcoming guests.

On the edge of town, he passed Jolie's house and looked for Quinn's truck but didn't see it. Quinn and Jolie were making things work, but Quinn had given up his nomad ways, working as Ian's eyes when it came to training dogs for their new company, Mad Dog Security. Quinn was sticking around, staying in town, which was no doubt why things were progressing with Jolie.

His hands fisted over the steering wheel before he hit it a few times with his palm. How could something so good could turn out so bad? It didn't make sense.

Maybe he was stubborn and set in his ways, but he liked his job. He was good at it. And he was careful, despite Tasha's words to the contrary.

He liked being in the field, knowing he made a difference in someone's life, even if it meant he put his on the line to protect them and see to it that they made it home to their families. That was *important*.

But was it more important than Tasha and the baby they had created?

He still pondered that question when he let himself into the gated entrance of the MacGregor house. He parked outside the kennel but didn't move, too tired and too angry to do more than glare into the night.

A light switched on inside the main house, drawing his attention. A glance in toward the kitchen sink showed Duncan there, the baby on his shoulder.

Muttering under his breath, Owen got out and shoved his hands into his pockets as he crossed the distance to the main house, the crust of ice and snow that had fallen at the higher elevation crunching under his feet.

Duncan must have seen him coming, because, by the time Owen made it to the kitchen door, it was open. He crossed the threshold but stopped in his tracks when he saw Duncan holding Bethany's daughter, Hollyn.

Something about the sight punched him in the gut, and even though he'd seen his boss and buddy holding Hollyn the other day, visited with them, now that he knew Tasha was pregnant…

"What are you doing here?" Duncan asked, pulling a chair from the table with his foot while holding a bottle to the baby's mouth.

The sound of Hollyn's sucking noises landed another punch, this one even harder than the last. Was he really going to miss out on moments as precious as this because of a job? He could work for Duncan in any number of ways. Maybe as a compromise he could look into doing something else.

"Owen?" Duncan stood and nodded his head toward the chair. "Have a seat. Looks like you need it more than we do."

In a way, he did. Legs weak, he fell onto the seat, wondering how seven pounds and eight ounces of baby could make him have such a huge change of heart.

"Take her. But if you drop her, I'll drop you," Duncan said, carefully handing Hollyn over with enough fuss to make Bethany proud.

Owen stared down into the tiny, sleepy eyes of his niece and felt his face get hot. Duncan would make an awesome father, but Bethany would still need her brother. This kid, her uncle.

His son or daughter, a father.

"Owen, what's going on?" Duncan demanded. "Say something."

"She's right," he answered, not taking his gaze off of the baby. A tiny hand fisted around his pinky where he held the bottle, and his heart swelled even more. "Tasha was right."

"I take it you're here because you two got into it," Duncan said, moving to the fridge to grab a couple of water bottles. Duncan carried them back to the table and opened them, setting one in front of Owen.

"She's pregnant," he said, sharing the news since Tasha hadn't told him he couldn't. Besides, he figured the *Besties* already knew, so why not tell Duncan? "But she wants nothing to do with me because of my job."

"Ah," Duncan said, leaning back in the seat and stretching his long legs out in front of him, crossing his ankles. "And now you've had a change of heart?"

Owen lifted his head and met Duncan's gaze. "Can you hold this little girl and not think twice before you put yourself in front of a bullet?"

A smile lifted one corner of his friend's mouth before Duncan chuckled.

"Here's the thing," Duncan said, his voice low. "We've served our time, paid our dues. I'm not going to ask any of my employees to do something I'm not willing to do myself, but I've also already done it. So have you. You want out, get out. But if you want to stay in, rest assured we can work around the assignments."

Owen looked from Duncan to Hollyn, at the sweet innocence that would only be little for a short period of time. "You need a better IT setup for tracking idiots like me who get themselves into trouble and can't find their way out."

"I agree," Duncan said with a nod. "Simon's a good hacker, but he can't fill your shoes when it comes to leading a team, cyber or otherwise," Duncan said. "He can't handle the pressure and caves at the first sign of a few tears. He needs to be in a room with his computers and nowhere else, which means I need a front man to lead things. Someone I can trust to head the division."

Owen looked at Duncan in surprise.

"I'm in the same position," Duncan said with a shrug. "I want to spend time with my family, and that means delegating some of the responsibility of the company to others— or as Bethany puts it, I have to stop being a control freak. What do you say? You interested?"

Owen pulled the empty bottle from his niece's lips and gently raised her to his chest. A loud burp immediately erupted from the tiny body, earning their laughter. "I think that's a yes."

Chapter 15

Tasha stood outside and smiled at the horse nickering to her baby. The colt was fifteen minutes old now, a beautiful spotted gray with black socks as well as a black mane and tail.

"Oh, I can't thank you enough," Mrs. Blevins said as she wiped more tears from her lined face. "Scared us to death when things just stopped."

"I can imagine. But they're fine now. And what a handsome boy," Tasha added, unable to take her eyes off the mother-and-son pair. It was moments like this that made the midnight phone calls worth every second of lost sleep and drive time. "I should head home, but I'll be back sometime later to check on them."

"Oh, hon, are you sure you won't just spend the night here? The spare bedroom's all made up," the woman said.

"And your son and his family are expected within— oh, six hours," she said, glancing at her watch and seeing that it was four in the morning. "I'll be fine. Besides, there's something about sleeping in your own bed, you know?"

"That's true. If I can tear myself away, I'm going to try to get some sleep before the kids get here. The little ones are always so happy to see their mommaw, but it wears me out."

"I'll bet," Tasha said with a tired grin, knowing from the woman's many stories that she had a total of seven grandchildren and another one on the way.

"Do you have any plans for Christmas? Are your parents coming to visit you?"

Tasha's smile fell, and she shook her head. "No, actually, but that's okay because they're celebrating their thirty-fifth anniversary on a *cruise*."

"How romantic! But sad for you. Please tell me you aren't spending Christmas alone?"

Realizing her answer dictated whether or not the woman insisted on Tasha joining the Blevins family for their holiday, Tasha shook her head. After all, technically, she wouldn't be alone, not with the baby. "No, I won't be. I have plans."

"Good, good. No one should ever be alone on Christmas."

Mrs. Blevins gave Tasha another hug and thanked her again before walking Tasha to the Jeep. She was exhausted and yet wide awake, her adrenaline still high due to the tricky delivery.

"Oh, look at that. That's a good sign," the older woman called from the walkway to the house.

"Oh?" Tasha asked, confused by the woman's words. "What is?"

Mrs. Blevins pointed toward the sky.

"A Blue Moon Christmas," the woman said. "My Irish grandmother always said it's a special happening, but on Christmas... Now is definitely the time to ask for miracles if you need any."

Tasha tossed her things into the passenger seat and climbed inside, shivering from the cold after being in the warmth of the temperature-controlled barn. The Jeep's heater cranked out cold air, and after letting the engine warm up a few minutes, she headed down the private mountain road away from the massive horse farm, taking things slowly since it had snowed during the night and her hours there.

Her thoughts drifted to Owen, and their conversation from last night replayed in her head. Why couldn't Owen see the danger he placed himself in? Understand how scared she got because of all that had happened? She couldn't focus on work and her family if she was constantly worrying about becoming a widow. It wasn't fair. Not to her, not to the baby.

She rounded a curve and, thanks to the light of the bright moon, managed to see the tree that had fallen across the road during the night. She jerked the wheel to the left, but the rear of the SUV slid on the snow and ice, her tires striking the tree with teeth-jarring force.

Tasha gasped when the Jeep tipped, vaguely aware of glass breaking, metal crunching, over and over until something stopped it.

She opened her eyes, dazedly batted at the airbag that had deployed. Something stung her eyes, and she lifted her fingers to the spot, pulling them away to see the blood. Her blood.

Mrs. Blevins's words filled her head, and Tasha fought the panic trying to overtake her.

Please, she prayed. *Please, God, I know I said I didn't think I wanted it but let me keep my baby. Please, give me this Christmas miracle.*

TASHA WINCED at the pain in her head.

"Can you tell me your name?" a too-loud voice demanded.

She frowned at the command and blinked up at the feminine face peering down at her. "*Laney?*"

Emma's EMT sister smiled.

"That's my name. Now how about you tell me yours?"

"Tasha," she muttered.

"Good. I hope you don't mind, but I broke protocol and called Em. She should be at the hospital when we get there."

"What happened? Oh… the tree."

"Yeah," Laney agreed. "I'm afraid it won the battle. Good thing you were a good bit down the mountain when it happened, or the temperature would've gotten you. Mrs. Blevins's family found you on their way to her house."

Mrs. Blevins. Delivering the colt. Prayers for — "My baby! Laney, please—" Tasha reached out and grasped one of Laney's hands. "My *baby.*"

"You're pregnant," Laney confirmed, her eyes widening just a bit.

Tears trickled down her face and into her hair, the many straps holding her in place, the neck brace, and the backboard she was tied to preventing her from wiping them away. "Please, save my baby. I want my baby. Please."

"Shh, Tasha, don't get so upset," Laney said, leaning over her. "Look, I don't see any signs of hemorrhaging, okay? Try to relax, and we'll find out about your baby soon."

The rest of the ambulance ride took place in a blur of questions and stomach-churning motion as the driver tackled the curvy roads down the mountain to town. Finally they rolled to a stop, and cold air blasted her cheeks.

"Here we go," Laney said, her voice filled with cheer and reassurance. "Try to relax, okay?"

The gurney began to move, and Tasha got a brief glimpse of snowflakes falling from the sky before Owen's face appeared above her. Her gaze locked with his, and more stupid tears appeared. She hated crying in front of people. Hated it.

"I love you, sweetheart. You're going to be fine. You hear me?"

"My baby…"

Owen pressed a quick kiss to her lips.

"Our baby will be fine."

Chapter 16

Owen paced the waiting room while the doctors examined Tasha, every turn amping up his anger at the entire situation.

Had he not gotten so angry...

Had he not listened to her and left...

He would've been there when the call had come in for the delivery. He could've driven her there. Driven her home. Maybe they would've still hit the tree, but... maybe not. "What's taking so long?"

"Sit down," Duncan ordered, "before you get us kicked out of here."

"What could be taking so long?" Owen demanded again.

"Better they be thorough than to rush," Bethany stated gently, carrying a tray of coffee into the waiting room.

Owen paced away and back again, choosing to ignore the fact the only cup remaining on the tray was marked decaf.

"Ugh," Morgan said, making a smacking noise with her mouth. "Jo-Jo, you've got the market cornered on coffee. This sucks."

Owen turned to pace away from them and nearly ran into Quinn. The man stood two inches shorter, but he was a solid eight inches broader and as immovable as a boulder.

"You're making Jolie more nervous than she already is," Quinn said. "Sit down."

Owen stared at the man, perplexed, until he realized what Quinn implied. Jolie had a tendency to want to self-harm when she became too overwhelmed to deal with her emotions, and if Tasha lost the baby…

"Owen Redd," a nurse called.

Owen beat feet to the nurses' station, aware of the nurse's glance at the others who followed.

"I take it you're all with the patient," the nurse said.

"Yeah, we are," Owen told her. "How is she?"

"The doctor wants her here for the next few hours, but she should be able to go home for Christmas," the woman said, handing a computer tablet over to a second nurse behind the desk.

"And the baby?" he asked.

"No sign of harm," a doctor said, joining the conversation. "She has instructions to take it easy while she recovers, but her tests are all good. She is one very lucky lady."

Relief left Owen weak and trembling. And all he could do was string a litany of *Thank you, God*s together in his head.

"You just going to stand there?" the older nurse said with a teasing smile. "She's asking to see you— but only one visitor at a time," she added with a stern look at the others.

Owen barely felt Duncan pounding him on the back, urging him to go. He stumbled through the swinging double doors but then stopped short of entering Tasha's hospital room, taking a moment to try to piece himself together after fearing the worst and shaking now that he knew she and the baby were okay.

He inhaled and forced himself across the threshold, careful not to make any noise in case she rested.

"I'm awake," Tasha said from the bed.

Owen moved to her side and seated himself on the edge before wrapping her carefully in his arms. "Just let me hold you. I need to hold you," he said, the words rough and low.

Her hands gripped his upper arms, her breath hot on his neck.

"I love you, Owen."

"I love you, too, sweetheart."

"I need to tell you something," she whispered.

"Later. Whatever it is can wait. Nothing matters right now but that you're safe."

"But…"

He leaned over the bed and closed his lips over hers, shushing her the best way he knew how. "Later," he said again. "I'm here and I'm not going anywhere."

THE DOCTORS RELEASED her late that evening. Owen drove her home in the Denali, then insisted on carrying her into the house and straight to bed.

"I've been asleep all day," she said in complaint.

"No, you've dozed off and on. And since I'm still going to have to wake you up throughout the night because of the concussion, you need to rest while you can."

"Great way to spend Christmas," she said with a grumble.

"At least now we're spending it together," he countered, earning a frown from her in response. "Tash—"

"Owen, I want to—"

He broke off before she did. Tasha blinked up at him from her pillow, her bruised temple stitched and held by butterfly bandages. "Me first."

"But—"

"No," he murmured, lowering his head and brushing her mouth with a kiss because he couldn't be this close and not kiss her after the last twenty-four hours. "Me first. I need to say something. Tash, I've been thinking… I came back here last night, but you weren't home. So I waited. And waited. I didn't know where you were, didn't know what had happened. I worried even though I told myself you were fine." He brushed her hair off her cheek and stared into her eyes. "And then your clinic opened, and your employees didn't know where you were, and I realized what a big deal it was for you to be out of touch. Which made me wonder if

Vargas was involved again, or if something had happened to you and the baby."

He had to stop and clear his throat, too choked up to speak for a long moment because he relived it all over again. "What I'm trying to say is that I got a very, *very* brief taste of what it's like for you when I go on assignment. I realized how it feels to be the one left behind in the dark, worrying and praying and not knowing."

"Sucks, doesn't it?" she murmured, a weak smile curling her mouth.

"Yeah, it does. But something else happened last night before I realized you were missing." He took her hand and lifted it to his lips, kissing her knuckles. "I held Beth's baby, fed her, and thought about what all I might miss out on if I continue to work as I do. All the things I don't want to miss."

Her fingers tightened around his.

"What are you saying?"

"I talked to Duncan last night, before your accident when you took twenty years off my life," he felt the need to stress. "Sweetheart, I didn't get it, but I do now. I want to spend my life with you and our baby, our family, and I don't want to miss a moment of it or have you constantly worried about my safety."

"But you can't quit. I mean— I don't want you to give up a job you love and resent *me* for it," she said. "Owen, I was driving home, and… I could've been killed. Just like that. I know I said all that stuff about your job, and it *is* dangerous, but I shouldn't have said what I did. The accident reminded me that we don't have guarantees, because we're not the ones in control. We're fooling ourselves if we think we are. Things happen."

He played with her fingers. "I'm glad you understand that, but it doesn't change my decision. I'm going to partner with Duncan and take a step back from field work."

"You won't regret it? You won't be angry with me?"

"For making me realize I don't want to miss out on us? No. Move over," he ordered, waiting patiently while she inched over to one side of the bed. He could tell she was sore and stiff from being banged around by the Jeep, but the moment she settled, he toed off his shoes and climbed into the bed beside her, tucking her close, her head under his chin.

"Oh, you feel good," she said, burying her face in his shirt and yawning.

"So do you," he told her, unable to imagine his life without her.

"I don't have a single present for you."

He kissed her forehead and snuggled her closer still. "Sweetheart, you just gave me exactly what I wanted for Christmas."

She smiled. "Guess Mrs. Blevins was right."

"About what?"

Tasha kissed him, slow and sweet. "Christmas is always special, but there is something extra special about this Christmas. But maybe I feel that way because I got my Christmas wish, too."

Epilogue
CHRISTMAS EVE, ONE YEAR LATER...

What are you two doing hiding back here in the corner?" Tasha asked Jolie and Morgan as she came to join them.

Jolie tilted her head to one side and smiled. "Just taking it all in."

"Amazing how fast things change, isn't it?" Emma said, joining the conversation. "Look at them."

As a group, they turned to watch the chaos on the living room floor of Emma and Ian's home. Their men were seated around the room, either in chairs or on the carpet, leaning against couches as they played with the children. Tissue paper, bags, boxes, and wrapping paper had been tossed about as presents were opened, the brightly colored ribbons and bows and sparkling tags gleaming beneath the lights of the tree and the mantel.

Morgan's two children from a previous marriage watched their stepfather's every movement as Knox opened one of the boxes of plastic, pretend food that went with the kitchen set little Camilla had received, while Knox's stepson waited patiently for his turn so Knox could help him with a remote race car. Bethany and Duncan's sweet Hollyn toddled about, carrying a doll and blanket, keeping Duncan and Bethany hopping up and down to retrieve her when something caught the baby's attention and she wandered off.

Emma's service dogs-in-training were also in the room, rolling in the crackling paper and wearing the bows Morgan's son had stuck to their sides and heads and wherever he could get them to stick as they romped around the room enjoying their new Christmas toys almost as much as the children.

Tasha's gaze slid to Owen, and she watched as he held a bottle to Ariza Kade's mouth, splitting his attention between his son and the action taking place around the room. His parents were due to visit tomorrow, and when they left, she and Owen were taking Kade to Florida for a week to visit and bask in the sun and surf. Her parents couldn't wait for time with their new grandson.

"Well, I don't know about y'all, but I can't imagine any sight prettier than that one," Morgan said in her southern twang. "Look at them. Have you ever seen so much testosterone look so *fine*?"

"There is definitely something to be said for a man holding a baby," Emma said, staring at her husband.

Tasha frowned at Em's choice of words and exchanged a glance with the others. "Em? Something you need to tell us?"

Em straightened and gave the *Besties* a pleased grin. "Yeah, there is. By next year, there's going to be another little one here for Christmas."

They screamed as a group, startling little Kade so badly he stopped taking his bottle long enough to let out a few whimpers before going back to it.

"Oh, Em, that's wonderful," Tasha said, hugging her friend tight. Emma was going to be such a wonderful mother. "I'm so happy for you. And Ian," she added. "He's okay?" she asked, knowing Ian's blindness left him struggling with issues of control and protectiveness where Emma was concerned. Now to have a baby...

Emma leaned her head on Tasha's shoulder. "He's adjusting. He doesn't like it that he won't be able to see the baby, but... I've reminded him that the most important thing is that he can love our child, but you'd better believe this baby will be the first to get his or her very own Mad Dog protection dog."

Jolie cleared her throat, gaining their attention. "Well, Ian's not the only one who will have some adjusting to do. There's actually going to be *two* more babies by next year."

All the screams had just started to erupt when Morgan held up her hands. "Wait! Wait! *Stop*. That's not right."

"What?" Emma asked, her smile fading.

Jolie looked befuddled— and upset that Morgan had ruined the cheer session. "What do you mean?"

"You're telling me you're *both* pregnant?" Morgan asked, splitting her attention between the two friends. "Right now? You're both pregnant right *now?*"

Emma nodded, as did Jolie.

Morgan burst out laughing and held up three fingers. "That makes three of us then."

This time, the roar was unstoppable, and the women hugged and laughed and talked all at once.

"What's going on over here?" Bethany asked, joining the group. "I went to get more punch and come back to discover everyone's screaming without me."

"Bethany, you've got to hear this," Emma said to her sister-in-law. "I'm pregnant."

"Seriously?" Bethany asked, her excitement tangible.

"I'm pregnant, too," Jolie added. "But then Morgan interrupted us and told us—"

"That I'm pregnant, too!" Morgan said, earning a toned-down version of the earlier cheer-fest. "By this time next year, the house will be *full* of babies."

LATER THAT EVENING, Tasha padded down the hall to the spare bedroom and peeked inside, leaning her shoulder against the doorway as she watched Owen in the nursery rocker, his son cradled against his big, bare chest in one thickly muscled arm, his other hand holding a book as he read to Kade. "I thought tonight was my turn."

He looked up with a sheepish expression. "I couldn't resist. And you were taking forever in the shower."

Uh-huh. A likely excuse. Tasha moved into the nursery and curled up on the love seat, watching as Kade's eyes grew heavier with every rock and every word. By the time Owen finished the story, Kade was fast asleep, his little mouth moving in a sucking motion.

Owen placed Kade in his crib, and Tasha moved to wrap her arms around her husband, leaning against him as they watched their son sleep.

"Come on. Now it's time for our Christmas celebration," Owen said softly, his lips in her hair.

They walked back to the master bedroom, pausing every now and again to kiss and turn off a light. Finally they made it to their bedroom, and Tasha sat on the edge of the bed, staring up at her husband's handsome face. "I love you."

"Is that right?" he murmured.

"Mmmhmm," she said with a nod, crooking her finger at him to come closer.

He kissed her forehead, a smile in his voice when he said, "Merry Christmas, Mrs. Redd."

"Merry Christmas." Her wedding rings sparkled in the dim light. Owen made her feel safe and silly and beautiful. Happy. All the little things that were so very important. "Did you ever think we'd find ourselves here?"

"Definitely," he murmured, giving her a playful leer.

She laughed and swatted his chest. "You know what I mean. Did you ever think we'd be this happy?"

"Yes. But I'm guessing you didn't," he murmured, his hand playing with the length of her hair.

She pressed her cheek to his chest, listening to the soothing beat of his heart. "It's not that I didn't want us to be," she said, staring at the lights of the Christmas tree flickering on and off in the other room. "I guess I was afraid it wasn't meant to happen for me. I lost faith when I should've stayed confident. I was so afraid I almost kept it from happening."

"But you didn't," he said. "And neither did I once I wised up."

She snuggled closer to him, reveling in his warmth on the chilly night. "Owen?"

Owen rolled so that he stared down at her, his expression so full of love and tenderness and desire that she caught her breath.

"Hmm?"

"I know we didn't plan to have Kade, but would you want to try to have another baby by, oh say… next Christmas?"

WANT MORE OF STONE RIVER? READ BELOW FOR A SNEAK PEEK AT ZACK DUPRE'S STORY IN SECOND CHANCES!

Rebecca Waites held too tightly to the tiny hand in her own and struggled to breathe despite the fist in her chest. "Remember what I said, okay? If you're good, and stay right here and play your games, when mommy's finished, we'll go for ice cream. As many scoops as you want. Okay?"

Becca stared down at her son's precious face, praying for the miracle that would result in the never-quiet behavior of a typical four-year-old.

"Bex? You made it! Oh, I'm so glad you're here!"

Becca turned at the sound of the nickname coming from her younger sibling, a smile forming on her lips because of Kaitlyn's squeal and how it echoed through the elegant old mansion where Kaitlyn's wedding reception would take place. "We're here. I told you before, no worries," she said, catching a nearly-flying Kaitlyn in her arms for a massive hug.

Kaity was four years younger and the only one who had ever called her Bex, the name born of Kaity's inability to say Rebecca or Becca when she began talking.

"They still don't know," Kaity whispered urgently into Becca's ear. "*When* are you going to tell them?"

Becca squeezed her sister before releasing her. "When the time is right."

"It's been a *year*. The time hasn't been right in a year?"

Kaity's big blue eyes reminded Becca of a doll she'd had as a child. Blond, blue-eyed and perfect in every way. Everyone loved

Kaity because she was as kind and good-hearted as she was beauti-ful. "Officially, it's only been six months since it was final," she said, referring to the day she and her husband of six years had divorced her to marry his mistress and raise his illegitimate--or his *normal* as Bryce liked to call him--son.

"Well, I hate the thought of them knowing as much as you, espe-cially since Mama's on the warpath. You have no need to worry about me turning into bridezilla because Wynonna Waites has it covered, trust me. Thank you *so much* for coming to take over the wedding planning. I know people usually contact you a year or two in advance, but David and I don't want to wait and Mama insists on a big wedding with all the fuss."

"It's-- I'm happy to help. I needed to get away from Charleston for a bit anyway. And since I had a cancellation..." Becca said, forcing another smile.

Fake it till you make it. Wasn't that the saying?

"Uh-oh. What now?"

Becca closed her tired eyes briefly and shook her head. Even Kaity didn't know about Eli's official diagnosis of selective mutism. It had taken years of doctor visits to rule out physical issues and autism as the reason her bright, beautiful boy didn't speak to anyone but her--and that was only on rare occasions. When he was ready he would talk, they said. "I'll tell you later. For now, get me up to speed on what's been done."

Kaity linked her arm through Becca's and tugged her toward the end of the long ballroom. As they walked away, Becca glanced over her shoulder to where Eli sat, head bowed and his concentra-tion fully on the video game in his hands.

Thankfully the room was devoid of any childish items of intrigue that Becca could see, so Eli should stay focused and not wander off.

"Well, I told you David and I wanted to elope and avoid all of this, but Mama insists and Daddy backs her because I'm--"

"*His last little girl,*" they said in unison.

"Exactly. So, big, elaborate, and over the top is apparently the theme," Kaity said.

"The theme being?" Becca asked, taking in the huge ballroom windows and ornate moldings. The Wickersham Estate and barely existing town of Stone River had escaped Sherman's march through Georgia, and over the years the family had added on and expanded the already massive house before gifting it to the historical society when the last living family member passed on.

"Black, white and tiffany blue," Kaity said. "Oh, I know it's been done a million times but I do so love the colors. Mama wanted all white, but Daddy reminded her of our plans to elope and Mama decided to go along with my color scheme."

"Nice of her to compromise," Becca said with a wry shake of her head. She loved her mother, truly, but Wynonna had a way of taking over and doing things her way. That boldness and determination was great for charity fundraisers and the like, but not a wedding where the bride and groom where already being held hostage for "the show."

"I know, right? Anyway, I've picked black on white damask--"

"Elegant," Becca added.

"With small touches of tiffany blue. To make Mama happy I told her we would only use white flowers."

Becca pulled her notebook tablet out of her large purse and began to take notes. "How many people?"

Kaity rolled her eyes. "Last count was 300 and Mama hadn't even gotten to the country club or her book club yet."

Becca smirked. "Four hundred it is."

Kaity groaned and crossed her arms over her front, tapping her foot against the antique marble floor.

"Please don't let this turn into a circus. I feel as though it already is. If only Mama would be happy with just a bridal tea or something."

"You know that's wishful thinking," Becca murmured, still making notes and drawing a quick sketch of the room. She'd take measurements of the windows, doors and floors to know exactly what space she had to work with.

Somewhere behind her, a door opened and closed and Becca vaguely heard Kaity suck in a sharp breath.

"Um, Bex? There's something else I haven't mentioned."

"Oh? What's that?"

"It's, um, about the photographer."

"What about it?" Becca asked.

"I've already hired someone. Actually, I've hired... *him*."

I hope you have enjoyed THEIR CHRISTMAS MIRA-CLE. Keep reading SECOND CHANCES.

Word of mouth and reviews are the two best ways an author has to gain attention for their books. While you're browsing the titles, please consider taking a moment to leave a short review of this book.

Thank you,

Kay

The Stone River Novels

WORTH THE WAIT

NOT BY SIGHT

MORE THAN LOVE (FORMERLY THROUGH THE VALLEY)

TO PROTECT HER (FORMERLY LEAD ME NOT)

CHRISTMAS AT HOLLY WOOD

THEIR CHRISTMAS MIRACLE

SECOND CHANCES

SIGN UP FOR KAY'S NEWSLETTER AND RECEIVE UPDATES ON NEW RELEASES, CONTESTS, PRE-RELEASE BOOK INFORMATION, EXCLUSIVES AND MORE!

- THE LAST GOODBYE
- LATTES AND LULLABYES
- MAP OF DREAMS
- WORTH THE RISK
- LOST LOVE FOUND

TAMING THE TULANES SERIES:

- SMALL TOWN SCANDAL
- THEIR SECRET BARGAIN
- CROSSING THE LINE
- THE NANNY'S SECRET
- SOMEONE TO TRUST

THE STONE RIVER SERIES:

- WORTH THE WAIT
- NOT BY SIGHT
- MORE THAN LOVE (FORMERLY THROUGH THE VALLEY)
- TO PROTECT HER (FORMERLY LEAD ME NOT)
- CHRISTMAS AT HOLLY WOOD
- THEIR CHRISTMAS MIRACLE
- SECOND CHANCES

SMALL TOWN SCANDALS SERIES:

- BRODY'S REDEMPTION
- FALLING FOR HER BOSS
- WITH THIS MAN

SECRET SANTA SERIES:

- SECRET SANTA
- SECRET SANTA II: A CHRISTMAS TO REMEMBER

SIGN UP FOR KAY'S NEWSLETTER AND RECEIVE FREE BOOKS, UPDATES ON NEW RELEASES, CONTESTS, PRE-RELEASE BOOK INFORMATION,

AUTHOR BIO

Kay Lyons always wanted to be a writer, ever since the age of seven or eight when she copied the pictures out of a Charlie Brown book and rewrote the story because she didn't like the plot. Through the years her stories have changed but one characteristic stayed true— they were all romances. Each and every one of her manuscripts included a love story.

Published in 2005 with Harlequin Enterprises, Kay's first release was a national bestseller. Kay has also been a HOLT Medallion, Book Buyers Best and RITA Award nominee. Look for her most recent novels with Kindred Spirits Publishing.

For more information regarding her work, please visit Kay at the following:

www.kaylyonsauthor.com

@KayLyonsAuthor (Twitter)

Kay Lyons Author (Facebook)

Author_Kay_Lyons (Instagram)

Kay Lyons, Author (Pinterest)

SIGN UP FOR KAY'S NEWSLETTER AND RECEIVE FREE BOOKS, UPDATES ON NEW RELEASES, CONTESTS, PRE-

RELEASE BOOK INFORMATION, EXCLUSIVES AND MORE!

KAY LYONS

Second
CHANCES

STONE RIVER BOOK SEVEN

Second Chances
A STONE RIVER NOVELLA

SIGN UP FOR KAY'S NEWSLETTER TO RECEIVE UPDATES ON NEW RELEASES, CONTESTS, PRE-RELEASE BOOK INFORMATION, EXCLUSIVES AND MORE!

Chapter 1

Rebecca Waites held too tightly to the tiny hand in her own and struggled to breathe despite the fist in her chest. "Remember what I said, okay? If you're good, and stay right here and play your games, when mommy's finished, we'll go for ice cream. As many scoops as you want. Okay?"

Becca stared down at her son's precious face, praying for the miracle that would result in the never-quiet behavior of a typical four-year-old.

"Bex? You made it! Oh, I'm so glad you're here!"

Becca turned at the sound of the nickname coming from her younger sibling, a smile forming on her lips because of Kaitlyn's squeal and how it echoed through the elegant old mansion where Kaitlyn's wedding reception would take place. "We're here. I told you before, no worries," she said, catching a nearly-flying Kaitlyn in her arms for a massive hug.

Kaity was four years younger and the only one who had ever called her Bex, the name born of Kaity's inability to say Rebecca or Becca when she began talking.

"They still don't know," Kaity whispered urgently into Becca's ear. "*When* are you going to tell them?"

Becca squeezed her sister before releasing her. "When the time is right."

"It's been a *year*. The time hasn't been right in a year?"

Kaity's big blue eyes reminded Becca of a doll she'd had as a child. Blond, blue-eyed and perfect in every way. Everyone loved Kaity because she was as kind and good-hearted as she was beautiful. "Officially, it's only been six months since it was final," she said, referring to the day she and her husband of six years had divorced her to marry his mistress and raise his illegitimate--or his *normal* as Bryce liked to call him--son.

"Well, I hate the thought of them knowing as much as you, especially since Mama's on the warpath. You have no need to worry about me turning into bridezilla because Wynonna Waites has it covered, trust me. Thank you *so much* for coming to take over the wedding planning. I know people usually contact you a year or two in advance, but David and I don't want to wait and Mama insists on a big wedding with all the fuss."

"It's-- I'm happy to help. I needed to get away from Charleston for a bit anyway. And since I had a cancellation..." Becca said, forcing another smile.

Fake it till you make it. Wasn't that the saying?

"Uh-oh. What now?"

Becca closed her tired eyes briefly and shook her head. Even Kaity didn't know about Eli's official diagnosis of selective mutism. It had taken years of doctor visits to rule out physical issues and autism as the reason her bright, beautiful boy didn't speak to anyone but her--and that was only on rare occasions. When he was ready he would talk, they said. "I'll tell you later. For now, get me up to speed on what's been done."

Kaity linked her arm through Becca's and tugged her toward the end of the long ballroom. As they walked away, Becca glanced over her shoulder to where Eli sat, head bowed and his concentration fully on the video game in his hands.

Thankfully the room was devoid of any childish items of intrigue that Becca could see, so Eli should stay focused and not wander off.

"Well, I told you David and I wanted to elope and avoid all of this, but Mama insists and Daddy backs her because I'm--"

"His last little girl," they said in unison.

"Exactly. So, big, elaborate, and over the top is apparently the theme," Kaity said.

"The theme being?" Becca asked, taking in the huge ballroom windows and ornate moldings. The Wickersham Estate and barely existing town of Stone River had escaped Sherman's march through Georgia, and over the years the family had added on and expanded the already massive house before gifting it to the historical society when the last living family member passed on.

"Black, white and tiffany blue," Kaity said. "Oh, I know it's been done a million times but I do so love the colors. Mama wanted all white, but Daddy reminded her of our plans to elope and Mama decided to go along with my color scheme."

"Nice of her to compromise," Becca said with a wry shake of her head. She loved her mother, truly, but Wynonna had a way of taking over and doing things her way. That boldness and determination was great for charity fundraisers and the like, but not a wedding where the bride and groom where already being held hostage for "the show."

"I know, right? Anyway, I've picked black on white damask--"

"Elegant," Becca added.

"With small touches of tiffany blue. To make Mama happy I told her we would only use white flowers."

Becca pulled her notebook tablet out of her large purse and began to take notes. "How many people?"

Kaity rolled her eyes. "Last count was 300 and Mama hadn't even gotten to the country club or her book club yet."

Becca smirked. "Four hundred it is."

Kaity groaned and crossed her arms over her front, tapping her foot against the antique marble floor.

"Please don't let this turn into a circus. I feel as though it already is. If only Mama would be happy with just a bridal tea or something."

"You know that's wishful thinking," Becca murmured, still

making notes and drawing a quick sketch of the room. She'd take measurements of the windows, doors and floors to know exactly what space she had to work with.

Somewhere behind her, a door opened and closed and Becca vaguely heard Kaity suck in a sharp breath.

"Um, Bex? There's something else I haven't mentioned."

"Oh? What's that?"

"It's, um, about the photographer."

"What about it?" Becca asked.

"I've already hired someone. Actually, I've hired... *him*."

ZACK DUPRE WATCHED as Rebecca turned to face him and waited for her to recognize him. It didn't take long. One second she wore a fake, welcoming smile, and the next she paled to the color of the antique white walls behind her. "Ladies," he said softly, never taking his eyes off of the elder sister.

"Bex, you remember Zack, right? Um, I mean, of course you do, but-- Zack is a fabulous photographer and he's agreed to be our wedding photographer."

Zack watched as Becca turned her surprised stare into a glare when she glanced at her little sister.

Kaity went on babbling about the photography awards he had won and how pleased she was to snag his services when he's usually booked a year or two in advance.

"Thankfully someone cancelled in his lineup as well," Kaity said. "I mean, I feel bad for them because it means no wedding, but what are the odds of both of you being available now? Perfect timing, isn't it?"

Zack wondered at Becca's thoughts, but her expression gave little away. He didn't imagine it was easy coming face-to-face with the man she'd tossed aside like trash ten years ago. Harder still to know she was going to have to work with him during all of the wedding preparations.

"Zack's taken our engagement photos and he's agreed to do a

comprehensive photo package for us. Oh, did I mention the magazine article?"

Zack watched as confusion gathered in Becca's blue-green eyes. While most men would probably find Kaitlyn the prettier of the two sisters, he considered Becca's bright gaze and reddish-brown hair more to his liking. He had ten years ago, too. Not that she had felt the same way. Apparently he was good-looking enough to fool around with on the sly, but socially unacceptable given how she'd run away at the first sign of trouble.

"No. You haven't mentioned a magazine article," Becca said, her tone almost hiding her upset at the situation, but not quite.

"Yikes. I'm sorry, Bex. I thought I had. Things have just been so crazy lately it must have slipped my mind. I can't remember who knows and who doesn't. Anyway, David and I are being featured in the magazine from proposal to marriage. He and daddy are the attorneys for the magazine publisher and when they heard about the proposal, well, the rest is history. I didn't think you'd mind since it's free publicity and you could use--uh, you know. All publicity is good publicity, isn't that what people say?" Kaitlyn ended awkwardly.

Zack wasn't sure what Kaitlyn had been about to say about Becca needing good publicity, but the silence that followed made it clear he needed to call in a favor and do some digging out of curiosity, if nothing else.

As a teenager under court-ordered community service, he'd worked for a blind woman who raised service dogs in training. The woman had wound up being his half-sister and she had later married a man whose brother owned an Altanta-based private security company.

As convoluted as it all seemed, things couldn't have worked out any better. He'd gained a loving family, and when he'd first started his photography business and bookings were slow, he'd worked for the security company.

The job was obviously meant to help out a family member in need, but he'd grown close to his brother-in-law's brother and all the men who worked for the company. They had become the brothers he'd never had and good men to look up to.

"Yes, of course. How exciting for you," Becca said. "And for you," she added, glancing at Zack. "A magazine spread is a big deal."

"Oh, it's nothing for Zack," Kaitlyn said with a friendly smile. "He's had lots of them."

Given what he knew of Becca's occupation he found himself slightly offended that she hadn't kept up on his successes. But then again, why would she? It wasn't like she'd expected him to become anything worthwhile, was it?

"Bex, you've had to have seen his work. It's been featured in bridal magazines, parenting magazines… His photos are the bomb."

A quick poke of satisfaction filled him when Becca's eyebrows rose and an expression of genuine surprise flickered across her face.

"That's wonderful. I'm happy for you," Becca murmured, making eye contact briefly.

"Not bad for a high school drop out, eh?" He hadn't meant to blurt out his thoughts but the words came without warning, bringing with them a wealth of anger.

He'd forgiven her, put the things she and her parents and said about him behind him and moved on. Built a good, satisfying life despite the way Becca had made him feel about his inadequacies, and lack of education and money. But it all came back to him in a rush of emotion he couldn't ignore. Apparently he had more issues to work on than he'd thought.

"Oh, please. No amount of schooling can teach art and the ability to have an eye for light and contrast and all the other phenomenal stuff in your photos," Kaitlyn said. "I'm serious," she said to Becca. "His work is *ah-mazing*. Oh—there's the manager of the Wickersham. I need to ask him a question. Be right back."

"Kaity, I'm the one who should be asking que—"

Becca broke off and closed her mouth with a pained sounding sigh as Kaitlyn took off toward the man, the flowy dress she wore reminding Zack of a butterfly.

Shifting his attention back to Becca, he stifled a laugh at the grumpy expression on her face. Looked like few things had changed between the sisters over the years.

When he and Becca had secretly dated, Becca had complained about Kaitlyn's flightiness and compared her sister to a hummingbird unable to light. Hummingbird, butterfly... He now saw what she'd meant.

"I-I-- I suppose I should get these measurements."

Becca turned to walk away but Zack snagged her arm, his grip on her elbow gentle but firm. "Are you going to be able to work with me? If not, speak now."

The muscles of her throat moved up and down as she swallowed hard. She avoided his gaze, but he noted the flush traveling from her neck to her face.

"I should be the one asking that question of you."

"So ask," he ordered, daring her. After everything that had happened over the course of that long ago summer, asking him the loaded question was the least she could do.

"Okay, fine. Do you have a problem working with-- Eli, *no!*"

Chapter 2

Becca blurted out the command before tearing lose of Zack's hold and putting her feet in motion. She raced across the room to where she'd left Eli sitting in an elegantly styled side chair, but even though she was quite certain Eli had heard her, her son continued to dig into a camera bag Zack had apparently left on the nearby table. *"Eli."*

Four inch heels didn't make for a fast trek across the large ballroom but Zack effortlessly jogged by her and made it to Eli's side in a matter of seconds.

"Hey, there, bud. Thanks for watching my stuff and keeping it safe. Mind if I take that?"

Finally coming close to where they stood, she watched as Zack deftly plucked an expensive looking lens from Eli's grasp.

"Eli, I told you to--"

"Pretty neat looking, huh?" Zack said, squatting down to be on Eli's level. "But they're not toys. I can show you what they do, but you have to promise you won't touch them unless I'm right beside of you to help you. Deal?"

Becca bit her inner lip and waited anxiously to see if Eli would respond to Zack's surprisingly gentle tone. Had Eli touched one of

Elliot's electronic gadgets he would've gone through the roof, yelling, grabbing at Eli's shoulders to impress upon the silent boy how dear and valuable the item was instead of realizing the most valuable asset he had stood trembling before him.

Tears stung her eyes as she heard Zack explain the lens took special photos and attached it to the camera dangling from his side with a twist of his fingers. That done, Zack flipped a switch and the digital screen brightened.

"Then all you do is point it and press this button," Zack said, aiming it at Becca.

The shutter clicked repeatedly before Becca could avert her face.

"See? There's your pretty mama."

She wanted to ask him to erase the photos but she deemed it unnecessary. Zack would have no problem erasing the images of her after all she'd put him through.

"But you heard me, right? No more messing around with my equipment."

Once more she waited for Eli to respond, nod, something, but he simply stared at Zack with the same big eyes that had stolen her heart the moment the doctor had placed him in her arms after delivering him.

"Sorry about that," Kaity called from the doorway. "I just had to ask a few questions. Uh... everything all right in here?"

Becca blinked the residual moisture from her eyes and nodded, pasting the same fake smile on her face as she had for the last year since her life had begun to implode. "Yes, it's fine. Zack was showing Eli his camera."

"Awesome. So, Zack, do you want to do the run through of shots and take a look around while Bex gets her measurements?"

"Sure. You're the boss," he said with a smile.

Zack rose and shouldered the heavy looking equipment bag after replacing the lens and latching everything for safe keeping.

"Okay, then," Kaity said, her expression revealing her curiosity as she split her attention between Becca and Zack. "Bex, you'll be here when we finish, right?"

Becca felt the intensity of Zack's gaze and knew he wondered if she would run away like she had in the past. "Of course."

Zack walked toward the door but Kaity hung back.

"If you run into Mama, don't mention Zack, okay?" Kaity made a face. "I wanted you to be here when I told her and Daddy who I hired. I mean, if you or Zack couldn't make things work then there was no need to tell Mama and Daddy and upset them, right? But so long as you and Zack are both okay with it, it'll be fine. I just know it."

Kaity turned and hurried after Zack before Becca could respond. Katy hadn't told their parents about Zack?

Her sister's positive attitude was more than a little far-fetched in this scenario, but now wasn't the time to confront her about the sneak-attack. A little warning would have gone a long way, but apparently she wasn't the only one Kaity had kept in the dark. Only Zack seemed to know what was happening, but then by accepting Kaity's invitation to scout potential photo opps, of course he would have to know he'd be required to deal with Kaity's family. "Oh, Kaity, what *are* you thinking?"

Their parents would explode when they discovered Kaity had hired Zack. So much so, Becca wouldn't be surprised if they threatened to not fund the wedding. Was Kaity ready for that?

She was fully aware of the blame and responsibility she carried for what had happened in the past with Zack, but her parents... They blamed him entirely, ignoring her statements about being just as culpable.

Recruiting Eli to help her with the measurements, she positioned him on one end of the long hall and stretched the tape, stopping periodically to note the floor to ceiling windows and grand French doors on the iPad she used to design the layouts. Thankfully, Eli dropped the tape several times, forcing her to start again and keep her too busy to dwell on what the next few weeks would bring having to work with Zack.

She'd finished designing the layout and had just saved it when the doors opened and her mother and father appeared.

"Becca? When did you arrive," her father asked, a smile on his sun-chapped lips as he crossed the room to where she and Eli waited for Kaity's return.

No doubt he was just coming in from the golf course given his attire.

"About an hour ago." She allowed her father to draw her against his chest for a hug, amazed as always by his ability to simply pretend the past never happened. How did people move on so easily? "Hi, Daddy. How are you?"

"Better now that my girls are both home. Now where's my little Eli?" George said, looking everywhere but at her son. Finally he fixed his gaze on Eli and smiled. "Why, that can't be Eli. You've grown a foot since I saw you last."

Kaity worried her lower lip with her teeth and prayed Eli would respond. At least do more than look at his grandfather with that blank stare he'd perfected over the last year.

"So? How's my grandson?"

George knelt in front of Eli but Eli didn't so much as blink.

"Um, Dad? Eli's really tired. It's been a long day."

Her father hesitated momentarily before he stood and nodded at her words, but Becca saw the glance he exchanged with her mother, their expressions as easy to read as her ex-husband's.

What's wrong with him?

Haven't we always suspected something was off?

How does this make the family look?

All those questions and more flickered across her parents' faces in a matter of seconds, recognizable only because she'd seen them on Elliot's so many times over the last four years.

"Of course," her father said, looking about the room with way more interest than necessary.

"Rebecca, I'm glad you're here," her mother said, moving close to place her hands on Rebecca's shoulders and air-kiss both cheeks. "Maybe you can talk some sense into your sister."

"Pardon?" Becca said, leery of facing her parents alone if they'd already discovered Zack Dupre was Kaity's choice of photographer.

"Kaitlyn is still threatening to elope, but I've told her again and again she simply can't. It's your job to make sure she doesn't take off halfway through the planning process."

"I'll do my best," she murmured, not blaming Kaity one bit for wanting to escape the chaos that some weddings became.

"You'll have to do better than that," her father said. "I'm not footing the bill for something that doesn't happen."

"Exactly," Wynonna agreed. "The timing of the wedding perfectly correlates with your father's announcement that he's running for State Representative. John, his political manager, says the wedding is a great way of showcasing George as..."

The large French doors opened and Kaity entered, Zack's deep, masculine voice drifting over Kaity's shoulder and across the marble floor to where they stood. But it wasn't until Zack followed Kaity into the building that Becca heard her mother gasp and her father released a sound similar to a growl.

"What is *he* doing here?" they asked in unison.

ZACK FELT like a bug under a microscope as every member of the Waites family stared at him. Even little Eli followed the adults' gaze and pinned Zack with his big brown eyes.

Seconds ticked by and no one moved. Finally Kaity cleared her throat and placed her hand on Zack's forearm.

"Here we go," Becca's younger sister murmured, gently squeezing his arm to get him moving toward the group.

"What's he doing here?" George asked, his tone low and rough coming as it was from between his clenched teeth.

"Kaitlyn, how smart of you to get an estimate from *all* the photographers in town," Wynonna said in a saccharine tone. "She will give you a call when she's received your estimate and has made her decision. You're free to go."

"Mama, I've *made* my decision," Kaity stated, glancing from Zack to Becca and back toward her parents. "And I've already hired Zack as my photographer. We were just going over some of the shots I'd like for him to take on the big day."

"Out of the question," her father said.

"Oh, Kaity, no. He simply won't do. I'm sure your work is perfectly acceptable," Wynonna hastily added. "But we know several photographers with far more experience and training."

"Mother, you're not listening," Kaity stated, lifting her chin. "I've already hired Zack," she repeated, each word receiving an extra second or two of emphasis. "The contract has been signed."

Becca had to give her parents credit. For two people who obviously wanted to explode in a fit of anger, they managed to remember their southern upbringing and somehow reined in their emotions. After all, it wouldn't do for George or Wynonna to be seen having a hissy fit.

"I'm sure Mr. Dupre would be happy to let you out of the contract. We'll pay him half the fee for his trouble. I'm sure that would suit you," her father said to Zack, his tone stiff and formal.

"I work for Kaitlyn," Zack stated. "I'll go along with whatever she decides."

George and Wynonna turned their combined gazes on to Kaity and Becca watched her sister square her shoulders and lift her chin.

Fearless Kaity. Becca had always envied Kaity her spirit.

"Daddy, Mama, the matter is decided. Zack's photos are the best. Mama, wait until you see them. He's won awards and-- and he even has art galleries wanting to host shows for his work."

The news had Becca shifting her gaze to Zack, and she noted that he looked surprised by Kaity's statement. Was it true? Or was he surprised by the fact Kaity defended him instead of caving to their disapproval the way she had ten years ago?

"Kaitlyn Georgette Allison Waites--"

"*Mama*," Becca said, gaining her mother's attention. A flutter of unease ran down Becca's spine in response to her mother's expression. "Obviously Kaity has her heart set on having Zack photograph her wedding, and contracts are binding as Daddy will tell you. Now, Kaity has already questioned Zack and I as to whether we are capable of working together during this period of time, and since we are both professionals, we've agreed to the arrangement."

"Rebecca--"

"Wise wedding planners always know to please the bride as much as possible. After all, a happy bride means a smooth wedding," Becca added. "Otherwise they tend to want to leave the fuss behind and elope."

Her father muttered something under his breath Becca wasn't able to make out, but it wasn't hard to guess given his expression. George wasn't one to curse but occasionally his temper won the battle between his anger and his good manners.

"I don't like this," Wynonna stated with a shake of her elegantly coiffed head. "I don't like it at all."

"Mama, the past is the past," Kaity said, splitting a glance between Zack and Becca. "Right, Bex?"

"Yes," Becca said, the response automatic.

Zack didn't respond verbally but he nodded his dark head once.

Becca pinned a smile to her lips and held it there, years of practice coming to her aid. "You see? Everything will be fine."

Fine. Things were a long way from fine but if ever her mantra of *fake it till you make it* needed to hold true, it was now.

Becca shifted her gaze and realized her father's stare bored a hole into her. Her resolve faltered beneath the intensity. Her father might be boisterous and loud at times but at his core she knew he loved her and Kaity with all of his heart. Knew he'd do anything for them. Had done whatever needed to provide for them and shelter them and...

Hide them.

Or rather, *her*. "I should, um... Eli's tired. I should get him settled."

"We will talk to you at home then," her father said.

"Actually, Daddy, Bex is staying with me," Kaity said.

"What? No," their mother said with a firm shake of her head.

"Mama, I need Bex with me for all of this wedding stuff. Besides, my condo is closer to town so it's easier on her and Eli. You wouldn't want her to have to drag Eli back and forth from your house, would you?" Kaity linked their arms. "Plus, with my work schedule we will have to plan at odd times. It will go much more smoothly if she stays with me. Right, Bex?"

Becca held all of their attention now and she fought the urge to squirm. Kaity had good intentions and Becca appreciated her sister running interference with the parents, but staying with her would only prolong the inevitable.

But when it came to answer, she couldn't deny Kaity's words because she needed more time to come up with a plan.

She pinned a smile to her lips and nodded. "What can I say? The bride is always right."

Chapter 3

Zack left Wickersham Hall as soon as he was able. He climbed inside his truck and slammed the door, wondering why he'd ever agreed to Kaitlyn's request. He'd known this would be a difficult job. He'd known he'd be forced to deal with George and Wynonna even though they were the last two people he ever wanted to have to talk to again in his life.

But he'd agreed. All for the chance to see Becca. Even if he still wasn't sure of why he wanted to see her at all.

He drove back to his studio, located near the veterinary clinic, but bypassed his turn. Several minutes later, he found himself sitting outside of the Shake Shak. Emma, his half-sister *and* cousin as weird and redneck as that sounded, spotted him from inside and motioned for him to come in.

"Hey! I was hoping you'd stop by," Emma said once he'd made it inside the old-fashioned diner. "How are you?"

Emma enveloped him in a hug, smelling of more than a little Shake Shak fry grease.

"Been busy. What are you doing here?" he asked, releasing her and following her urging to seat himself on one of the bar stools facing the ice cream machines.

"Dad and Helen are off on an anniversary trip and I told him I would check in on things."

In the years since finding out that Frank Wyatt was his father, Zack had formed a strange relationship with the man. Not exactly something anyone would call father-son but more... mentor? Counselor?

Emma was largely responsible for the change, hiring Zack to work at the Shak despite her father's upset, and getting them together as often as possible just to form a connection. Eventually the awkwardness lessened and they began to talk man-to-man. And as strange as it had seemed at the time, he'd eventually been able to forgive Frank and his biological mother for making the decisions they had and was able to focus on the here and now.

Emma returned from refilling a patron's soda glass and settled herself back behind the counter.

"Well? Don't just sit there. I know today was the day you met with Kaity Waites and her family. How'd it go?"

He lifted an eyebrow. "I didn't tell you that."

"Yeah, well, I have my ways," she said, laughing softly. "Oh, come on. You know everything happening in Stone River flows through here at some point. Besides, the wedding is *the event of the season*," she added with a smile, shoving a folded newspaper across the counter to where he sat. "Everyone is talking about it. The wedding, the magazine spread... Sally Mitchell said her daughter called her earlier and told Sally she'd spotted you and Kaity walking the grounds at Wicker," she said, using the locals' nickname for the old estate. "And *then* she saw you inside talking to the Waites family... Including Becca."

Kaity's big blue eyes stared up at him from the newspaper. He'd taken the photo of Kaity and her fiancé, but looking at it now he saw it as a man and not a photographer. Would he ever find someone who would make him look as happy as the couple on the page?

"Hey," Emma said, nudging his hand with hers. "You okay?"

Zack shifted his gaze from the newspaper to Emma and shook his head. "Yeah."

"Your mouth says yes but your body says no. That bad, huh?"

Several seconds passed before he was able to speak what was on his mind. "She has a kid," he said, careful to keep his voice low so none of the other customers could overhear.

Emma had been around that fateful summer and knew of his and Becca's... fling. Emma knew he'd taken the brunt of all that had happened, and also knew how badly he'd been hurt because of the accusations of being a gold digger and using Becca to try to get money from the family. "She has this big ring on her finger. It was just-- Seeing her and her son-- Knowing she married someone else when I wasn't even good enough for her to..."

"Listen to me," Emma said. "You are the best, and that was her loss, you hear me? You don't need to prove yourself to anyone, Zack."

"Still--"

"I get what you're saying. No matter how many times you tell yourself it doesn't matter, you still wonder. But that won't get you anywhere."

"I know. But in this case, I know exactly what he had that I didn't--money, a name, connections. Everything Miss Waites apparently wanted in a husband."

Had a part of him actually hoped for some impossible scenario where Becca came running into his arms and apologized for leaving him? Yeah, right. Things like that only ever happened in books and sappy movies. "I don't know what I expected but it was more than her pretending nothing had ever happened between us."

"She may have pretended but I'm sure it wasn't easy for her, either. Just remember that when you decide."

He glanced up and found Emma's eyes trained on him. How amazing was it that when he'd met her she was totally blind but now... "Decide what? What do you mean?"

"I mean, thinking about having to deal with Becca as part of the wedding party as well as the wedding planner is one thing, but actually seeing her face-to-face is another. Will you be able to handle being around her after all that was said and done?"

"I signed the contract. Besides, life goes on, right? Turn the other cheek? Forgive and forget?"

"Zack, just consider something, okay? You were both so young. As hard as it is, remember to look at things from a grown man's perspective rather than a teenage boy's, okay?"

Yeah, they'd been young. But not too young. He'd been nineteen at the time, nearly twenty, to Becca's seventeen. But she'd finished her senior year of high school and seemed more mature than most of the girls her age, different than the other girls who lived in the affluent area of Rose Hill. But it had all been a lie.

"I'm not defending her. Not at all. But it's never easy standing up to your family. I know that all too well," Emma said. "And... so do you."

Emma referred to her overprotective father and sister and how they'd sheltered her during her years of blindness, but the second reference named his adoptive father, a drunk and abuser who never had a kind word for either of his kids. But the circumstances between the two scenarios were polar opposites.

Weren't they?

"I certainly can't imagine how difficult it would be to stand up to George and Wynonna Waites."

"They are a force to be reckoned with," he murmured, wondering if maybe he _had_ been a little unreasonable when it came to his expectations of Becca at such a young age. But he'd loved her with everything inside of him and he'd thought she'd felt the same-- until the night George had caught Zack sneaking into their Rose Hill house.

He'd only wanted to see Becca, to try to talk to her and get answers about why she'd been avoiding him. But George had threatened to have him arrested and prosecuted for stalking his daughter along with breaking and entering. With a misdemeanor assault charge for punching a perv coming onto his fourteen-year-old little sister already on his record, Zack knew the man could send him to jail with no problem. George had that much power with the small town legal system.

It was go away--or get put away. Not that Becca had seemed to care either way.

"So what's she like now?" Emma asked. "Is she as pretty as ever? What did you talk about when you saw each other?"

Zack rubbed a hand along his chin and pondered Emma's questions. "She looked beautiful."

"That's it? That's all you have to say after not seeing her for ten years?"

Zack stared down at the fifties-style Formica counter in front of him. Yeah, that was all he had to say.

Because he couldn't say that with one look into Becca's beautiful face he'd realized he'd never stopped loving her.

SEEING Zack again had brought out every memory, every regret. Every *what if* question she'd ever pondered since leaving Stone River ten years ago.

Becca pressed her fingertips to her forehead and prayed for relief from the headache beating against her brain. Stress headaches had become the norm since her divorce and she'd quickly discovered finding a quiet spot in which to breathe and say a quick prayer was the best medicine.

Too bad "quiet" wasn't available at the moment--and wouldn't be until after the wedding was over.

"You can do this, right?" Kaity asked, her tone soft. "I mean, I know the wedding has turned into a circus and it's become crazy large, but you can pull this together? Our wedding day won't actually *be* a circus, will it?"

After leaving Wickersham Hall, Becca had followed behind Kaity's sporty BMW to the condo she'd purchased the moment she began earning a living as an RN. The only problem was that Wynonna had followed them as well and now stood across the spacious open-concept apartment talking loudly on her cell phone.

"I've got this," Becca said automatically, lowering her hand and pasting on a smile.

"That poor man," Kaity whispered after a bit, her gaze on their mother. "Little did he know what he took on when he bid on mama's landscaping job."

Becca smiled despite the pain. It might sound to some as though they only saw the bad in their mother, but truth be told Wynonna Waites was a fabulous chairwoman. If elected, she could run the White House and get it financially in the black in no time. She was purposeful and focused, charitable. Her only problem was being so driven she sometimes forgot the toll the work took on others. "He'll be fine. Mama's a good tipper, if nothing else."

"True. And I have to say the thoughts of a bridal shower in the new design sound wonderful."

"Even though it means a fuss?" Becca teased.

Kaity laughed and nodded. "Okay, fine. I confess, I was a *little* sad at the thought of eloping and not wearing the white dress and doing the whole wedding thing."

"Well, now you get the best of both worlds-- the wedding without the hassle."

"Thanks to you. Becca, thank you so much. I'll never forget this. Or your courage in having to work with Zack after what he tried to do."

Becca stilled, the pen in her hand pausing over the paper where she made notes. "Pardon?"

Kaity looked perplexed by Becca's response.

"You know... the way he tried to take advantage Mama and Daddy that summer."

"Is that what they told you?"

Kaity expression changed from sympathy to startled confusion in the blink of an eye, but before she could answer Becca's question, Wynonna ended her phone call and joined them.

"Well, it took some doing, but the garden and patio *will* be finished in two weeks."

Wynonna settled herself at the table with her daughters, her bracelets jingling with her movements.

Kaity looked to Becca, questions in her gaze, and Becca inhaled shakily. "Well, that's good to hear. I thought while we wait for Eli to wake up from his nap, we could go over the bridal shower preferences and I'll get the ball rolling. Also, I need a list of potential bands for the wedding and--"

"First, Rebecca, we will talk some sense into your sister. Tell her you're not willing to work with that man."

"Really, Mama? Are we back to that again?" Kaity asked, immediately going on the defensive. "People change. Zack was a kid then but he's a grown man now, a good man. If God can forgive him, I would think you can, too. Especially when we all attend the same church."

Wynonna fluffed her hair and avoided eye contact.

"I agree," Becca interjected, forcing herself to say the words and somehow find the courage to mean them. "Kaity's right. Zack and I... It was a long time ago. Besides, the odds of getting another photographer on such short notice is slim to none, and if Zack's professional reputation is even remotely accurate, Kaity has done very well scoring him as her photographer."

"It's all true," Kaity said. "And the magazine is sooo happy to have Zack doing the photo spread. All the I's have been dotted and the T's crossed. Breaking the contract would be a nightmare, like I told Daddy. Now, can we please move on?" Kaity asked with a tilt of her pointy chin.

Wynonna looked highly displeased but didn't comment further.

Becca knew her mother would continue to fight against using Zack, but for now at least the issue was settled. "So, the bridal shower. Are you thinking of a garden party, formal tea, a themed event or something else?" she asked Kaity.

Kaity practically squirmed in her seat in excitement. "A winter wonderland. That will work perfectly with Mama's new patio and garden, don't you think?"

"Yes. It's perfect." But had Kaity considered the fact she was inviting Zack into the lion's den? Zack would have to come to Rose Hill for the event. Walk into the very house he wasn't welcomed into ten years ago.

One glance at Kaity's expression caused Becca to still.

Her sister knew exactly what she was doing. And with a sudden jab of awareness, so did Becca.

Kaity had hired Zack, begged Becca to come there--because like any bride in love, she wanted to matchmake.

The pleased grin on Kaity's face confirmed it.

Lord, help me. What have I gotten myself into?

Chapter 4

The next day, Zack leaned against the wall of the bridal salon, feeling very much like the rooster in a hen house. Everywhere he looked he was surrounded by women. Women in white desperate to find the perfect dress. Women in black running here and there hunting the next potential gown, all the while calming fears and handing out tissues to mamas and grandmamas unprepared to let their babies go.

Then there were the women seated across from him wearing black sparkling shirts that read *Bridesmaid, Maid of Honor, and Mother of the Bride.*

While Kaity's girlfriends had opted to wear their shirts with blinged-out blue jeans, Becca wore black slacks that made her look much too thin, while Wynonna wore a white shirt beneath her T-shirt along with several strands of pearls. The sight was such a southern trademark, he lifted his camera near his chest as though checking a setting and focused on the image on the screen, letting the shutter click several times.

Becca had her head down and was scribbling notes in a binder. He couldn't imagine keeping track of all the details of a wedding this size, but she seemed to be in her element when it came to organizing.

As though sensing his perusal, Becca lifted her head and their gazes met. His finger tightened automatically and once more the shutter clicked. He removed his finger from the button, hoping the nearly-silent whirl of the camera couldn't be heard given the noise of music and chatter and laughter in the salon.

But the phone call he'd received enroute to the location had shaken him and now he wondered...

Leave things be. Focus on the job and let sleeping dogs lie.

"Here we go, ladies," one of the black-clad workers said as she followed Kaity into the mirrored area where her bridal party sat.

Due to the wedding date being so close at hand, apparently Kaity was being forced to buy "off the rack," which upset Wynonna to no end. From what Zack had gathered from the bits and pieces of conversation he'd overheard, that meant available dresses were considerably numbered.

Who knew all this wedding stuff was so complicated?

Zack lifted his camera, snapping several shots of Kaity's reflection in the mirror from over her shoulder to get both the front and back of the massive ballgown.

"It's beautiful," Kaity murmured, but a frown pinched her eyebrows overtop of her nose. "But..."

"If there's a "but" then it's not the one," Becca quickly interjected before Wynonna could comment.

The dress had been Wynonna's choice from the wall of available gowns, but Zack agreed with Becca's statement. The dress swallowed Kaity and took away from the bride because of its size.

"Girls?" Kaity asked.

The bridal party shook their heads, each woman giving Wynonna a pained smile of apology.

While Kaity and the attendant retreated to the dressing room to change, Zack found himself watching Eli. He'd almost forgotten Becca's son had come along, but given the boy's silence it was easy to misplace him.

Zack frowned, realizing that he had yet to hear the boy make *any* sound. That wasn't normal. Not for a kid Eli's age. Emma and her besties had quite a few munchkins running around and quiet was never a word that could be used to describe any of them. But Eli...

Zack watched as the boy played with several cars on the floor of the salon. In typical kid fashion, he spun on his knees as he drove them, sometimes crashing them before starting all over again.

Kaity reappeared in several more gowns. All were beautiful but one by one they were rejected for being too simple, too fussy, too sparkly, the skirts too full. It made Zack appreciate the fact that all he had to do to prepare for his job as photographer was put on his tuxedo.

"Well?" Kaity asked, entering the showing area once more.

Zack turned and straightened from his slouched position, taken in by the sweet beauty of the woman in front of him. Zack lifted his camera and took more photos, his mind working overtime on how he could layout this portion of the magazine spread to best feature the bride.

Oohs and ahhs sounded from the ladies in waiting and he quickly swung his camera around to capture the moment. But it was Becca's expression that caused his heart to still before it picked up speed. Tears brightened her eyes and made them sparkle like the majestic blue-green of the ocean, her expression happy, yet sad and wistful.

"Say something," Kaity said. "This is Becca's pick. What do you think?"

All the women spoke at once, detailing what they loved about the dress.

"That's the one."

"Oh, Kaity, it's perfect!"

"Just gorgeous."

"Mama?" Kaity asked, tensing a bit as she faced Wynonna.

"It's beautiful, Kaity. Quite breathtaking. I didn't expect to find something so beautiful under the time constraints. Your sister chose well."

Kaity beamed and Zack captured the shot, going on to take several more as the attendant and her manager brought out a veil and earrings. In a matter of minutes Kaity was decked out in full wedding attire and Zack continued to shoot the moment, careful to get the expressions of the ladies in the background as well as when Kaity said yes to the dress.

When the moment was over Zack watched as the ladies stood and began gathering up their things. Wynonna left the area entirely to pay for the gown, and the bridesmaids chatted with Becca about the luncheon to follow before heading off to go to the restaurant.

Kaity gathered her binder and placed it in a large tote bag.

"I could see you in that dress."

Becca turned, looking visibly startled by his words but no more so than he was to have blurted them out. It was true, though. The dress looked beautiful on Kaity but in his mind he'd pictured Becca wearing the gown and--

"I have to go."

"You have to wait on Kaity," Zack countered, stepping in front of her when she looked ready to bolt.

"Zack..."

"What? It was just a statement."

"One you have no business saying to me."

"Why not? It's not like we didn't talk about getting married."

Becca closed her eyes and kept them shut for several seconds. Behind her, Eli continued to play, oblivious as kids usually were when engrossed in something.

"Please don't..."

"Remember when you told me about your dream? How we had gotten married and you wore a white dress and--"

"Stop it," she said, lowering her voice and looking around nervously.

"Why?" He watched her closely, noted the changes ten years had taken on her.

"Because it's-- We can't go back. It's too late. It was too late then but it's even more impossible now."

The tip of her nose turned pink and he saw the battle waging behind her eyes. Her words created a fist in his gut, and he wished he could read her mind. "It's never too late, Becca. Especially since you're not married anymore."

KAITY <u>TOLD</u> YOU?" Becca demanded. How could she? Why would she?

"Sit down."

"No, I--" The dizziness creeping up on her truly hit her and she found herself grateful for Zack's hold on her arm, firmly but gently guiding her into one of the seats behind her. "I can't believe she'd--"

"Kaity didn't tell me about the divorce."

She shook her head, confused.

"I made a phone call," Zack admitted. "That was all it took."

"But-- how? To whom?"

Zack quickly explained the connection between his newfound family and the security business ran by Duncan MacGregor.

"You're-- Mrs. *Dibbs*?" she asked, thoroughly flabbergasted by the fact one of the nicest, sweetest elementary teachers she'd ever had was capable of such a thing. An affair and-- to give Zack up for adoption?

Zack nodded, his expression grim as he stared at her.

"Look, none of that matters now. Why do you still wear his ring after what the guy did to you?"

Becca floundered beneath the weight of Zack's stare and the heavy awareness of what he now knew. If he was aware of the divorce, it stood to reason he was also aware of Eli's condition. "Please, I can't talk about this. Not now. Not here. Kaity will be out any second. And my mother... They don't-- She doesn't... Zack, please."

The way she fumbled for words must have triggered Zack's suspicions because his frown deepened and a sound of frustration emerged from his throat.

"Are you telling me that they don't know you're divorced?"

"Shhh!" Becca stared into Zack's face and prayed. She prayed for help. Prayed for the words. Prayed for deliverance from the mess she'd made of her life. "No," she whispered, glancing over her shoulder. "They don't. K-Kaity knows some but not all. Zack, please. You can't say anything."

"You're not going to tell them?" he asked, sounding incredulous.

"I am. I *will*. But when the time is right," she said, using the same lame excuse she'd used with her sister and hating herself for it. "I have to... work up to it. There's just so much happening right now. The wedding, the *holidays*..."

"You haven't changed at all, have you? You're still the same girl with no backbone."

Becca drew back against the seat, the words cutting through her like a knife. "That's easy for you to say. You don't know what it's like. You didn't grow up in a family like mine where the expectations and demands are *so* high, you--you don't ever want to disappoint."

"They're adults. Disappointment is a fact of life. Face it, Becca, you haven't told them because you still can't stand up to them. You're a grown woman but nothing's changed, has it?"

"I'm ready--and starving," Kaity said as she walked down the wall from the dressing area. "Do you think we can-- Oh."

Zack stood from where he'd seated himself beside of her during the exchange and stalked over to where he'd left his camera bag by the mirrors.

"Um... is everything okay?" Kaity asked, splitting her attention between them.

"Fine," Zack said. "I'll see you at the restaurant."

Becca remained seated, her legs trembling too hard to hold her weight.

"What just happened?" Kaity asked, taking the seat Zack had vacated before stalking out of the viewing area.

"Nothing."

"Don't give me that. Bex, talk to me."

Becca lifted her head and met her sister's gaze. "He knows."

Kaity's eyes widened for a moment before a smile spread across her face. "Really? That's perfect!"

"No, Kaity, that isn't perfect. None of this is *perfect*," Becca argued. "What are you doing? How could you hire Zack? Couldn't you have talked to me about it first?"

"I could have. But you would've said no."

"For good reason!" she said, struggling to keep her voice down. "I don't know why after the total disaster ten years ago, but I know you're trying to matchmake. Don't deny it."

"I wasn't going to," Kaity said boldly, lifting a hand to smooth Becca's hair. "Bex, you did what Mama and Daddy wanted you to do back then and I don't blame you. But what I do know is it's time to do what *you* want to do. To live *your* life. I just want you to be happy and when I talked to you and you sounded so sad on the phone, I don't know... It just made me wonder if things were different now. And since you and Zack are both single..."

"You think we could pick up where we left off," she said, shaking her head in disbelief. Kaity didn't know the whole story. She didn't, otherwise she'd know just how impossible that statement was.

Even if her mother and father would accept Zack into the family--which would never happen--there were the lies she'd told. The things she'd said to him. All because she lacked the backbone to stand up for herself, as Zack had pointed out.

"Bex, you were happy with him. I know I was young that summer but... I've never seen you like that. And I've definitely not seen you like that since then. Yes, you were happy with your marriage until you found out about the affair and all the awful stuff, but during your marriage? I never saw you light up about Elliot the way you did just *talking* about Zack."

"I was a stupid kid." Becca stared down at her hands, at the obnoxiously large ring on her left hand. She'd asked for something small and simple, vintage, but Elliot had insisted on large and gaudy to impress his boss and friends. Another example of how money couldn't buy happiness.

"You were in love," Kaity said. "Love isn't stupid."

"Oh, Kaity. Even if I were interested in Zack--which I'm not--Mama and Daddy would never--"

"Bex, it's not their life. You married a man they approved of and look what happened? I know this is all weird and sudden for you, but I've gotten to know Zack a little better over the last couple of years. The rough kid Daddy saw isn't there anymore. He's a grown man with a flourishing business, he goes to church with his sister and family. Things are different now. If I can see the changes, maybe Daddy and Mama can, too."

It wasn't possible. It just wasn't.

Because Zack would never forgive her if he knew the real truth of why and how she'd left him.

Chapter 5

Later that evening, Zack lifted his hand to knock on the door of Kaity's condo but hesitated.

What was he doing?

He turned away and retraced his steps down the hall but stopped again.

Had he really walked up to the door only to turn around leave like a coward?

He paced the hallway, hoping none of the neighbors saw him acting so strangely and called the cops.

Once more he found himself in front of Kaity's door but this time he forced himself to knock before he could chicken out.

Silence followed and he glanced at his phone for the time. Nine-thirty. Was it too late?

The luncheon had gone as well as could be expected with Wynonna glaring at him when she wasn't smiling for the camera. He didn't get anymore time alone with Becca at the restaurant and, by the end of the day, he couldn't stand not having the answers he craved.

A noise sounded on the other side of the door. A footstep, a gasp? He stared into the peep hole, sensing Becca on the other side. "Let me in. We need to talk."

"It's late. Eli is asleep," Becca murmured, her words muffled by the wooden panel between them.

"I won't stay long. Let me in."

Seconds passed and he could almost feel her mind churning over his words. Finally the locks clicked and the door opened.

Becca took several steps back, avoiding his gaze but no longer barring his path. "Thanks."

"You shouldn't be here."

Zack moved deeper into the luxurious condo, taking in the feminine furnishings and art on the walls. "We need to talk. Face-to-face."

"Zack, please. I'm too tired for this."

He turned and faced her once more, noting her white-knuckled grip on the doorknob and the pallor of her face. "Shut the door and I won't stay long."

Her body language screamed reluctance but she did as ordered. He stayed on the far side of the room, watching as she moved to stand behind a chair.

"What do you want?"

"Is Kaity here?" He wanted privacy for this conversation and Kaity was too curious for her own good.

"No. She and David went to a movie."

He nodded, not sure what else to do in response since he doubted she would approve of him liking that they were virtually alone with Eli asleep in a bedroom.

"Zack, what do you want?"

"Answers," he said simply. "For the last ten years I've gone through every scenario I can think of as to why things ended between us the way that they did. How we had plans one minute, and were at each other's throats the next."

She wet her lips, looking nervous and ill at ease.

"Things just... happened."

"Like what?" he asked, the words bursting out of him. "You said you were happy. That you *loved* me. What happened?"

"I was *seventeen*. That's what happened."

"Your age doesn't change what you said or what we shared. Did you mean any of it?"

"Yes, I-I did but..."

"But I wasn't rich enough? My family wasn't good enough?"

"I know it probably seemed that way but... Zack, when we were together all I wanted was to be with you. I couldn't think straight because I was so blinded by love and... lust," she added, knowing it had to be said. "But once we were apart and I began thinking about marriage and jobs and trying to live--"

"You realized I couldn't keep you in the lifestyle you were accustomed to." He heard the bitterness in his tone despite his efforts to stay calm and simply unearth the truth.

"I *realized*," she countered, "we both had dreams and if we stayed together *neither one of us* would achieve them because we would be too busy just trying to survive and feed ourselves."

Something about the way she said the words, her expression, sank the truth of them into his soul. That summer he'd been scraping for every dollar, dreaming of being a photographer but not having any experience or training. It had taken a lot of work, odd jobs, time and effort and instruction to get to where he was today. Had they run away and gotten married...

He ran a hand over his chin and face, rubbing hard to ease the ache in his jaw from gritting his teeth. "Tell me about the guy you married."

"He doesn't matter anymore. He's no longer in our lives as I'm sure you discovered since you had me investigated."

Zack faced her once more, taking in her crossed arms and the jut of her chin. "It wasn't that in depth."

"Then why did you bother to do it?"

"I wanted to know more about you."

"You couldn't have simply asked?"

He shrugged and walked over the window overlooking the pool area. "He doesn't come around to see his son?"

"No," she said simply.

Zack frowned at her lack of explanation and decided to settle in for a while. Getting the answers he wanted obviously wasn't going to be easy.

He seated himself on the comfortable couch and waited for her to join him. It took several long seconds before she released her grip on the back of the chair before she moved around it to perch on the edge. "Ever?" he asked, keeping them on topic.

"No."

"Do you receive child support?"

"No. When it became obvious that Elliot didn't... want to see Eli the way a father should, I made a deal with him. He would pay no child support and in exchange I got full custody."

He couldn't imagine giving up a child for any reason. But having been given up as a child himself, he had strong opinions about the subject. "Eli's better off with you."

"I think so, too," she said simply.

"What does Eli say about all of this?" He watched as she swallowed hard and smoothed her fingers over the material of her shirt.

The seconds stretched on and Becca jumped to her feet to move to the window where he'd stood earlier.

"Eli hasn't said anything," she whispered.

"He doesn't ask about his father? Ask why he isn't around?"

He moved toward her to better see her expression, reflected in the glass. The anguish he saw on her features caused his lungs to squeeze.

"Eli has selective mutism. He talks to me sometimes, but no one else. Ever."

Things began to make a little more sense as to why Becca and Eli were staying with Kaity instead of in the house in Rose Hill. "How do your parents do with him?"

"Not well but it could be worse. They haven't heard the official diagnosis, something else I haven't told them, but they know there's an issue."

She turned her head to glance at him, arms wrapped tightly around her body.

"I'm sorry, Zack. About everything. If you believe nothing else, please know I truly, truly never meant to hurt you. I just wanted... to do what was best for us both."

He didn't reach out on a conscious level. One second he stood in front of her and the next he pulled her into his arms, folded her against his chest. The embrace was one of shared experiences, sadness, forgiveness. Everything he'd wanted from her and needed for the last ten years.

"Oh!"

Zack loosened his hold when Becca shoved against his chest to separate them once she heard Kaity's arrival.

"You guys!" Kaity said with a gush, a huge smile on her face. "See, Bex? *I told you* Zack would forgive you for not telling him about the baby."

Zack struggled to process Kaity's words as he stared down into Becca's wide-eyed and fearful expression. "What baby?" The truth sank in and his knees weakened. "You're pregnant?"

THIS COULDN'T BE HAPPENING. Not now. Not like this.

Becca's stomach churned and she pressed a hand to her middle, trying to stop the topsy-turvy roller coaster twisting her insides.

"Oh, no. No, she's not-- I mean. Oh, Bex, I'm so..."

Kaity's words trailed off but Becca scarcely heard her, unable to shift her attention from Zack's expression.

What else did you expect?

"I'm *so* sorry. I'm-- I'm going to bed," Kaity said before racing down the hallway and shutting the door with a gentle slam.

Zack continued his narrow-eyed stare, searching her gaze. Emotions flickered rapidly over his face. Confusion changing to real-ization and then...

"It was *my baby?*"

"I'm..." She had to stop and swallow and even then her voice emerged hoarse and thready. "Zack... let me explain."

"You had a--*my*--baby?"

He left go of her arms so abruptly that she stumbled backward, stopping only when her body bumped into the balcony door behind her. She watched him, saw every ounce of pain and disgust and anger rushing through him. "No. I mean--yes, I did, but--"

"Which is it? You can't seem to make up your mind. Are you saying you left Stone River knowing you were pregnant with my baby and you didn't see fit to tell me?"

Her heart broke all over again as the memories flooded back. "Y-yes," she whispered.

A rough sound left his chest, not quite a growl or a huff but a combination of the two.

"You didn't think I had a right to know?"

"I wasn't thinking clearly. I was completely overwhelmed. Zack... please, try to understand."

"What was it? Boy or girl? Where is he or she?" Zack muttered something unintelligible beneath his hand. "Becca, they're ten years old and I've *missed* their childhood."

"No," she said, leaning heavily against the door for support. "No, they're not. You h-haven't. The baby's gone. I-I lost it. Her," she corrected, closing her eyes because of the tears stinging them and the way her chest squeezed until every breath took effort. "She didn't make it. I-I have a clotting condition b-but I didn't know it then. I wasn't on medication for it so she didn't develop properly and..." She tightened her arms around her belly, remembering that last night. She'd stayed up, rocking the baby she knew she wouldn't bring home from the hospital. "She died inside of me a-at four months."

Becca inhaled shakily, her breath catching in her throat and chest, eyes dry. She'd cried. She'd mourned. Now it was Zack's turn, not hers. "I'm sorry."

"Are you? Because I think it's funny you say that since you obviously weren't sorry enough to tell me about her at the time."

The verbal blow crushed what was left of her resolve and her shoulders sagged. She deserved everything he said to her. Everything and more.

He raked a hand through his hair and paced away from her,

every step seemingly more angry than the last.

"Start at the beginning."

Zack faced her once more, anguish and fury marking his handsome features.

Unable to handle the way he looked at her, she faced the window, the night sky a beautiful deep purple. "We... weren't always as careful as we... should have been." They should have abstained entirely but that was water under the bridge now. Many mistakes had been made. Too many to count.

"Obviously," he said. "Becca, why didn't you tell me? Why did you leave town?"

"I had to."

"Your parents made you? Forced you?"

She'd faced him in time to see him straighten to his full height, his hands fisting at his sides.

It would be all too easy to blame her parents and tell Zack they had, in fact, forced her to go away. They had jumped on the idea at the time, too angry and embarrassed by her behavior and the consequences to say anything else. But now that the truth had come to light, she had to be honest. Anything else would only deepen the hole she'd dug for herself ten years ago when she'd run away. "Not exactly."

"For the love of-- Becca, spit it out. What happened?"

"Daddy told me that he'd threatened to have you arrested and... that he'd offered you money to stop seeing me."

"I didn't take it."

"You also didn't tell me," she countered, "so I wasn't the only one keeping secrets."

"Not telling you that your father tried to bribe me isn't the same as not telling me I was to be a father."

"Agreed," she murmured. "But once I heard the news... It combined with the overwhelming fact I was seventeen and pregnant-- It was too much for me. I panicked. I thought... I thought about everything you'd told me, about your dreams and how you wanted to be a photographer. How much it cost and your plans to have your own studio... Daddy said it was only a matter of time before you took him up on his offer, and I believed it."

"That wouldn't have happened, Becca. Ever. Look, I understand it was a shock and you were scared. I get it, but what about later once the shock had worn off? Why not tell me then? Why didn't you call me? Come home?"

"So you would do what, get down on one knee?"

"It's not like we hadn't talked about the future."

She moved toward the couch, her legs trembling so badly she felt the need to sit down. "Zack, we daydreamed about a future but that didn't make it real. My parents would never have accepted a relationship between us, and even though I wanted to be with you, *marriage*... I wasn't ready to walk away from my family and that was exactly what it would have meant if I stayed with you."

Becca shook her head, all of the fear and panic filled her, just like it had back then. "I knew you'd want to do what was right. I knew you'd want to be a father because of the lousy childhood you had growing up, but how could we have survived? How could we have fed a baby and paid bills? All I had was a high school diploma and you..."

"Didn't even have that. Nor did I live up to your families' standards--or yours, apparently," he bit out. "Becca, I would have done anything I had to do to provide for you."

"*Exactly*. I knew you would, Zack. But that would've meant giving up your dreams and getting a job at the factory or something."

"Don't. Don't sit there and pretend you lied to me in some twisted belief it was best for me."

"But it was. I didn't want to hurt you but someone had to be realistic. We had *everything* stacked against us. What were the odds we would've made a marriage work under those circumstances?"

"We could have if you had only been willing to try. Instead you were too busy worrying about losing face with your parents and your country club friends because you had gone slumming with me."

Becca closed her eyes and lowered her head to her hands, her elbows digging into her knees. "No."

"Yes."

She jumped, startled when he grasped her hands and pulled them from her face. He now sat on the coffee table facing her, his knees bracketing hers, his hold on her hands making escape impossible.

"Look me in the eyes and tell me you weren't more embarrassed and scared of losing your Daddy's money than in love with me."

She blinked at his words, at the intensity of his gaze, but once more she found herself unable to do more than nod. The truth was a bitter pill, but she wanted Zack's forgiveness and telling him the truth was the only way to get it. "That...I would be lying if I said I didn't think about that, too. I'm s-sorry."

"I don't want to hear excuses."

"It's the truth. I have so many regrets, made so many mistakes. There are so many things I wish I could change but I can't. I want you to forgive me, but before you say anything you have to know everything."

She watched as Zack turned to stone. The grip of his hands hardened over hers and his nostrils flared with his breathing.

"What else haven't you told me?"

Becca swallowed hard, knowing that Zack would never forgive her for being so weak and shallow. "After Daddy told me about the offer he made to you, I thought about it," she whispered. "Zack, when Daddy and Mama found out about the pregnancy... Things were *so bad*. I couldn't look them in the eyes. I couldn't stand the expressions they wore. But more than anything, I didn't want to force you to give up your dreams any more than I wanted to give up mine, s-so I told Daddy I would go away to school, stay away from you, away from Stone River, if he made me the same offer. You didn't t-take the money... but I did. Zack—please forgive me."

Zack's eyes widened slightly. He leaned away from her as her words sank in. The slide of his calloused hands over her skin left fire in its wake, and she waited for his anger to erupt. For the accusations and insults to begin like they always did whenever she and Elliot fought.

Zack stood. He stared down at her a long moment then turned and moved toward the door with near-silent strides. He paused on the threshold and she waited anxiously, watching, hoping, he would speak. Say something to end the torturous thoughts in her head.

But he stepped into the hall without a word and closed the door behind him with a deafening *snick* of sound louder than any slam.

Chapter 6

A heavy weight appeared on his legs as Zack lay in his bed early Sunday morning. He didn't bother opening his eyes, playing the well-known game Moses, an eighty-pound Lab, liked to play to start their day.

Seconds later, Moses inched his way up Zack's legs to his chest and resettled like a giant stuffed animal. Still, Zack didn't move. Moses released a sound somewhere between a complaint and a sigh, his large paws gently kneading Zack's shoulders.

Given the cue, Zack finally lifted his hands and began to pet the large dog, scratching all the places Moses liked best. "What am I going to do with you? Lazy dog. Can't even start your morning without a massage."

Moses snuffled out another sigh before doing his daily doggy roll so that Zack scratched his belly, a yawn stretching Moses' jaws wide and very close to Zack's ear since the dog was on top of him. "Sorry about the late nights and no sleep. You can catch up while I'm gone."

Moses yawned again, rolling onto the bed beside of Zack, sprawling out in the middle of the mattress and getting comfortable.

"Kicking me out of my own bed. Some best friend you are," Zack grumbled, performing his own roll toward the side of the bed.

His gaze landed on a photography book across the room and he seconds later he found himself flipping through the pages until the slip of stiff card stock appeared, the four smiling photos of him and Becca taken inside of a photo booth mocking him.

He stared at the delicate lines of her face, the bow of her mouth and fullness of her lower lip. The way she stared at him in the third photo, smiling at him instead of the camera.

Zack shoved the strip back into the spine of the book and shut it with a snap, earning a grunt from Moses because of the disturbance.

The coffee pot called to him and Zack made his way to the kitchen, pouring himself a cup of the strong, black brew before sitting down at the table and opening his Bible to read the scripture this morning's class would cover.

But after a few minutes he pinched the bridge of his nose and shoved the book away. Ever since last night he hadn't been able to find the words. Couldn't focus on the scripture in front of him. Couldn't do anything but think of Becca and how she'd betrayed him. Left him.

Like the selfish, entitled, rich--

The old coffee mug popped, scalding coffee flowing onto his fingers, wrist and hand. Zack gasped at the pain and shoved his chair back from the table, slinging off the burning liquid as well as he could while rushing to the sink and faucet.

The cold water cooled the sting but as soon as he removed his hand from beneath the spray, the pain returned, throbbing with every beat of his love-battered heart.

TWO AND A HALF HOURS LATER, Zack sat in the church pew between his half-sisters Emma and Laney, every cell in his body aware of Becca and her son sitting one aisle over toward the front beside of her family.

Throughout the sermon his gaze strayed toward the left and lingered on what he could see of her pretty profile. That was the kicker. Despite all that she'd done, he still found himself drawn to her. Not just physically, but on a deeper level. He'd known the exact moment she'd entered the church because, after ten long years, they were still connected in some intrinsic way.

Emma elbowed him, jerking him out of his thoughts and back to the moment at hand. He followed everyone else and stood, bowed his head when the minister asked an elder to lead the closing prayer.

Zack closed his eyes, tried to concentrate on the man's words but his mind wouldn't stop whirling, the anger and disappointment he felt at being so wrong about Rebecca eating away at him.

Church dismissed and since his exit was blocked by his half-sisters and their families, he turned his back on Becca and asked Emma's husband about his latest guard dog-in-training while the mothers gathered their brood of offspring and chatted with friends.

After a bit, his awareness of Becca dimmed and he knew she'd left the building.

Zack said his goodbyes to his sisters, escaping the pew once everyone got moving toward the exit. "Nice sermon today, Preacher."

The minister's hand tightened on Zack's.

"Thank you. Zack? I was wondering if you had some time? Just a few moments after everyone leaves."

The minister had been wanting a group photo of the entire congregation and with the holidays coming up, Zack figured the man wanted to discuss the details. "Sure. I'll wait inside."

Zack retraced his steps down the aisle of the old church, admiring the the vaulted, beamed ceilings and stained glass window in the peak as he always did. Thanks to Emma and Laney and the men in their lives, Zack had been asked, pressed, begged and bargained into attending church there. And joining them had been the best decision he'd ever made.

"Thanks for waiting," Minister Jones said as he joined Zack.

"No problem. What can I help you with?"

"Actually, I was wondering the same thing," the man stated, looking at Zack with a knowing expression.

"Pardon?"

"For the last nine years or so, you've been here nearly every Sunday service. It took a while, but you eventually began to sing and pray and interact with the others. But today I noticed your attention was elsewhere. Something wrong?"

The man had always been astute. Zack figured such a gift either came with the job or quickly learned. "I'm fine."

"I see. Well, may I remind you that you're in a church--on Sunday, no less."

Duly scolded, Zack sighed. "Fine. You caught me. I've got something weighing on me."

"I'm here to help if you'd like to talk about it."

Zack stared at the stained glass cross high in the church. "How do you forgive the unforgivable?" he finally murmured. "I know I'm supposed to, but I'm not sure it's something I'm capable of."

"We're all capable of forgiveness. But that doesn't make it easy."

"You're a pretty easy-going guy," Zack said. "You probably don't think twice about it."

Zack watched as the minister shifted on the pew and--for maybe the first time--saw the minister as a man.

"You might think so, but you would be wrong," the man said. "I have my own difficulties with sin. I love serving my Lord, but I would be lying if I said I didn't admire some of the cars parked in the lot outside."

"Sorry, Padre, but coveting a car doesn't rank high as a sin in my book."

"So, tell me, then, what is unforgivable in your 'book'?"

Caught in a trap of his own making, Zack stood, exited the pew and moved several paces closer to the stained glass window. "I guess the word would be... betrayal. And before you say it, I know Jesus was betrayed in the worst ways possible and He still managed to forgive, but it's pretty obvious none of us are Him. So how do we get to that place? How do we let it go when the pain will *never* go away?"

"It might help to know more of the circumstances involved. Can you give me more information to go on?"

He could--but he doubted Becca would appreciate it if he did. "No."

"Well, in that case, I suppose I would try to put myself in the other person's shoes and pray for the insight needed to see things from their perspective. Changing our point of view of the situation can sometimes help us see things in a new light."

He'd tried that. The night Becca had told him about the baby and nearly every waking moment since, he'd tried to understand things from her angle. But try as he might, it never worked. Even though the baby had died and would have regardless of him being aware of its existence, that precious time of knowing, that experience, had been taken from him. *Becca* had taken it from him.

And that theft was something he could never forget--or forgive.

SUNDAY DINNERS AT HER PARENTS' house were always interesting. Thankfully Kaity and David were there to lighten the tension filling the formal dining room.

Elda, the housekeeper and cook and former nanny, had prepared Kaity and Becca's favorites to celebrate having both of "her girls" under the same roof once again. The table was loaded down with fried chicken, mashed potatoes, green beans, corn, cole slaw, macaroni salad and more. Dessert awaited them on the side-board, the antique piece of furniture lined with no less than three different flavors of fresh-baked pies.

"Eat, eat, Miss Becca," Elda urged, refilling Becca's water glass. "You're too skinny. Men like women with a little meat on their bones."

"Well, if I eat anymore, Elda, I won't be able to fit into my wedding gown," Kaity said with a smile, pushing her plate away.

Elda tsked but smiled, obviously taking Kaity's words as a compliment.

"Eli, how about we do some fishing at the pond once we've had our pie?" George asked.

Becca looked from her father to Eli and noted that Eli either didn't hear the question or purposefully ignored it.

"Eli, would you like to go fishing?" Becca pressed.

Eli tucked his chin to his chest but didn't respond otherwise.

Becca glanced at her father and noted the frown lines around his mouth had deepened. "Maybe instead of fishing you guys could check out the old playhouse in the backyard?"

"That's a good idea," her father said. "We will," he continued, not bothering to form it as a question. "Eat up, son."

Eli wouldn't lift his head and Becca worried her lower lip between her teeth, what little appetite she'd had disappearing and rapidly making her regret what she'd eaten so far.

The conversation changed over to wedding details and plans, but Becca noted her father's gaze remained on Eli, worry etched on his craggy features. Her father was a brusque man. His occupation as an attorney and judge had earned him a formidable reputation. Her father wasn't afraid to tackle any challenge and often did, like a bull charging the red cape at full speed.

But how was she going to explain Eli's diagnosis to a man who wouldn't understand what it's like to be afraid? Too afraid to speak?

Once dessert was completed, they left the table and headed outside to the back patio while David and her father walked with Eli to the playhouse in the thick limbs of the Japanese Elm. The leaves had fallen weeks ago and the air had a distinct chill and dampness to it. She'd changed Eli out of his church clothes and into play clothes, adding a sweatshirt for warmth.

Despite having the wedding binder open on her lap, Becca had a hard time concentrating on the conversation about the reception food choices because she was so fixated on her father and David attempting to interact with Eli.

"Hey. What is up with you?" Kaity asked.

Becca jerked to awareness and realized her mother had disappeared from the table.

"She went to get her glasses. Why she doesn't just wear them is beyond me. It would drive me crazy having to go get them all the time. Now," Kaity's voice lowered, "what is going on with Eli?"

"What do you mean?" Becca asked, buying time as her mind scrambled to form the words needed to explain his diagnosis.

"Seriously, Bex? Okay, fine. I'll play along. Does Eli *ever* speak?"

The moment of truth had come and even though she knew it would happen eventually, she still wasn't prepared. "Not very often," she revealed softly. Continuing required a deep breath and hard swallow. "He's been diagnosed as having Selective Mutism. He can talk. He just doesn't."

"Oh, Bex. Why haven't you said anything? Has this always been going on or is this new? Please don't tell me this is because of your divorce."

"You're getting a *divorce*?"

Kaity's eyes widened and she shook her head in apology for not having noticed their mother's return.

"I have *got* to stop talking," Kaity murmured. "I'm so sorry, Bex."

Becca squeezed her sister's hand and shrugged. "Had to happen sometime. It's fine."

"Rebecca, explain. And, Kaity, you will answer for why you've been keeping something like this from me."

"Mama, please, don't make it worse," Kaity said as she scooted her chair away from the patio table. "Besides, it wasn't my news to tell."

The metal legs scraping against the concrete grated on Becca's veins. She couldn't face her mother so instead she focused on Eli. David had plucked Eli up and helped her son settle onto a board swing attached to a branch beneath the playhouse. For the first time in a long time, Eli smiled when David put the swing in motion.

"Rebecca?"

Her mother's tone demanded answers but Becca also heard concern in the depths. But was it concern for her? Or concern that Becca's marital failure might tarnish the Judge and Mrs. Waites' image? "I'd rather not have to repeat this conversation," she murmured. "Can it wait until I can talk to you and Daddy together, please?"

"How about I go take over for Dad? David and I can keep Eli occupied for a while," Kaity said, leaving the table before Becca could even respond.

"Rebecca, are you getting a divorce?" her mother queried.

Becca stared down at her clasped fingers and said a quick prayer for God to give her the words to explain things to her parents. They loved her. They were wonderful parents who would truly do anything for their children. But sometimes they just didn't get it. "Wait for Dad."

Wynonna walked to the edge of the patio and waited for George to rejoin them. Becca looked up just as her dad spotted the expression on her mother's face and realized something was very wrong.

"What's going on?" George asked. "Kaity said you needed me."

"Daddy—sit down. Please," Becca added, remembering her manners and the fact one didn't go about ordering one's father around.

George seated himself in the chair Kaity had vacated before lacing his fingers together over his nearly flat stomach. The judge spent an hour every single morning in the gym and it showed.

"What's going on, Rebecca? Is something wrong?"

"She's getting a divorce," her mother said, the words sounding teary and strained.

Her father's thick eyebrows lowered as he narrowed his gaze on her and Becca resisted the urge to squirm.

"Is this true?" George asked.

"No," Becca said, knowing her father preferred facts. "It's not."

"Rebecca, I distinctly heard your sister say--"

"I'm not *getting* a divorce," she interjected, rudely interrupting her mother and earning another glare for it, "because... I've already gotten one. It's been final for six months."

Silence descended. Even poor Elda who had been about to clear the dishes stood frozen just inside the patio door, her hands clasped in front of her.

"Six months," her father repeated.

"Rebecca." Wynonna stared at her in horror. "Why didn't you tell us?"

"Because I couldn't. The time never seemed right and-- and I wasn't sure what to say."

"What happened?" George demanded. "Did you try counseling?"

Becca managed a smile at Elda and motioned for the older woman to join them at the table. Elda had been around before Becca or Kaity had been born and was more family than employee. She needed to hear this too. "Apparently Elliot was seeing another woman while dating me. Someone his family didn't approve of and who didn't--couldn't--help his career or image in any way. So, he married me, but never broke things off with her."

"Oh, my poor dear," Elda said, tears streaming down her lined cheeks.

"It gets better," she murmured, her tone more than a little bitter despite her efforts to remain unmoved. "When I got pregnant with Eli, she was also pregnant. She had a boy as well."

Her father abruptly stood, the chair scooting backward so quickly it nearly tipped over.

"Long story short, when it became clear that Eli has a problem, Elliot decided he wanted out. He wanted to raise his 'normal' son and be with the woman he really loved instead of me and Eli."

"What's wrong with my grandson?"

The hoarseness in her father's voice relayed his worry and upset, and that was the only reason Becca was able to keep her emotions in check. "Nothing is physically wrong with him." She held up her hand, ending her father's attempt to interrupt before it gathered steam. "Nothing is wrong, but he does have Selective Mutism."

Becca swallowed hard, aware of Kaity's concerned glances from across the yard because they bored a hole into her back. Her parents and Elda looked shellshocked and as devastated as she'd felt when she'd first heard the diagnosis. "Eli doesn't talk to anyone but me--and that's only sometimes."

"What about his father?" Wynonna asked. "Surely he talked to Elliot?"

"No. Elliot never had much to do with Eli. Eli was usually asleep when his father left for work and in bed when Elliot got home. He golfed on weekends or spent time with his other family. Apparently seeing the difference between Eli and his other son cemented the fact that Eli had a problem and Elliot couldn't handle it."

Her father moved to stand at the stone pillars lining the edge of the patio, leaning against the wrought iron railing overlooking the lawn. Elda wiped her eyes with the edge of her old-fashioned apron, and Wynonna leaned sideways in her chair to comfort the older woman.

Becca split her attention between the three of them, noting her father's bent head and sagging shoulders, how her mother focused on comforting Elda. "I'm sorry," she whispered. "I didn't tell you any of this because I had hoped things would get better. Maybe not with the marriage, but with Eli."

"But why doesn't he talk?" Wynonna asked.

Becca held her mother's gaze. "I've been asking myself that for the last four years, Mama. But I still don't know the answer." At least not any she was willing to share.

Chapter 7

The following morning, Zack patted his leg for Moses to come to him and rubbed the dog's head before sending Moses to his large comfy bed in the corner of the studio. Generally, the dog was better behaved than many of the kids brought to his studio for photos, but Moses' size had a tendency to make non-dog owning mama's nervous until they got to know Moses' personality.

The security system chimed that the front door had been opened and Zack braced himself for another run in with Becca, the first face-to-face meeting after their devastating conversation.

"Zack?" Kaity called.

"Back here."

Zack listened closely, discerning multiple sets of footsteps making their way toward the rear of the old house turned business.

"Nice place you have here," David said as he entered the room.

Zack thanked the man and turned, his gut clenching at the sight of Becca and her son hovering near the back of the house. "It's served me well."

Becca stayed quiet, her gaze on the many prints hanging on the walls throughout the waiting area, hall and back section of the room.

"You guys ready to start?" Zack asked.

"Actually, I wanted to show you something," Kaity said, motioning for him to step closer to her. "I know this is our engagement session, but I wanted to see if you would take a few of these shots as well--with my Maid of Honor."

Zack stared at Kaity's too-innocent expression. Leave it to her to come up with something to force Becca's presence on him. "I'm sure something can be worked out. What do you have in mind?"

While he looked at images saved on Kaity's phone, Zack tracked Becca's movements in his peripheral vision. She moved from image to image, staring at them like one would a work of art in a gallery.

Pride filled him along with the sense of accomplishment. Coming from nothing and building his business hadn't been easy but he was fully aware of the change in his life once he'd gotten himself on track. His behavior, training, church. Doors once closed to him were suddenly open and people treated him with growing respect for the direction his life had taken.

But how could he forgive her for leaving town knowing she carried his baby? He'd had a right to know. A right to be there when she--

"Zack? Are you sure you're okay?" Kaity asked, a worried pinch to her pretty features. "If you need to reschedule, we can."

He shook his head and forced his mind to focus. "No, I'm fine. Sorry. Just distracted. Let's get started."

Zack led the couple to a settee he had positioned in front of a backdrop. "Let's start with the formal ones. It will help you loosen up and get comfortable."

In short order he was snapping photos, aware of Becca behind him, watching, but able to concentrate on his task as he adjusted angles, lighting and the couple themselves.

After a few sitting and standing shots, Zack told David to recline on the couch and then had Kaity perch on the edge by David's side, arms resting on his chest leaning against him as David kissed her forehead. He tried a few other poses that Kaity had requested then moved on to ideas he'd had incorporating the theme she'd picked for her wedding.

"I think that should do it for you, David. You're free," Zack said to the younger man, noting the guy's visible relief. Zack smiled and clapped a hand on David's back as he stopped long enough to thank Zack and kiss his fiancé goodbye before heading out the door.

"Now it's our turn," Kaity said, clapping softly. "Bex, come on. Zack is awesome."

Zack turned and found Becca staring at her son. The boy had crawled onto Moses' large dog bed and sat leaning against Moses' chest while flipping through the pages of a kids' book.

Without a word, Zack lifted the camera and took several shots of the sweet moment.

"Bex?" Kaity whispered softly. "Is Eli reading?"

Zack tilted his head and sure enough he heard the boy whispering to the dog. But wasn't he a little young to actually be reading?

"It's his favorite book," Becca told them, her eyes sparkling with unshed tears. "I've read it to him hundreds of times."

"But he's speaking, right? I'm not just hearing things?" Kaity asked.

Speaking became too much for Becca because she pressed her fingertips to her mouth and simply nodded.

Kaity moved to stand beside her sister and wrapped her arms around Becca, leaning her head against her sister's. Realizing that the lighting was perfect, Zack quickly raised his camera and snapped several shots, including the one where the sisters shifted their gazes to him.

"Don't move," he ordered, slowly walking around them and taking shots from several different angles. He photographed them up close, capturing their beautiful faces. He zoomed in on their hands and how their fingers were laced and holding tight to the other.

Zack stilled, only then noticing the lack of rings on Becca's left hand. He lowered the camera, his gaze shifting to Becca's. His expression must have revealed the many questions racing through his mind because she shook her head slightly, a silent plea to leave things be for the time being. "Okay, come on, ladies," he murmured, the awareness of her ringless state giving him a burst of energy because it made him--what? Happy? Pleased that she'd removed the ring of a man unworthy of her or their son?

"What now?" Kaity asked, giving Becca one last squeeze before releasing her.

"How about we have some fun?" He moved to the opposite side of the room and flipped on the radio to his favorite station.

Growing up in the home of an abusive alcoholic, Zack had seen and heard things no kid should ever witness. He hoped, if nothing else, playing the uplifting music would raise some spirits while in his studio. After all, no one ever knew what went on behind closed doors and the music coming out of his sound system might be the only good thing his clients heard that day.

He paused, his mind shifting to Eli. Had the boy experienced bad things in his home? Had his sad excuse for a father said horrible things to Eli and his mother? Was that why the kid didn't speak?

Zack positioned the sisters back to back looking toward him. He loved the play of big sister to little sister in that Becca stood two inches taller than Kaity, Becca's hair dark to Kaity's light. From there he moved them from pose to pose, setting aside his thoughts of Becca's ex to concentrate on the present.

One of his favorite songs came on and in unison the sisters stated their love for it as well. Kaity laced her fingers with Becca's and began dancing, earning smiles and laughter from her too serious elder sibling.

Zack captured the moments as they came, loving the spontaneity of the photographs over the standard poses. Eventually Moses' left his bed to join the fun and Eli followed the dog, staring up at his mother and aunt with more than a bit of bemusement as they wrapped a prop scarf around Moses' neck and danced around him.

The silliness prompted smiles from Eli and eventually a shy-sounding chuckle.

Hearing Eli, Becca and Kaity increased their antics in an obvious attempt to get the boy to laugh full-out, tugging the child onto the backdrop and giving him an old hat to wear. After a while, Zack sat back on his haunches, camera lowered, and simply watched the silliness, the sight too special not to experience it in the moment rather than secondhand from behind a lens.

A tone sounded from the direction of the ladies' purses and Kaity whirled around, rushing toward her bag.

"Oh, that's my alarm! I have to go so I'm not late for work. I'll see you in the morning, monkey," she said to Eli. "And, Zack, thank you so much for making this fun."

"Kaity, you drove us," Becca said. "Did you forget?"

"Oh, sorry! Zack, you'll see them back to the condo, right?"

Whirlwind Kaity didn't wait for his response. She grabbed her bag and raced out the door with a flighty wave. Becca stared after her sister like a deer in headlights.

He wasn't much better. Kaity had obviously hoped the time alone with Becca would help settle some things, but he wasn't sure that was possible. If it would ever be possible.

He'd been able to lose himself in his work while taking the pictures, but now all the tension and anger boiled to the surface like lava.

"I'll call a cab," she murmured. "Eli, grab your toys, please. We have to go."

"I'll drive you," he said, sounding less than gracious even to his own ears. One of the last things the minister had told Zack was to put himself in her shoes and imagine how she'd felt at the time. Imagine what had driven her to make the decisions she'd made.

"I don't want to take you away from your work. Eli?"

"Becca, let him play. Give me a few minutes to shut everything down and we'll go." He didn't give her a chance to respond but stalked away to his office for a much needed break from the thoughts tumbling through his head and the awareness of his ongoing attraction to Becca despite their past issues.

He packed up his computer so he could get caught up on some editing and turned when he heard a noise in the doorway of his office. Eli stood staring at Zack with his big eyes, his small hand holding onto Moses' fur like a lifeline. "You like him, don't you?"

Eli nodded.

"Well, I can tell Moses likes you, too," he said, grabbing a couple of items from the desk drawer before approaching the boy and the dog. Zack knelt before them and ran his free hand over Moses' head. "You wanna know how I can tell?"

Another nod from the child lifted the weight of Zack's anger from his shoulders and eased the fist in his stomach. "I can tell because Moses brought you in here to get his treat. See, if he behaves himself all day while I'm working, he gets a special treat before we leave. And since you've been so good while I took all those pictures, he thinks you deserve something special, too. Would you like that?"

Zack waited, hoping to get more than a nod from the boy.

Eli nodded shyly and lifted his hand to take the small digital camera Zack revealed but Zack pulled back and held it just out of reach. "What was that? Did you say something? I couldn't hear you."

"Thank you," Eli said again, this time using his voice instead of simply mouthing the words.

Such a simple thing and yet the sound of Eli speaking--knowing how precious an act it actually was--ripped through Zack.

So much had happened between him and Becca but in this moment, none of it seemed as important as this.

BECCA WAS silent on the trip back to Kaity's condo, her thoughts jumbled and chaotic. Eli sat in the backseat of Zack's large SUV with Moses, both looking happy as larks as Eli carefully played with the small, older camera, Moses at his side devouring his treat.

Earlier in Zack's studio she'd taken a phone call about a potential job in Charleston, but during those brief minutes on the phone Eli and Moses had disappeared. When she'd found them...

Eli had talked to Zack. He'd talked!

So why did she feel so angry? Hurt? Almost... betrayed?

It made no sense. Eli had spoken to someone other than herself and she was beyond thrilled at the fact. But why did it have to be Zack? Why not Kaity or her parents?

"I don't understand," she murmured.

"What was that?" Zack steered the large vehicle onto the condo's lot but instead of pulling up at the front entrance and letting them out, he drove to a spot and parked.

"You don't have to see us in," she told him, hurrying to open the door and exit. She opened the rear passenger door as well and unbuckled Eli from his booster seat, which Kaity had oh-so-thoughtfully left behind in Zack's SUV before taking off for work, unfastening the seat from the buckles and straps and hauling it out only to have Zack take it from her to carry. "I can..."

Only then did she notice Zack had also shouldered the oversized backpack containing his laptop as well as a camera--and held Eli's hand while Eli grasped Moses' leash.

Kaity's comment about getting to know Zack the last two years blasted through her head with dawning awareness. "You live here."

A hint of a smile tugged at the corners of his firm mouth and he nodded.

"For the last five years or so."

In unison they moved toward the complex and the crazy thought of what they looked like struck Becca. How many families looked just like them?

But they weren't a family and never would be.

Once they crossed the parking lot onto the concrete walkway, Moses tugged at his leash to go to the bushes. She wasn't sure if Eli followed or was tugged along for the walk by the big dog but he went as well.

"He's really taken to Moses," she said softly. "I think I'll have to check into getting him a pet when we return home."

Zack remained quiet for several long seconds.

"Dogs are great. I never had a dog until I worked for Emma. Now I can't imagine life without one."

Zack turned and stared down at her, leaving Becca struggling with the urge to squirm. Zack was so handsome, always had been. Why couldn't they have met now? They could have had a fresh start without the baggage and emotional heartbreak dividing them.

"You're angry," she whispered. "And you have every right to be. But please know I thought I was doing what was best for all of us."

"That wasn't your call to make."

Zack was careful to keep his voice just as soft and low as hers and she was thankful for the consideration. Little ears had good hearing and this wasn't something Eli would understand at his age. "I know. In hindsight, I see that now."

"If you just would have told me..."

"I wanted to. Zack, you have no idea how much I wanted you to show up at my door. How much I needed you with me, especially when things... went wrong. I was so scared," she whispered. "But I can't go back in time. I don't even know if I would change things." In her heart of hearts, she knew that different decisions would still have had the same outcome. She'd inadvertently spared Zack the pain ten years ago, but he felt it now. "We weren't ready for that kind of responsibility. If we had been... maybe I wouldn't have had the miscarriage. Maybe something would've happened to alter our lives but--"

"But we'll never know because you didn't give us the chance. Moses," he called, patting his leg. "Let's go."

The ride up the elevator was even more uncomfortable than the drive home had been and once the elevator doors opened, she stepped off and turned to retrieve the car seat only to nearly run into Zack. "I'll take that."

"I'll leave it at the door," he said.

His long legs quickly ate up the distance down the hall and she dragged her feet as she followed, Eli and Moses' jogging behind Zack to try and keep up.

Zack left the car seat outside of Kaity's door and said goodbye to Eli by ruffling Eli's hair, earning a smile from Eli and a look of adoration.

"Take care of that camera now. It's old but it takes really good pictures."

Eli nodded solemnly.

"Let me know when you've filled up the card and we'll sort through them and print a few of them for you to keep."

Becca leaned against Kaity's door, trembling internally because of the kindness and generosity Zack showed her son. She wasn't surprised by it. Tough guy Zack had always had a soft side. That's one of the things that had drawn her to him in the first place.

And yet she'd been so sure they would crash and burn as a couple. Sure that it was only a matter of time until Zack got fed up with her attitude and insistence on secrecy because of her parents' snobbishness toward him, and walked out.

Was she wrong? Could they have made it even scraping by dollar by dollar and trying to raise a baby when they were kids themselves?

She faced the door and dug the key Kaity had given her from the zippered pocket of her tote bag, unlocking the door and setting the heavy tote and her purse inside while Zack said goodbye to Eli.

When she went to retrieve the car seat she expected to find Zack and Moses at the elevator but instead they had walked further down the hallway and Zack was in the process of unlocking a door. Not only did Zack live in the complex, but right next door to Kaity?

And right next door to you until this wedding is over. If you want something to change, you have to try.

"Zack, do you have plans for dinner?" She wasn't sure who was more surprised by her question, Zack or herself. But once the words emerged from her mouth it wasn't like she could retract the offer. "You and Moses are welcome to join us," she said, desperate enough to forge a bond of forgiveness that she used Eli's hopeful expression as leverage. "I've become a decent cook."

Eli reached out, snagged Moses' leash from Zack's hand and hurried toward Kaity's apartment.

Zack stood silent for a long moment as the two disappeared inside and then sighed.

"Guess that means we accept."

Chapter 8

If someone had told Zack he'd hang out with Becca and actually manage to enjoy himself after all she'd said and done, he would've called them crazy.

Right now he felt like the crazy one, though, because that was exactly what had happened last night--and somehow carried over into the following day.

Last night's dinner had been Eli's favorite of spaghetti with Italian bread followed by pudding for dessert. Zack and Moses had even wound up staying *after* dinner long enough to play with Eli while Becca tidied up.

But today the agenda included cake tasting--and ballroom dancing later in the evening--with George and Wynonna along for kicks and giggles. Not that Zack figured he'd be laughing much.

"Oh. My. Word. Bex, you've got to try this one," Kaity said around a mouthful of cake.

Zack noticed that the bride looked tired but after working all night and only catching a couple of hours of sleep before hitting the bakery, who wouldn't be?

"No thanks. This is all you. Even David said so."

"He just wants to stay skinny for his tuxedo fitting. My dress won't fit if I keep this up. Zack?"

Not about to turn down cake, he lowered his camera and stepped forward to accept the sample slice the baker offered him. He seated himself beside of Kaity, opposite of Becca, and noticed her gaze drop to the plate in his hands. "Sure you don't want this?"

She shook her head and he frowned. Life was too short not to eat cake. And she was certainly skinny enough to afford the calories.

"Oh, this is it," Kaity said. "This is the one. And the coconut icebox cake. I want those two flavors and red velvet for David's groom's cake."

"I'll go get the design books then," the baker said to Kaity.

"I'll help you. Eli and I both need to wash our hands after all the icing we managed to smear on ourselves, right, Eli? Be right back, Bex."

Becca looked uncomfortable being abandoned by her sister yet again and studiously made a notation in her wedding binder, the act taking too much focus.

He wiped his mouth with the napkin and shifted from his seat to what had been Kaity's. "Try it. You won't regret it."

"I'm sure I wouldn't but no."

Zack shrugged and sat back in the padded chair, scarfing down another bite of the delicious cake. "Suit yourself. I'm curious, though."

"I'd think you would have more important things to wonder about than my not wanting cake."

There it was again. That bite of sass and coolness he'd been subjected to all morning along with silent glares. "I find it strange that you're the one upset with me when I've been so...forgiving."

Sitting so close to her, he heard Becca suck in a sharp breath.

"You've forgiven me?"

"I'd like to say yes but I'm not quite there yet," he said, sliding a glance over his shoulder to make sure no one was around to hear their discussion. "I'm still angry as all get out that you kept me in the dark and denied me the chance to know my child. But, despite that, I thought we'd made some progress last night toward being able to get along without having to pretend so much. What changed?"

"Everything..."

Becca stared down at her hands and when the waiting stretched from seconds to nearly a minute, he reached out and took one of her hands in his. "Becca, talk to me."

She shook her head, blinking rapidly, until she finally took a deep breath, straightened her shoulders and lifted her head.

"It's silly and stupid and petty. And I'm a horrible person for feeling this way."

"Feeling what way?"

"Zack... He *talked* to you."

Still confused, he stayed silent, willing her to continue.

"Eli is so loved by my family and friends and yet he won't speak to them. Only me--and now *you*?"

Zack removed his hand from hers. "First I'm not good enough to be father to my own child and now you're angry because I'm not good enough for your kid to *talk* to?"

"What? No."

"That's exactly what it sounds like," he said, standing and getting as far away from her as physically possible in the small room.

"Zack..."

He held up his hand and thankfully she got quiet, giving him the time he needed to process and work through the anger nearly over-whelming him.

Eyes closed, he braced a hand on the window frame. He was a grown man, no longer the kid from nowhere who had nothing to offer her. Her comment shouldn't hurt as much as it did.

"Zack."

She touched his back, lightly at first and then firmly, using both hands to brace herself and lean against him. When he felt her head against his shoulder blade he tried to remember what it was like not to love her. Want her.

The realization that he couldn't was a slap in the face he didn't need on top of everything else.

"I'm sorry for how it sounded when I said that. For how my

words hurt you. You are a *good* man. You always have been and I know that. Wait," she said, fingers clenching into the layered flannel over thermal shirt he wore. "The lack of... faith I had in myself... That had nothing to do with whether or not you were a good man or whether I believed you would be a good father. I know you would've been."

"Except for the fact I was dirt poor," he murmured. "I guess I didn't realize it bothered you so much."

"We were so *young*. And I am deeply sorry for the way I handled things."

"Are you?"

Silence followed the question.

"I'm sorry for my part in you not knowing your baby, for taking that away from you. But I'm not sorry for going away with the end goal being to give our baby a better future with parents who desperately desired a child and couldn't have one instead of two unprepared kids who weren't ready for that responsibility. It was more than not having money, Zack. It really was. I couldn't stand the thought that we would have ended up resenting each other, maybe *hating* each other, and what kind of life would that have been for a baby? Tell me you understand that. Will you at least *try* to understand that?"

He inhaled a steadying breath and turned to face her. Her beautiful gaze held his and for a moment Zack saw into her soul. All of the pain, the fear and hurt and sadness. She held nothing back and in that moment, forgiveness filled him, rushing through his body like waves crashing over the shore.

He lifted his hand to her face and tilted her head higher, lowering his head but stopping just short of kissing her even though his body wanted to do nothing else.

When she didn't pull away or tell him no, he closed the distance and brushed his lips over hers. Memories crowded his brain as he deepened the kiss and the only thing he could truly focus on was how right it felt. How right it had always felt.

But what about her upset over Eli talking to him? The nagging thought intruded on the tender moment and he ended the kiss, pulling away from her. "Why don't you want Eli talking to me?"

Her eyes had a dreamy quality to them and he liked the fact that he'd caused it more than he probably should have.

"Oh, Zack. It's not that I don't want him talking to you. I'm thrilled that he's talking to someone other than me. It's just... Last night after you left Kaity's apartment, when I put Eli to bed... We always read a story at bedtime. It's our thing. But last night-- All he wanted was for you to come back. That's when I realized I have to be very, *very* careful. The last thing I want is for him to get attached to you when we'll be leaving right after the wedding. He's had enough to deal with in his young life, and with his issues, I don't want to add to it."

It made sense. Protecting her son was what any loving mother would do. Not that he'd ever had any experience in that area. His biological mother had given him up and his adoptive mother had left him and her blood daughter behind with an abusive alcoholic to raise them. *You've got a good mama, kid.*

And truth be told, he didn't want to do anything to hurt Eli or his mother despite everything that had happened. After all, Becca had gone through the adult version of everything Eli had experienced as well and wore the results on her too thin frame and in her battle-weary expression. "Okay."

"Okay?"

He lifted his hand, using a single finger to smooth the pinch from her eyebrows. "I get it. You don't want Eli getting attached and getting hurt because you plan to leave after the wedding. But what if you didn't leave?"

"What? Why wouldn't we go back?"

"Because Eli's father gave up his parental rights and you have family and friends here who are more than willing to fill the void in his life."

"I have a business in Charleston."

"You can relocate. Becca.... stay," he said, holding her gaze and praying she saw everything she needed to see. "Give me a chance to show you how much things have changed."

OH! Daddy, I'm so sorry I keep stepping on your toes." Becca smiled in apology at her father and tried to calm the flutters in her pulse due to Zack's steady observation of her. Shouldn't he be photographing the bride?

Her father kept up the gliding pace of the dance, twirling her around despite her clumsiness.

"I should've worn my steel-toed boots."

A laugh caught Becca by surprise as she met her father's amused gaze. "Like you've ever owned a pair of steel-toed boots."

A flicker of something--regret?--passed over his features but when she opened her mouth to ask him about it, he noisily cleared his throat. "How are the wedding plans coming? Have you emptied the account I set up for you yet?"

Still struggling to remember the proper steps, she stared down at her feet and shook her head. "No, but if there's anything leftover, I'll let you know."

Her father chuckled and squeezed her hand tight. "That's my girl."

One-two-three, one-two-three. Why was Zack still watching her?

"Rebecca..."

She lifted her head to gaze at her father and managed not to stumble. Graceful, she wasn't. "Yes, Daddy?" *Stop staring. Just stop already so I can focus.*

"You've had a good life, haven't you?"

Becca stumbled and her father tightened his arms to keep her from falling. "Yes, of course. Why would you ask that?"

He exhaled and the deep sigh blew the curl by her cheek, causing it to tickle.

"I've just wondered if maybe... Well, we're both old enough to know money doesn't bring happiness."

"That it doesn't." She and Elliot had made a good living but happy wasn't a word to describe their marriage. At first things went well but then...

"Do you know I used to *own* a pair of steel-toed boots?"

She gaped at him for a moment before looking down at their feet, taking in his Brooks Brothers suit, power tie and designer shoes. "You did? Was it part of a costume?"

This time a low chuckle rumbled out of his chest, the sound more than a little wry.

"No, it wasn't part of a costume. Believe it or not, I used to work construction."

This time she really did gape at him. "Seriously?"

Her father nodded, his eyes narrowing in his amusement at her question.

"It's true. I didn't receive the inheritance from your grandfather until I was 25 and despite him having plenty of money to send us kids to school, he decided it was best if we earned our education. Well, I didn't think he was serious, so I made decent grades but nothing scholarship-worthy."

"I see. Daddy, why are you telling me this?"

"Because after all of these years, the man without money is the same man now with money."

She frowned, not following her father's words. "Daddy, I'm sure you have a point to all of this but..."

"I've noticed you keep looking at the photographer. Any special reason as to why?"

Becca stiffened and in the process stumbled again. "N-no. I'm just... watching to see what pictures he takes of Kaity."

Her father leaned low and brushed his lips across her forehead.

"Don't ever play cards, sweetheart."

"Daddy..."

"You still have feelings for him," her father stated, his tone grim.

She had to mull over her answer, even though it was a statement and not a question. "I... loved him. I know you and Mama always thought it wasn't real and just a teenage summer crush but it was more. And that was *before* we shared something so precious as..." Her voice broke and she had to stop and clear her throat. But her father's hands tightened over her and at her waist and she knew he understood. "But you were right. We were too young and the timing was all wrong."

"God's timing is never wrong, Becca-boo."

"No, but-- He also took our baby home so it wasn't meant to be. Zack was so angry when I told him the truth. But now he says... He says he's forgiven me."

They danced several steps in silence.

"You don't believe him?"

"No, I-I do. But I've made a life in Charleston," she continued softly. "Even if I worked out all of the details with my business and my life there with Eli... there's still you and Mama, and I know for a fact you can barely stand being in the same room with him right now."

"I wouldn't say it's quite that bad."

"But it's pretty close."

"I'll let you in on a little secret," her father said, lowering his head so that he could speak into her ear. "Father's aren't supposed to like the men in his daughters' lives, at least not right off."

"Well, I might not be eighteen anymore but I couldn't go against your wishes back then and I still can't."

"Is that why you kept your divorce a secret?"

She lowered her lashes in an attempt to hide her thoughts. "I knew you'd be disappointed."

"I'm disappointed that after all we've been through you didn't feel you could come to me when things began going downhill."

"I'm sorry. I wanted to. But--"

"But your mother and I haven't made it easy for that to happen, have we?"

Becca inhaled and shrugged. "You expect a lot of yourself so... I'd say it's normal to expect a lot of us."

"Life isn't about expectations, Becca. It's about love."

"I know. But that's why I couldn't tell you I had screwed up again. Family means everything. You taught me that."

"Okay, everyone. Time to pair up with your partner for the night," the instructor called. "Bride and groom, parents, bridal party. Oh, I love how you are already couples," the woman said.

Until she turned to her left and saw Becca standing there alone.

"Are we missing a groomsman?"

"Yeah, sorry," David said with a grimace in Becca's direction. "He had a work emergency and had to leave."

"Well," the instructor said, her attention shifting to Zack. "It looks like you will have to be our fill-in once again, Mr. Dupre."

"Oh, um..." Becca shook her head, but Zack immediately set his camera down and walked toward her. Becca saw Kaity's smile turn positively blinding, but more than anything else, she felt her parents' scrutiny. Especially her father's.

"Don't worry," the instructor said. "Mr. Dupre is now a pro at this. How many times have you had to step in for the bridal parties you've photographed?"

"Too many to count," Zack said, moving to a stop before her.

The intensity of his gaze left Becca struggling to breathe properly, but before she could make an excuse to untangle herself from the awkwardness of the dance with her parents watching, the instructor walked over to the sound system and told them to take their positions.

Zack took her hand in his and place his other hand at her waist. Becca stared up at him, transported back in time to a hot summer night when they had danced under the stars.

"Relax. I'm halfway decent at this," Zack murmured.

The music started and right on cue Zack began to lead her in the steps. He wasn't "decent." He had a natural masculine rhythm and grace that left her gliding across the floor despite her two left feet.

"Look at me," Zack ordered. "Don't count the steps. Just move to the music."

She followed his instructions, the act easier since Zack was such a good leading partner.

"Have you given any thought to my question?"

"It's all I've thought about." Zack kept them moving, guiding her through the steps and around the wooden floor of the studio.

The song came to an end and Zack brought them to a stop, only then did she realize they were the center of attention and that the other dancers had stepped aside to watch them. She'd been so lost in the moment she hadn't realized they had become a spectacle. "Oh... Oh, um."

Kaity's eyebrows rested high on her forehead and she began clapping, grinning all the while, and the others joined in, a few of the groomsmen whistling and saying that Zack had put them to shame.

A flush crept into her face, her cheeks blazing hot. One glance at her frowning parents sent a cold blast through her and she felt like a teenager all over again.

Chapter 9

Zack stared at the numerous images on the screen in front of him, all of them having one thing—person—in common.

Over the course of the last couple of weeks, he'd spent a lot of time taking photographs for the upcoming magazine spread as well as for Kaity's wedding album. But it was the photos that wouldn't make it into either of those things that kept him fascinated more than they should.

You're getting awfully close to stalking.

He released the mouse and sat back in his home office chair with a disgruntled sigh. He'd actually been accused of stalking once as a teenager trying to teach himself the techniques he'd read about in books and magazines. Then, his subject had been his blind, court-ordered boss. At the time, however, she'd simply been the person he had access to in all shades of light, and he'd been desperate to learn.

But what was his excuse now?

He stared at the many images of Becca on the screen in front of him, studying the play of light and shadow, the angles, the openness and honesty on her face when he managed to catch her unaware.

The pain and heartbreak she hid from so many but the camera revealed.

His phone buzzed with a text message he ignored. As great as technology was, he hated the feeling of always being available. Sometimes people needed to check out of reality for a while. Take time to sit back and recharge and not be at the world's instant call.

The phone buzzed again. And then again.

Eyes shut, he ignored the irritating device. *I still love her. Doesn't that mean anything?*

The constant buzzing of a phone call ended his prayer and he picked up the phone with a jerk of his arm. "Dupre."

"Zack? It's Becca."

He sat forward in the chair with a snap, the irony of the situation not lost on him. "Hey. What's up?"

"Is Eli over there?" she asked quickly, noise crackling over the phone as though she was in motion.

"What? No. Why? What's going on?"

"His sleep schedule has been so messed up since we got here so when he fell asleep playing, I just let him nap. I left the room to make some phone calls and when I came back he was gone. I've searched the entire apartment and he's *not here.*"

Her panic sent adrenaline racing through Zack in response. "I'll be right there."

He sent the rolling chair flying backward when he stood and left his spare bedroom office. He hurried through his apartment, not even taking the time to don the shoes he'd left by the door.

Becca waited for him in the hallway.

"Where can he be?"

"He's got to be around here somewhere. He probably just fell back to sleep."

"But where? The apartment is empty."

"Did you check the closets? Kitchen cabinets?" He'd spent plenty of time hanging out in closets and cabinets as a kid. Playing, hiding from his drunk step-father. Getting locked inside when the old man simply didn't want to deal with raising a couple kids on his own.

Becca followed him back into her sister's apartment and they began to search for the child, but with every empty space they found, Zack's panic grew. The kid didn't talk. Would he scream if he'd wandered out of the apartment and got snatched up by some perv?

They looked under the beds and in the linen closets, anywhere and everywhere a small child could be.

"Eliiii?"

He turned to find Becca standing in the middle of Kaity's apartment, her arms wrapped around her front and a look of stark terror on her beautiful face. Zack crossed the room and pulled her into his arms, against his chest. He hugged her tightly, kissed the top of her head. "Stay calm. He's here. We just have to keep looking. Panicking isn't going to help."

"I know but--"

He released her long enough to raise his hands to her face, gently tilting her head so that she had to look at him. "He's fine. I'll help you find him."

A low whine sounded and Zack recognized it as belonging to Moses. But where was he? The dog usually didn't let Zack out of his sight whenever they were home and all the while they'd been looking for Eli, Moses would normally have been right there... "Moses."

"What?"

Zack whistled and called Moses' name and once again the dog let out another low whine. "Come with me."

Becca followed closely behind him as Zack hurried back down the hall to his apartment. "I've been in the spare bedroom working for hours. Moses was with me but then disappeared."

"You think they're together? How did Eli get inside?"

Zack glanced over his shoulder. "I don't lock my door. Compared to where I grew up, this place is Fort Knox."

He smiled at the way Becca's eyes widened and hurried into his apartment to scan the room. "Moses?"

A soft snuffling sound came from the direction of the kitchen. The open concept apartment was spacious but the kitchen was tucked back into a corner with a small seating area that shared a fireplace with the living room. He hurried around the couch and sure enough Moses was curled up on his big bed--around a sleeping Eli.

Zack stopped in his tracks when he spotted the two of them, the overwhelming amount of tension and fear leaving his body in a rush of air. "Look."

Becca gasped softly and he turned to see her hand over her mouth, the tears sparkling in her eyes turning the orbs into liquid aquamarine.

He put his arm around her and hugged her close to his side. "He's fine. Breathe."

She nodded, blinking hard to rid herself of the tears, and wrapped her arm around his waist. They stood there like that a long time, marveling over the dog and how Moses didn't move as though afraid he would wake Eli.

"That dog is amazing," Becca whispered.

Unable to help himself, Zack leaned over her and kissed the top of her head once again. "So are you."

MAYBE IT WASN'T WISE, Becca mused, but when Zack had invited her to stay at his apartment and hang out while Eli napped, she'd accepted, more than a little exhausted by the scare and more than a little comforted by Zack's presence.

Zack had insisted on making dinner while she waited. She'd offered to help cook but Zack had claimed his kitchen to be his own. He now stood behind the granite-topped island dressed in jeans and a t-shirt with a kitchen towel slung over his shoulder for convenience. The image was... appealing, to say the least.

Had Elliot ever made her a meal? Cooked for her after a long, hard day?

Don't compare the two. That isn't right.

It wasn't. And she forced her thoughts away from her ex and her... what? Friend?

"You look awfully serious in there. What's going through that pretty head of yours?"

She scrambled for a response, unwilling to share the fact she pondered their relationship status. "Nothing. Just thinking."

"About?"

Remembering his earlier words, she focused on them. "What made you think to check the closets?" she asked, staring into the flames of the fire from her position on his couch.

Christmas carols played on his big screen television, the music a soothing balm to her raw nerves.

"Looks like someone's waking up."

She fixed her attention on Eli and saw her son roll onto his stomach, his head still propped by Moses' large body. Eli looked sleepy-eyed but calm and more content than when he'd finally crashed earlier.

Zack turned his back to her as he flipped the steaks over on the stove-top grille.

"Experience," he said, keeping his voice low and even. "Spent more than a little time there for one reason or another."

A reference to his past. Another small hint of what had gone on behind closed doors. "You never said much about your life at home. Not when we were together."

"Not much to tell."

She shifted to settle more comfortably on the large leather couch, not fooled for an instant. "Oh, but I think there is. Especially if you're bringing it up now."

He turned his head and shot a look over his shoulder in her direction, their eyes meeting and holding for a long moment until he refocused his attention on his tasks.

"Maybe I have a reason."

"Oh?"

He nodded, winked at her. "Being the tough kid from the wrong side of the tracks didn't work back then. Now it's time for a new plan of attack."

A thrill jolted through her because of his words and the interest visible in his eyes. "A plan of attack? I think you might be spending too much time with the military people in your family."

He grinned, the smile transforming his features. He was a handsome man, no two ways about it.

"The easy answer is that I know what I want for my life, and I know what <u>not</u> to do because of how I grew up. Some people wind up following the same path as those who raise them, and that's their choice, but there are others, like me, who veer the opposite direction out of the sheer determination to be different. Better. No kid of mine will ever be in a closet unless it's to play there by choice."

Her heart broke over the pain of his childhood but she also knew that he wouldn't be the man standing before her if not for that pain. "I admire that." The words appeared out of nowhere but they were no less true. Ten years ago, her father had angrily filled her in about Zack's home life and reputation so she knew about the arrests, the drinking, the domestic violence calls and CPS checkups. But to compare that angry, sullen teenager to the man before her...

"Come and get it," he said, wiping his hands on the towel.

"It smells wonderful." She got to her feet and padded across the room, earning a head lift from Moses who was still in position with Eli.

"Let's eat in there," he said, indicating the table with a nod of his head.

Before long all three of them were settled into seats with Moses sitting pretty by Zack's chair waiting patiently for a handout.

She picked up her fork, only then realizing Zack had stretched both hands across the table for her--and Eli--to grasp.

"I'm feeling thankful. Okay if we say grace?"

Her heart picked up speed at the sweetness of it all, and she had to swallow hard as she nodded. "Yes. Eli? Let's pray first."

She waited until Eli lowered his head and shut his eyes before doing the same, feeling Zack's scrutiny for several seconds.

"Lord, thank you for the blessing of this food and the company I share it with," Zack said. "Thank you for watching over Eli when he left his mother's care, and for Moses keeping track of the boy and out of harm's way. Thank you, Lord, for bringing Becca home to Stone River. Amen."

"Ah-men," Eli whispered.

Becca gasped and looked at Eli only to find her son engrossed in stabbing a piece of his already-cut steak. She turned to Zack and saw him staring at her son until he gave his head a slight shake, indicating, she believed, that she shouldn't make a big deal out of Eli speaking. But it was a big deal. And yet another sign that her son was bonding with Zack.

She and Zack talked about the wedding plans and Christmas as they ate. Zack's half-sister held a gathering at her home atop a mountain. The younger sister he had been raised with was married and living in San Antonio with her military husband so she and Zack would be sharing a phone call instead of hugs.

Since Kaity and David would be leaving for their honeymoon, Becca told Zack she and Eli would remain in Kaity's apartment until the holidays were over.

"And then? You still haven't answered the question I asked about staying in Stone River."

"I'm not...sure," she said, torn between the two worlds in which she lived. She loved spending time with Zack here in his apartment by a cozy fire, but the reality of staying in Stone River... Dealing with her family...

"It's not an easy decision."

"No. It isn't. Thank you for understanding that."

"I do. And I'll abide by whatever you decide--so long as you make the decision based on your feelings and no one else's."

He knew. Zack knew being with him would cause her to have words with her parents, but the decision was hers to make and one she would have to fight to defend should she decide to stay.

But was she ready? Was she prepared for that on top of everything else?

Or would it be best to go back to Charleston and live her life without the man sitting across from her?

Chapter 10

You want me to do what?" Zack asked, staring down at Kaity's bright smile. It was early. Too early. Especially after a sleepless night spent tossing and turning and thinking about a particular woman.

"Come with us to Nashville. It will be fun! We're combining the bachelorette and bachelor parties and taking a road trip to Nashville. Everyone's going so you have to go, too."

He wiped a hand over his face and turned, leaving the door open for Kaity to come in or stay as she chose to do. "I need coffee."

Not surprisingly, Kaity entered his apartment full of pep and cheery smiles. "Didn't you work last night?"

"Yes," she said, grinning, "but I'm too excited to be tired. Come on, don't be a grump. It's *Nashville*. And it's Christmas. Do you have any idea of how beautiful it will be?"

"How did you get reservations for so many people at the last minute?"

"We booked the last few available rooms. The girls are all staying in a suite together and so are the guys. But you get a regular room, Daddy's treat."

I'll bet ol' George loved that. Zack shook his head an yet another attempt to clear the cobwebs from his brain and removed the old-fashioned coffee pot from its resting place, grateful to whomever had invented the timing mechanism. "Does your father know he's paying for this?"

Katy grinned and shrugged.

"I guess that's part of the package when he insisted Mama get her way and they host a wedding. The bride's gotta be happy, right?"

Zack sipped the steaming brew, mentally shaking his head at Kaity's antics.

"So will you?"

"Turn down a free trip to Nashville? No."

"Awesome!" Kaity clapped her hands together and beamed like the happy bride she was. "You won't regret it. The hotel is so beautiful! I can't wait to see the pictures you take inside the atriums."

"Thanks for inviting me to tag along," he said, offering a cup of coffee she quickly declined with a shake of her head. "I'd better get back to my place. I guess Bex had a rough night with Eli."

The comment woke him up faster than the coffee. "What happened?"

"Apparently Eli napped yesterday because he was so worn out and then couldn't sleep last night. He woke up in the dark and had a meltdown because Bex was so tired she'd forgotten to leave a night-light on for him."

"I see."

"So... I heard he napped over here," Kaity murmured, leaning against the door frame, her sudden hurry to get back to her apartment put on hold. "And you fixed dinner?"

"Don't get excited. Nothing happened."

"Nothing?"

"We talked. Ate. That's about it."

Katie's gaze narrowed on his and she searched his face for a long moment.

"Uh uh. I don't buy it. You *talked*, yeah, but something else happened, didn't it? Tell me!"

He took another long draw on the coffee and smiled at her impatience. "Physically, no, nothing happened. But I think it was a good evening. We shared a meal, good conversation, played with Eli. Nothing too heavy or emotional."

"You sly dog."

He drew back, confused. "What?"

"You're sweet talking her."

He grinned and lifted his cup in a salute. "Honey, not vinegar."

Katy laughed and glanced over her shoulder towards her open apartment door.

"Okay, so now you can sweet talk her amongst the Christmas lights and decorations and beauty of Nashville. Bring your A-game and *romance* her."

IT TOOK him a couple of hours to pack a bag, gather his equipment, and to drive Moses up the mountain to Emma and her husband, Ian's, house to stay while he was gone. Thankfully Emma had plenty of room in the barn-turned-kennel, and Emma was all too eager to help out.

Kaity had messaged him and asked him to ride with her fiancé and Becca, but he didn't like the feeling of not having a vehicle available. He did join the caravan for the drive to Nashville, and more than a few times caught Becca looking back from the backseat of David's car.

The drive went quickly and in a matter of hours they were rolling onto the hotel's massive parking lot.

Zack self-parked and shouldered his camera bags, overprotective of the valuable equipment it had taken him so long to acquire.

The group had checked in and their bags were being loaded onto a bell cart when George and Wynona spotted him entering the lobby. They weren't the only ones to see him. Eli saw Zack as well and the little boy left his mama's side and ran over to Zack, grinning from ear to ear as he shyly held up what looked to be an old camera bag.

Zack knelt down and waited patiently for the boy to unzip and open the top, and inside was the digital camera Zack had given the child. "What is this? Ah, buddy, that's just great. You're a professional now. Are you going to take pictures of your Aunt Kaity, too?"

Eli nodded, that little-boy grin tugging at Zack's heartstrings.

"He insisted on having a bag for his camera," Becca said, joining them. "So Kaity let him have an old one of hers."

"It's perfect," Zack said, sharing a smile with Becca because he knew what it meant to her to have Eli expressing his joy over something. "I'll show him some tricks to take pictures while we're here. You can be my assistant if you want to."

Eli quickly looked at his mom for approval.

"So long as you behave for Zack, that's fine. You just can't get in his way, okay? He has to take a lot of important pictures that's going to go into a book about Aunt Kaity's wedding, so you have to be a very good boy."

Eli nodded, his expression even more serious than the norm.

"I'm sure he'll be good. Right, kiddo?" Zack winked at Eli and the kid grinned, the first big smile Zack had ever seen from the boy.

"Well, we had better go get settled," Becca said, lowering her hand to Eli's shoulder. "Ready?"

"Zack," Kaity said, David at her side. "Here's your room key. Everything's taken care of. You're on the fifth floor."

Zack accepted the key and the folded paper map of the hotel's layout. He'd looked online to get a general idea of the scope but until he explored, the map would come in handy. "Thanks."

"No problem. See you later at the restaurant, right?"

"I'll be there," he said. Becca turned away and followed the soon-to-be bride. He watched them go, his gaze lingering on the sweetness of Becca holding Eli's hand as they walked through the crowd of people in the lobby.

When they were no longer in view, Zack glanced around, locking gazes with Becca's father.

Zack lifted his chin in a nod and readjusted the heavy backpacks he carried, deciding now would be a good time to make his escape before he found himself cornered by the father of the bride and Maid of Honor.

It didn't take long for him to unpack and settle in. His room was nicely furnished and decorated and after a shower and change of clothes, he grabbed his gear and headed back downstairs.

He explored one of the atriums within the hotel before searching the map for his destination. Dinner would be interesting since he would be sharing a table with a man who'd sworn revenge if Zack didn't stay away from his family.

Zack found the restaurant easily enough and paused a moment to don the suit jacket he carried with him. He'd guess the upscale restaurant's clientele were more comfortable in boardrooms and charity balls, and even with the jacket on, Zack knew he stood out as the hired help thanks to the camera bags.

"Zack," Kaity said, her smile as warm and welcoming as her tone of voice. "You found it."

Kaity never judged. It was one of the things he loved most about her. "Hey. I thought I would beat everyone. Sorry if I'm late."

"No, no. You're right on time. Everyone is just arriving. But I should warn you..."

"Warn me about what?"

Kaity made a face and tilted her head to the left. Zack looked over her shoulder and saw Wynonna rushing toward a handsome, thirty-something man, a smile on her face.

"Elliot! I'm so glad you decided to join us." Wynonna made a show of hugging her now ex son-in-law. "Christmases are meant for families, and ours should be together."

"I feel the same way. I wouldn't miss it," Becca's ex-husband said.

Silence descended amongst the group as Becca and Eli's presence became known. Zack noted the shock on her face and realized she had no idea that her ex would be in attendance. A small part of him relaxed at the sight, but just as quickly he reminded himself that he was the outsider in this scenario, not the ex-husband who spotted Becca and his son and crossed the room in hurried strides, lowering his head to kiss Becca's cheek.

"Elliot, what are you doing here?" Becca said.

The words were low, hoarsely spoken but Zack heard them and waited for the man's response.

"I'm here because I love you. I've finally come to my senses, Becca. I want you back. I want my family to be whole again." He turned and indicated the people and festively decorated restaurant around them. "What better time than Christmas to work this whole mess out and start over again?"

Chapter 11

This is what going to Oz feels like.

Becca stared at her ex-husband, the swirl of the room and the thickness of her sweater bringing so much heat that sweat broke out on her forehead. "You... *what?*"

"None of that now, Elliot," her mother chided. "There's plenty of time to talk later when you and Becca are alone. In the meantime, let's just celebrate the fact that you're with us. Right, Becca?"

Becca closed her mouth and tried to gather what was left of her scattered wits, aware that Zack watched her every move.

When she didn't--couldn't--answer, her mother widened her too cheery smile and waved a hand toward the table and the wait staff ready to take their orders.

"Shall we?"

Elliot grasped her elbow in a gentle but firm grip and made it clear he was going to escort her. She refused to make a scene, so she went along with his urging toward the table. "You didn't say hello to your son," she murmured along the way.

A glance up into Elliot's features revealed his dislike of the reminder but he managed what seemed to be a genuine smile at Eli once they reached the table. Elliot pulled out her chair and once seated, he plucked Eli up and bounced him gently in his arms.

"Hey, kiddo. Have you missed me?" Elliot asked his son.

Eli blinked at his father, not responding otherwise. She wanted to remind Elliot that his son might have missed him more if he'd actually spent quality time with Eli before abandoning him, but bit her tongue to keep the peace. She didn't want an audience, most especially not their son, if she and Elliot were going to have words. The fact that he showed up out of the blue now? Here? Wanted them back?

Elliot's mouth tightened at his son's lack of response but he lowered Eli gently onto the waiting booster seat beside of her, taking the chair on the opposite side of Eli. Normally Elliot always left her to handle Eli on her own, but this time he placed their son between them and the surprise of it wasn't unpleasant. Could he have really changed? Come to his senses?

And if he had?

"Zack, would you take some pictures of us gathered around the table," her mother asked. "I think that would be lovely."

Becca shot a quelling glance at her mother, realizing suddenly what her mother was up to. The invitation to join them at the hotel had to have come from Wynonna.

"Of course," Zack murmured, opening his bag to get his camera.

Zack stood at the end of the long table and prepared to take the photos when Elliot placed his arm around Eli's chair, his hand atop her shoulder. She stiffened at his touch but short of scooting away there was little she could do but pin a smile to her stiff lips.

Dinner proved to be trying and awkward. Throughout the evening Elliot continued to brush his hand against her shoulder or neck, and no amount of glaring at him made him stop. He turned on the charm, too, and she got a glimpse of the man she'd fallen in love with. The one who'd treated her well and worked hard, the one who'd made their life *good*.

Before destroying it.

The dinner was superb but she had little appetite and pushed her food around on her plate. Every time she looked up she found Zack watching her, his expression dark.

The group left the table to relax in the restaurant's library lounge. The smell of books and leather filled the air, bringing back memories of her playing in her father's home office as a child while he worked on briefs or prepped for court cases.

"I'll watch Eli while you two go for a walk," Wynonna said. "It's so beautiful here at Christmas. You simply must see all the decorations."

Becca opened her mouth to protest but quickly thought better of it. She needed to talk to Elliot. Needed to know why he'd really shown up here and what had prompted his change of attitude.

Elliot took her arm once again and guided her toward the door of the lounge. She felt Zack studying her every step of the way.

Once they exited the restaurant, Elliot wrapped her hand over his arm and led her toward the sparkling lights and sounds of a waterfall. The hotel was breathtaking during the day but at night... The lights twinkled, carols played softly in the background and everywhere she looked Christmas gleamed shiny and bright.

"I'm sorry," Elliot said, drawing her attention back to him. "I need to say that first."

"Sorry for what, exactly?" If he was indeed sorry, she needed to hear the words.

"I'm sorry I got so messed up that I put them first. Before my family, my life."

"You told me *they* were your life."

Elliot winced. "I'm sorry. I shouldn't have said that."

"No, you shouldn't have. So what happened? Why are you here?" She extracted her arm from his and walked to the railing, staring at the beauty around her with unseeing eyes.

"Your mother invited me. I... ran into her and told her that Mason isn't my son after all. That I regretted leaving and I dreaded the thought of spending the holidays alone. She said I should meet up with you here."

Becca closed her eyes briefly, the news not bringing the relief or pleasure it probably should have. "Mason not being your biological son still doesn't mean you didn't cheat on me in the first place. You lived a whole other life while you were married to me. *Years*, Elliot. And then you chose them."

"I regret it. I do. I was scared, okay? Eli... I couldn't handle him not talking. It got to me. That's why I worked so much and..."

"Cheated? You're blaming your son for the fact you couldn't stay faithful? Seriously?"

Elliot ran both hands through his hair before lowering his arms to his sides.

"I messed up, okay? I was out of my head with work and stress and grief. We fought all the time. You know we did."

"I deserve someone who can be faithful and honest with me at all times, no matter the circumstances."

"Do you want me to grovel? I will. Becca, please. Give me a second chance. Let me make it up to you."

"And how do you propose to do that?" She stared into Elliot's face, still handsome and strong, the angles of his cheeks and jawline giving him a very Roman look. Women stared when they saw him, and together, she knew they had made a striking couple. None of which mattered when it came to living day-to-day as husband and wife. Looks faded but character remained. Could she ever trust him again?

"I don't know yet, but I'll figure out a way. Becca, please. Let's start over again. We can date. Whatever you want. Will you give me another chance?"

THE OTHER BRIDESMAIDS were asleep in the two bedrooms, but Becca had curled up on the couch in the sitting area to stare at the wall and try to make sense of it all.

A soft knock sounded on the door, startling her. Who would be knocking at this hour?

She tiptoed to the door, uneasy with the thought of Elliot wanting to talk again so soon, and glanced through the peep hole.

Zack stood on the other side and as she watched, he turned to walk away.

Becca hurried to unlock the door and open it. "Zack?" She fumbled with the tie on her robe, securing it with trembling hands. "Is something wrong?"

He'd turned at the sound of his name, his gaze dark as it slid over her frame and left a tingle in its wake.

"I'm sorry to bother you so late. I...hope I didn't wake you."

"No. I wasn't— What are you doing here?"

Zack shoved his hands into the pockets of his slacks.

"Your ex... He wants to reconcile, doesn't he?"

She crossed her arms over her front in an attempt to self-comfort. "He does."

"And?"

And? "I told him I would have to think about it."

"I see."

"I didn't say yes."

"You didn't say no, either," Zack countered. "But I'm going to make things a little easier for you by taking myself out of the running."

"What? Zack..."

"I saw the way you welcomed him back."

"I wasn't going to make a scene in the middle of the restaurant."

"You didn't have to. But you could have moved away when he touched you. You could have immediately said no when he asked you to reconcile. The fact that you didn't says more than you think. I'm not going to be the guy waiting to find out if I'm good enough. Not this time."

She sucked in a sharp breath. Her feelings for Zack had grown so much in the small amount of time she had been back in Stone River and she'd thought he felt the same. But if he did, how could he give up on them so easily? "So that's it? You're done? You're walking away again?"

"Not again— this time. You walked away the first time, and I refuse to stand around while you do it again."

"My mother invited him, Zack. I didn't know Elliot was going to be here."

Zack took a step closer before he stopped, looking as though he'd hit a wall and bounced back a step.

"You said it yourself--you have a life in Charleston that you're not sure you want to give up. He's part of that life, not to mention Eli's father. I was angry at you for denying me that right but I would be a hypocrite if I did the same to him."

She closed her eyes, squeezed them tight against the burn. How could everything be so messed up? "Zack... Just give me time to think. Please."

"That's exactly what I'm doing, Becca. I'm giving you time and space so you can be with your husband. Once the wedding is over we will never have to see each other again."

THE NEXT DAY Zack snapped a photograph of a particularly beautiful Christmas arrangement when he heard a familiar laugh. He followed the sound with his camera, zooming in on the beautiful brunette immediately.

Becca knelt next to Eli on the waiting area for the indoor boat launch and tickled Eli with the red-hatted moose he carried. When Eli smiled, Becca laughed again and the sight filled Zack with bitter-sweet emotion.

"She's beautiful when she smiles."

Zack turned, surprised to find Becca's father standing close by. How had he approached without Zack noticing?

He didn't respond, unsure of what to say to the man since agreeing might not be in his best interests.

"Eli wanted a souvenir and a boat ride before we left."

"That's understandable. That boat is a kid-magnet."

"I think Rebecca used it as an excuse to go off with Eli on her own. Her eyes were red this morning, like she'd had a sleepless night," her father said. "It's good to see her smiling now."

"She has a lot on her mind."

"Agreed. Elliot and her mother very much want Rebecca to reconcile. I was told you've taken yourself out of the picture."

The man moved closer to where Zack stood, a file in one hand and his briefcase in another.

"I don't know that I was ever *in* the picture," Zack murmured, "but it seemed like the thing to do."

"It's something a gentleman would do for the woman he cares for."

Another laugh caught his attention and he returned his gaze to Becca. The boat had pulled up to the launch and emptied, and the line in front of Becca and Eli started to move as the next group of passengers climbed aboard. "Is there something you want to say?"

"Ten years ago I gambled on something. The odds were in my favor and I knew without a doubt I was right, knew I'd win. But time has proven me wrong and when I'm wrong, I'm man enough to admit it."

Zack stiffened, his elbows digging into the railing on which he leaned.

"You had everything stacked against you. Bad home life, criminal record. You were a young punk kid who couldn't keep himself out of trouble and all I saw was you taking advantage of my baby girl. I thought I knew exactly where you'd end up. I figured it was only a matter of time."

Zack didn't look at George Waites. Couldn't. His hands gripped the camera so tightly his knuckles whitened.

"I see people in my courtroom again and again because they can't let go of the past long enough to build a future, but somehow you've managed to do that. That means I lost that bet I made years ago."

Eli was next in line, his mama behind him. Becca held onto one of Eli's small hands, urging the shy child forward whenever he hesitated.

A man hustled down the ramp toward the boat. It took Zack only a second to identify Elliot before the man jumped line, his voice echoing up to where Zack stood as Elliot cited wanting to ride with his wife and son and thanking the people allowing it to happen.

Within a matter of seconds the last of the passengers boarded the boat and the ride began with Eli sitting on his mama's lap, Elliot beside of them with his arm around Becca's shoulders. They were the very image of a happy, well-to-do family.

"But I still want what's best for my daughter," George murmured.

"I understand." The words rolled from Zack's mouth but the lump of anger and pain and heartbreak made them rough.

"I hope you do." George handed Zack the file. "I'm counting on you to do what's right for Becca and Eli."

Zack watched the man walk away before glancing down at the file in his hand. One flip of the cover revealed his name and several photos of him taken from a telephoto lens.

He snapped the file closed and shoved it into his open camera pack. He wished more than anything he could toss it in the trash but that single glance had made it clear the file contained every kernel of personal information on him George's PI had been able to dig up.

All the personal progress, all the training... all of his success. None of it mattered. He was still the kid from the wrong side of town, unworthy of Judge Waite's daughter.

Chapter 12

Back in Stone River, the days before the wedding flew by with last minute details, floral appointments, and the rehearsal dinner. Becca didn't see much of Zack, but Elliot found numerous excuses to join her as she raced about town and dealt with the chaos.

Elliot stayed at a hotel, but every day he appeared at Kaity's door to help Becca with Eli. She had to give him credit. Elliot showed a newfound patience with their son that she hadn't witnessed before. Not since Eli's babyhood when their son's lack of speech hadn't been a known issue.

Sleepless nights turned into even longer days as Becca saw the old Elliot. The man she'd fallen in love with, the man who'd been so proud introducing their son to friends and coworkers.

But had Elliot truly had a change of heart? How could she be sure? The last thing she wanted to do was give into the moment because of the pressure she felt from her mother to reconcile only to wake up and realize nothing had changed.

Becca glared down at the mass of ribbon and tulle she'd gathered for Kaity's bow bouquet from all the gifts given to her at the bridal shower this afternoon. At least seventy-five women had attended the shower, most of whom made it clear they would welcome advances from Zack. Instead of keeping a list of gifts and gift-givers, she'd found herself distracted by Zack's presence as he circled the patio to take photos at various angles, and every female turned to smile at him as he walked by.

"You're deep in thought," her father murmured from behind her.

She'd escaped the noise and chatter of the patio for the quiet peace of the den, more than eager to leave behind the sight of Zack surrounded by females. "Just trying to focus on all that needs done."

George slowly joined her and Becca felt the intensity of his gaze searching her face.

"I thought showers were supposed be refreshing."

She slanted a wry look at her father. "Funny, Daddy. What are you trying to say?"

"You look tired, sweetheart."

"It's not easy throwing together a wedding in such a short amount of time. I'm fine, though."

"Are you?" George shoved his hands into the pockets of his suit pants. "This wouldn't have anything to do with Elliot's return would it?"

"Some."

"Becca, I know your mother has made it clear she thinks you and Elliot should try again, but is that what you want?"

She blinked at her father, taken aback by the fact he seemed genuinely torn by the thought. "I thought you and Mama loved Elliot."

"We love you, Becca."

"He's Eli's father."

"He is. But he's also a man who's been unfaithful to you."

"I know. I can't stand the thought of it. It hurts so much and I feel... For a long time I felt inferior but I know that it was his issue and not mine. Elliot seems to be trying really hard, though. He seems remorseful and regretful of all the things he did."

"And you believe him?"

She closed her eyes, frustrated by the bit of ribbon unwilling to do what she wanted it to. "I don't know. I'm not sure what to think."

Her father moved closer and placed his hand on her shoulder, gently but firmly turning her so that she faced him.

"Forgiveness doesn't necessarily mean remarrying, Rebecca. Not if that isn't what you want."

Once more she was left nearly speechless by her father's words. He very much believed in the longevity of marriage and honoring the vows taken at the altar. Was he really suggesting... "You once told me you and Elliot were cut from the same cloth."

George winced at the reminder and drew her to over to a chair, urging her to sit down.

"Daddy, I have things I have to do. I should get back to the shower."

"This won't take long. Sit."

She frowned at the order but did as she was told. Her father seated himself on the edge of the adjacent chair and leaned toward her.

"Do you love him?"

"I... loved the man I thought he was."

"I'm not asking if you love Elliot."

Becca silently thanked her father for forcing her to sit given how weak-kneed his words left her. "P-pardon?"

Her father tilted his elegantly grayed head to one side, a hint of a smile curling one corner of his mouth. "Zack isn't the man he used to be, either."

She couldn't hide her surprise that her father would say such a thing. When had her father changed his mind about Zack? What had changed his mind? "No... he isn't."

"So the question remains... Who do you love? Who do *you* want to be with?"

"Daddy, it's not that simple. You know it's not." Nothing could be that simple. She'd built a life with Elliot. Built a home. She had to consider Eli, too. Children needed their fathers in their lives. Didn't they?

Elliot had given up his parental rights and, yes, that was lousy and horrible of him. But Elliot now said it was all a mistake, that he regretted everything. He'd apologized repeatedly, was doing his best to win her back. And her first priority was to do what was best for Eli. That was her duty and responsibility as a mother.

Her father patted her hand with one of his.

"I believe that's the kicker, sweetheart. Love is meant to be easy. We're the ones who make it complicated."

"Becca?" someone called. One of Kaity's work friends stuck her head inside the den and smiled at them. "Sorry to interrupt but Kaity needs you."

"I'll be right there," Becca called, eager for the distraction. She removed her hand from beneath her father's grip. "Zack has taken himself out of the picture. Even if my feelings for him were stronger than what I shared with Elliot, it doesn't matter because Zack walked away. He's made his feelings clear."

"Ahhh, sweetheart. You're going to make me into a maudlin romantic, aren't you?"

"I'm sorry?"

Her father stood when she did and stared down at her with a bittersweet expression.

"True love means putting the other person's happiness above their own--even if it means letting them go. Think about that when you consider your options, sweetheart."

Her father's words stayed with her the rest of the afternoon and the following days, all the way up to the evening of the rehearsal dinner when Zack appeared right on time to photograph the events. Zack had left the shower during the time she'd spent in the den, but during the rehearsal whenever she tried to talk to him, Zack either moved away or else Elliot appeared.

Finally dinner was over and Elliot drove Becca and Eli back to Kaity's condo. Elliot rode up the elevator with them and walked them to the door.

"Tomorrow's going to be another busy day," she said needlessly, feeling the urge to babble because she was so aware of Zack's door just down the hallway. Was he home? Like at the shower, Zack had taken the requisite photos and then disappeared, leaving the family to finish the celebration.

Was her father right in what he said about loving someone so much you let them go? Put their happiness before your own? Is that what Zack was doing? She wanted to ask him, talk to him, but it seemed he didn't want to be anywhere near her.

"I'd like to talk to you, Becca. Alone."

"Eli, go on in and brush your teeth," she said. "I'll be in to tuck you in soon."

Eli was so tired he shuffled his way into the apartment without hesitation or even a backward glance at his father.

"Have you given any thought to what I asked?"

"Some."

"And?"

"Elliot, I need more time."

"How much time? I'd like to announce our reconciliation after the wedding. That way it's truly a celebration."

She blinked at him, astounded by his selfishness. "Absolutely not. It's Kaity and David's day."

"They wouldn't mind. And I know your parents wouldn't mind. But," Elliot added, staring down at her and apparently recognizing the horrified look on her face. "I'll wait. If that's what you want."

"That would be best. Especially since I haven't agreed."

Elliot placed his hands on her upper arms and drew her close before he lowered his head.

"But you will. You know it's what everyone wants for us."

Becca tensed at his words and stiffened even more when Elliot brushed his lips across hers. He tried to deepen the kiss but she broke contact immediately, turning her head to the side. The elevator dinged and she tried to step back but Elliot's grip on her arms tightened just a tad, holding her in place.

Zack exited the elevator but paused when he spotted them. She could only imagine what he thought seeing them like that. "Z-zack..."

"Goodnight." Zack dipped his head in a nod, his long strides taking him to his door in two seconds flat.

"Goodnight," Elliot said. "Come on, sweetheart. Let's go inside and tuck in our son."

WHAT'S GOT YOU SO GRUMPY?"

Zack looked up from his breakfast plate at the Shake Shak and stared into his biological father's eyes. The last ten years since the truth of Frank Wyatt's paternity had come to light had been rocky. But with Emma's help Zack and Frank could now speak to each other without it turning into a shouting match, unlike earlier conversations. "Busy day ahead."

And after a long night tossing and turning because he couldn't get the image of Becca in her ex-husband's arms out of his head, nor could he erase the echo of the man's words. Today was going to be a long day.

"Ah. That Becca girl."

Zack glared at the man responsible for his existence and wondered if this conversation was going to resemble those of their first. He wouldn't mind letting off a little steam. "Coffee. To go."

Frank smirked and took his time pouring a large cup, taking still more time to locate and add a sleeve and lid.

"You know, if you want some advice—"

"I don't."

"—I say go for it. That girl—woman—she'd be getting a good thing."

Zack was in the process of standing up when Frank's words sank in. He paused, half up and half seated, unable to move because of the impact.

"I know I'm not responsible for you turning out the way you have. I know that's because of Ian and Duncan and the rest of his crew taking you under their wing. But I can see how much you've grown and changed. You're a good man. Any woman would be lucky to snag you, son."

Frank set the cup on the counter and waved off Zack's fumbling attempt to retrieve his wallet once he'd made it fully to his feet.

"On the house. You didn't eat much of it anyway."

Zack hesitated but then shoved the wallet back into his pants. "Thanks."

Zack grabbed the uneaten bacon off of his plate and carried it out of the diner. Moses waited expectantly in the SUV, licking his chops at the treat in Zack's hand.

It took only minutes to arrive at the downtown church where the ceremony would take place. Zack gripped the wheel and braced himself for the day.

Seeing Becca and her ex locked in an embrace the moment the elevator doors had opened last night had turned Zack's stomach. Had Becca invited her ex inside last night to talk? Had Elliot stayed the night? Zack hadn't allowed himself to stare out of the peephole of his apartment door to find out.

Zack parked near the rear entry of the large church and gathered his gear. Moses hopped out of the cab, tail wagging because he knew he was welcome to wait out the day on the minister's large couch.

He shut Moses in the office for a long snooze and headed out into the sanctuary to set up his equipment. He'd nearly finished when he heard voices coming from the front entry.

"Becca, how about I take Eli somewhere here and play with him until it's time," Elliot said. "You do your thing and we'll be out of the way."

"Are you sure?" Becca stared up at her ex, breathtakingly beautiful in a floor-length black gown.

"Of course I am. I wouldn't have offered to babysit if I wasn't willing."

Zack ground his teeth together, wanting to speak up and point out that it wasn't babysitting when it was your own kid. Watching over your child was a parental duty, a privilege, not *babysitting*.

Somehow he managed to keep his mouth shut. Elliot disappeared with his son and Becca went full-tilt wedding planner complete with a headset microphone to connect her to the videographer and others. Zack found himself pausing to watch her in amazement.

Becca was in her element. She stood in the back of the church and spoke into the headset, using her hands and arms to direct the others like a conductor guiding an orchestra.

Reeling himself in, Zack bent to retrieve his big camera bag to carry with him to the ladies' area for bridal preparation pictures. The bag was open, and when he lifted it, the file folder George Waites had given him in Nashville fell to the floor, the contents scattering.

Zack stared down at the mess, caught off guard by the sight of himself in the photos. But when he knelt to gather the scattered papers, he was more surprised by the fact he wasn't the only one featured in the file like he'd thought.

He shuffled through the pages and found photos of him and his family leaving this very church after service. Photos of him helping Emma out with her PAWS Class at the local university. Photos of him and Moses heading into and out of his apartment building alone.

But the photos of Elliot...

The images and investigative reports depicted a man with a secret side. There were images of Elliot kissing different women as they left what appeared to be his home given the man's lack of clothing. Pictures shot through what appeared to be his office window in which he was literally caught in the act. There was a copy of a DUI charge that had been "handled" according to the report. Page after page of information and evidence, all dated down to the day before Elliot's reappearance.

It wasn't until that moment that George Waites' words sank in. The man had *apologized* to Zack in Nashville. Owned up to believing the odds stacked against Zack and how he'd tried to protect his daughter.

How he only wanted the best for his daughter.

A chill rolled through Zack and he lifted his head, staring at the far end of the church and the cross high in the stained glass window. Had he not been so stubborn and looked at the file sooner instead of thinking the worst about George Waites...

You got me, didn't You?

Voices came from the entry and Zack realized some of the guests had actually started to arrive, no doubt hoping to get the best seats for what would be the most talked about wedding in town for quite some time.

He needed to get a move on. Needed to hurry to the brides' chambers.

Zack shoved the papers and file into his bag and zipped it closed. He had to talk to Becca but it would have to wait. He had a wedding to shoot first.

Chapter 13

Becca ripped off her headset and handed it to her assistant mere seconds before the doors opened for the processional to begin.

She followed the others and walked up the aisle when it was her turn, somehow forcing a smile for the camera and the man behind it. It was like she walked toward the altar for him, and her mind ran rampant with images of her in a beautiful dress and Zack in a black tux like the one he now wore.

Zack remained in position and Becca had to walk by him to get to her spot. She couldn't be certain, but as she passed she could've sworn Zack murmured something like *my beautiful Becca.*

It was her imagination. It had to be. She and Zack hadn't spoken in days except for brief, professional exchanges about certain photos Kaity wanted taken.

Becca watched Eli shyly hurry down the aisle carrying the Bible tied with faux rings. Once at the front, he ran the last few steps towards Becca and stood close by her side, his face turned into her long skirt.

Kaity made her grand entrance and walked beside their father down the aisle. Her father winked at Becca along the way, and she smiled, vaguely aware of Zack moving along the shadows capturing the moment.

The ceremony began and, as the minister asked Kaity and David to say their vows, Becca found her gaze wandering to the man behind the camera then on to the man sitting beside her mother on the front pew.

Her chest squeezed and she fought off the wave of unease that filled her. Elliot wanted her but, truth be told, she wasn't sure she could ever trust him. She could trust Zack, but he obviously didn't care as much for her as she did for him or he wouldn't have walked away so easily.

"Becca?"

Becca snapped to attention when Kaity whispered her name. Her sister had turned to retrieve her bouquet but in her dazed state, Becca wasn't letting go.

The receiving line was endless but finally the last of the guests walked through and the wedding party quickly reentered the sanctuary for family photos while the guests enjoyed hors d'oeuvres and drinks at the Wickersham until the bride and groom arrived.

Zack remained professional, even when Elliot insisted on crashing one of the family portraits because he would soon be family again.

Becca was mortified. She wouldn't allow Elliot to push his way back into her life unless she wanted him there, but she wasn't going to cause a scene here. It was only one picture, after all.

Eli needed to go to the bathroom and Elliot volunteered to take him. Becca continued to pose for the many photos with the bride and her family, and finally Zack completed the long list of must-have shots, releasing them to go to the reception.

"I'll go get Eli," Becca said. "Elliot must be having trouble with him or they would've been back by now."

Becca hurried toward the bathroom area but several knocks and even pushing the door open to call into the room proved pointless. They weren't there. But where were they?

She moved further down the hallway, not stopping until she heard cheers from the end of an adjoining hall. She followed the noise, pushing the already open wooden panel into the room to see Elliot and several of the ushers, a combination of Kaity and David's younger cousins, standing in front of a large television.

"Yessssss!"

"Now that's what I'm talking about!"

"Pay up, loser," Elliot said to one of the eldest, holding out his hand.

"Yeah, yeah."

Becca visually searched the room but didn't see Eli anywhere. "Elliot?"

The guys turned as a group, all of them wearing guilty expressions.

"Is it time to go to the reception?" one of them asked.

She nodded, the group scattering around both sides of the couch to leave the room. "Where's Eli?"

Elliot counted the money in his hands, grinning. "He's around here somewhere."

"He ran out," the youngest of her distant cousins murmured to Becca as he approached her and the door. "Elliot yelled at him and he started crying."

"Yelled at him for what?" she demanded in a low voice.

The young man grimaced. "Eli had an accident."

Becca stood where she was, hands fisted, fuming, waiting for the room to clear. The moment she was alone with Elliot she asked, "You didn't take him straight to the bathroom?"

"Oh, come on, Becca. He's old enough to hold it a few minutes."

"Yes, he is. He's also *four* and he'd held it during the last several *hours*. How could you yell at him when you're the one at fault for not taking him to the bathroom like you said you would?"

Elliot pocketed the money, a put-out expression on his face. "He's fine. You can change his clothes at the reception."

She could? Why wouldn't Elliot do it since he was the one who created the problem in the first place? "Where is he?"

Elliot looked around the room and shrugged. "Probably in the bathroom."

"I just came from there. He didn't answer me when I called."

A huff of a laugh left Elliot.

"Like that's unusual. Come on, I'll help you look."

Elliot's lack of caring and consideration, his lack of empathy, tore through her. "You haven't changed at all, have you?"

"Oh, come on, Bec. Are we really going to do this now? I'm sorry I yelled at him, okay?"

"No, it's not okay because you don't mean it. It's just words to you. You've been on your best behavior here, trying to win us back, but nothing has changed. Stay here and count your money. I'll find him. You've done more than enough to us both already."

"Hey. Don't take that attitude and walk away from me. Becca!"

"We're done," she said, relief flooding her body. It was like a weight had been lifted from her and she was able to breathe for the first time since Elliot had reappeared in her life. "I should've known better. I'm an idiot for letting you get by with putting on such a show! Go home, Elliot."

"Becca, he had an accident. That's no reason to call it off between us."

"But it is. You put a game and betting ahead of your son. You yelled at him, and then yelled at me, when you're the one who's at fault. We don't need that in our lives."

"You're not going to take my son away from me."

"You *gave* him away, remember? I have the papers to prove it."

Elliot locked his jaw until a muscle began to twitch.

"This isn't over," Elliot growled.

"Oh, but it is," Zack said.

Becca turned, only then realizing Zack stood behind her and looked every bit as angry and upset as she felt.

Elliot cursed and stalked toward them and Zack gently tugged her backward so that she stood behind him and the huge camera bag he had hanging from his shoulder.

"Stay out of this," Elliot said to Zack. "You're only here because you're paid to be here."

Zack shrugged off the camera bag and removed a file folder from within the depths, shoving it against Elliot's chest. "You're done. Stay away from Becca and *our* son."

ZACK HEARD Becca gasp at his words and watched as Elliot reluctantly accepted the file and glanced inside, a red hue flooding up his neck, into his face.

"Have I made myself clear?" Zack snatched the file back so Elliot wouldn't be tempted to destroy the evidence.

"Is there a problem here?" George asked, joining the group.

"Not anymore," Zack said. "It's been handled thanks to your research."

"Elliot was just leaving," Becca added, her voice hoarse from the strain of her emotions.

Elliot scurried away like the rat he was, and Zack came face-to-face with Becca.

"Research?" she asked, motioning to the file.

"It's nothing," Zack and her father said in unison.

"Oh, you will show me that," she stated unequivocally.

"Later," Zack promised. "It can wait until later. Let's go find Eli."

"This church is huge. He could be anywhere," she said. "He gets very upset when he has an accident. Elliot yelling at him would've only made it worse."

Her eyes sparkled with unshed tears and Zack could only imagine all of the emotions rolling through her at the moment. "You check around here," he told George. "I've got an idea of where he might be. Come on," he said to Becca.

Zack took her hand in his and tugged her along behind him through the twists and turns of the large church, not stopping until they made it to the rear near the office where he'd left Moses.

"It's empty," Becca said. "Oh, where is he? Should we call the police?"

Zack heard a low thudding noise and lifted his finger to his lips to silence Becca. "Listen."

They followed the sound of the noise, crossing the room toward the large desk. Zack had to move the heavy chair out of the way, but once he did he saw fur--and two tiny dress shoes sticking out from beneath the edge.

Zack knelt down, Becca bending over his back, to see Eli hiding beneath the desk hugging his knees. Tears stained his little face and he smelled a bit, but Moses had curled protectively around the boy.

Moses' tail thudded against the privacy panel of the wooden desk in greeting, and Zack automatically reached out to pet the dog. "Good boy, Mo."

Eli sniffled and lowered his legs as though to climb out from beneath the desk. Zack helped him by scooping the boy up and holding him so that his mama could shower him with kisses without mussing her dress.

"I'm sorry," Eli whispered.

"Oh, sweetie. I know it was an accident. Let's get you changed, huh? Then we'll go to the party and have cake and you can play with Moses as much as you want. Does that sound fun?"

Zack watched as Becca wiped the tears from her son's cheeks and kissed him until Eli smiled and nodded.

His heart tugged at the sight, and he couldn't wait until things between them were settled so that he could kiss Becca with just as much enthusiasm.

BECCA ALLOWED Zack to lead her out of the ballroom and into the cold night air of the balcony. He didn't stop there, though. Holding her hand, he tucked her against his side and steered her down the concrete steps toward the beautifully lit fountain. "Where are we going?"

"Somewhere where I have you to myself."

"Hmm... I'm not sure that's allowed since we're both working."

He stopped at the edge of the fountain and drew her against his chest.

"Are you cold?"

"Not with you here to warm me."

Zack apparently liked that answer because he lowered his head and kissed her.

"Becca?"

"Mmm?"

"I love you."

Pure joy filled her and flooded her body with warmth. "I love you, too. I didn't realize it before... I focused on all the mistakes we've made and how dark that time was. But I should have been focusing on how far we've come."

Zack lowered his head and kissed her again, staying forehead-to-forehead and nose-to-nose when it ended.

"I can't believe I was so stupid. I was going to give you up again. All because I thought it would be better for you. But all I want is to spend the rest of my life with you and Eli. Becca, will you marry me?"

She opened her mouth to respond but nothing would come out. The words, her voice--they weren't there. But she knew her answer. Knew that babbling questions and fears would get her nowhere and this was probably God's way of keeping her from screwing things up--again.

"Becca?"

A laugh burst out of her and the tears in her eyes leaked out as she nodded vigorously.

"You will? That's a yes?"

She used her hold on his neck to tug him low and kissed him with all of the intensity she couldn't express verbally. Yes, she would marry him. Yes, she wanted to spend her life with him. Yes, yes, yes!

Maybe Eli had it right. Maybe words weren't always needed. Maybe, sometimes, she needed to be quiet, and listen. Otherwise, how could she see the second chance she'd been given?

Epilogue

One year later...

BECCA GENTLY SQUEEZED the tiny hand in hers and smiled despite the tears leaking from her eyes. "So? What do you think, Eli?"

Eli let go of Zack's neck and reached for Becca and the newborn in her arms. Zack carefully lowered their son to the bed beside of her and then grabbed his camera to capture Eli's response to his very new baby sister.

"She's mine?"

Zack's low chuckle joined Becca's and she held the baby to one side to kiss her firstborn. "She's your baby sister, yes. She's a wonderful Christmas present, don't you think?"

Eli ran his hand carefully over the baby's tobogganed head before snuggling against her side with a vigorous nod. Becca shifted her gaze to Zack's, not even caring that the camera shutter whirled in her direction so soon after a twelve hour labor and delivery.

She placed her cheek against Eli's head, his hair smelling of baby shampoo and little boy mystery smells. Eli still wasn't as talkative as most of the kids in his preschool class but he was talking more and more every day. He'd also served as Zack's unofficial best man when she and Zack had married last New Year's Eve. Elliot wasn't happy with the news but he'd quickly recovered in the arms of a tall, skinny blond, quickly losing interest in the son he'd claimed to want so badly.

In the year since she'd remarried, relocated her business to Stone River, gotten pregnant, purchased a house large enough to accommodate their growing family, and fallen deeper and deeper in love with Zack.

Zack lowered set the camera aside and climbed into the hospital bed with them.

"Merry Christmas," he said to Becca, kissing her temple.

"Merry Christmas to you," she said in return, tilting her head back on Zack's shoulder to accept the kiss he gave her.

"Mama?"

"Hmm?" she said, smiling against Zack's lips when she had to end the contact. "What, honey?"

"You weren't supposed to have the baby yet. Santa won't know to bring her presents."

Staring up at Zack, she saw him wink at her and grin. "That's because she *is* a present. She's mine and daddy's surprise present this year."

I hope you have enjoyed the Stone River series. Listed below are links to all of the books. Please feel free to share the links on social media, with friends, and family.

- WORTH THE WAIT
- NOT BY SIGHT
- MORE THAN LOVE (FORMERLY THROUGH THE VALLEY)
- TO PROTECT HER (FORMERLY LEAD ME NOT)
- CHRISTMAS AT HOLLY WOOD
- THEIR CHRISTMAS MIRACLE
- SECOND CHANCES

Word of mouth and reviews are the two best ways an author has to gain attention for their books. While you're browsing the titles, please consider taking a moment to leave a short review of this book.

Thank you,

Kay

The Stone River Novels

SIGN UP FOR KAY'S NEWSLETTER AND RECEIVE FREE BOOKS, UPDATES ON NEW RELEASES, CONTESTS, PRE-RELEASE BOOK INFORMATION, EXCLUSIVES AND MORE!

Other titles by Kay Lyons:

MAKE ME A MATCH SERIES:

- ROMANCE RESET
- RULES OF ENGAGEMENT
- THE MATCHMAKER'S SECRET
- PERFECTLY MISMATCHED
- BY THE BOOK

MONTANA SECRETS SERIES:

- HEALING HER COWBOY
- IT HAD TO BE YOU
- HERS TO KEEP
- MILLION DOLLAR STANDOFF
- HIS CHRISTMAS WISH
- THEIR SECRET SON

THE SEASIDE SISTERS SERIES:

- THE LAST GOODBYE
- LATTES AND LULLABYES
- MAP OF DREAMS
- WORTH THE RISK
- LOST LOVE FOUND

TAMING THE TULANES SERIES:

- SMALL TOWN SCANDAL
- THEIR SECRET BARGAIN
- CROSSING THE LINE
- THE NANNY'S SECRET
- SOMEONE TO TRUST

- WORTH THE WAIT
- NOT BY SIGHT
- MORE THAN LOVE (FORMERLY THROUGH THE VALLEY)
- TO PROTECT HER (FORMERLY LEAD ME NOT)
- CHRISTMAS AT HOLLY WOOD
- THEIR CHRISTMAS MIRACLE
- SECOND CHANCES

SMALL TOWN SCANDALS SERIES:

- BRODY'S REDEMPTION
- FALLING FOR HER BOSS
- WITH THIS MAN

SECRET SANTA SERIES:

- SECRET SANTA
- SECRET SANTA II: A CHRISTMAS TO REMEMBER

AUTHOR BIO

Kay Lyons always wanted to be a writer, ever since the age of seven or eight when she copied the pictures out of a Charlie Brown book and rewrote the story because she didn't like the plot. Through the years her stories have changed but one characteristic stayed true— they were all romances. Each and every one of her manuscripts included a love story.

Published in 2005 with Harlequin Enterprises, Kay's first release was a national bestseller. Kay has also been a HOLT Medallion, Book Buyers Best and RITA Award nominee. Look for her most recent novels with Kindred Spirits Publishing.

For more information regarding her work, please visit Kay at the following:

www.kaylyonsauthor.com

@KayLyonsAuthor (Twitter)

Kay Lyons Author (Facebook)

Author_Kay_Lyons (Instagram)

Kay Lyons, Author (Pinterest)

SIGN UP FOR KAY'S NEWSLETTER AND RECEIVE FREE BOOKS, UPDATES ON NEW RELEASES, CONTESTS, PRE-

RELEASE BOOK INFORMATION, EXCLUSIVES AND MORE!